HOLLYWOOD DEAD

HOLLYWOOD DEAD

Aaron Amadeus

Commonwealth Books Inc.,

A Commonwealth Publications Paperback
HOLLYWOOD DEAD
This edition published 2022
by Commonwealth Books

Copyright © 2022 by Aaron Amadeus / James W Haddad
Published in the United States by Commonwealth Books Inc., New York

Library of Congress Control Number: 2022934522

ISBN: :978-1-892986-40-5 (trade
ISBN: :978-1-892986-37-5 (E-Pub)

This work is a novel and any similarities to actual persons or events is purely coincidental.

First Commonwealth Printing, April 2022

PUBLISIHED BY COMMONWEALTH BOOKS, INC.,
www.commonwealthbooksinc.com
www.commonwealthbooks@aol.com

Manufactured in the United States of America

1

My name is Benjamin Becker, and I wasn't what one would call an "average" teenage boy. While I wasn't in any kind of hurry to have sex of any kind for the first time, every other boy in school was rushing to lose his virginity. I didn't know why. There were plenty of other things to focus on, but apparently, *most* teenage boys tend to think of only one thing. I wasn't one of them.

Fast-forward ten years, and not only was I still a virgin, but I still wasn't in a hurry to lose it. Being a Christian partly played into that, with the whole "no sex until marriage" mindset, but girls with awful attitudes were also a huge reason. I grew up in Bemidji, Minnesota, and, with the exception of my best friend, Callie McCormick, whom I met at summer camp when we were eight, 90% of the girls I knew were horrible and rude.

I used to be a nice guy. When one deals with as many disrespectful people as I did, though, certain defense mechanisms become acquired. Mine happened to be that I was an asshole. If someone was rude to me, my automatic reaction was to be rude right back—ten times worse.

Don't mess with me.

My father, Nicholas Becker, was a freelance graphic designer who worked on major projects, like designing movie posters for the romantic comedy *Ain't No Mountain High* and the horror film *Christmastime Is Fear*. He made enough to support me and my sisters, Brandi and Bianca, comfortably, but, when I turned fifteen, he received a job offer that required a move to New Braunfels, Texas with a company where he'd have steady work. We moved the summer before my sophomore year of high school.

Freshman year at Bemidji Township High was torture. If it hadn't been for Callie, I didn't think I would have survived. I was afraid that what I called my "second freshman year," would suck. To my surprise, it was actually good.

I met my best friend, Brady Remer, in the first week. We bonded quickly over our shared interest in the paranormal, and my high-school career was made. Brady was the king of the popular clique, and, by association, I made it to the top, too. It was nice, even though the real world didn't give a damn how popular anyone was in high school.

I graduated at the top ten percent of my class and went to Texas State University the following fall, earning my associate degree in graphic design (following in my father's footsteps) when I was twenty.

I started looking for my own place to live. I began the search alone, but Brady suggested we find a house together, and, since we were best friends for four years, that sounded like a good idea. We found a nice three-bedroom place in San Antonio within our budget and decided to get it. That worked well with my job with the San Antonio Zoo, and I wouldn't have to drive forty-five minutes to work each day. That saved a lot on gas and wear and tear on my car.

My schedule was set for Monday through Thursday, nine to five, off Saturday and Sundays, and working alternating Fridays. In addition to being a zookeeper, I had a syndicated TV series I filmed every other weekend called *The Banshee Busters*. It was like *Ghost Adventures* in the sense that we went to haunted locations around the U.S., sometimes the world, and we filmed everything ourselves, although we stayed away from places with documented demonic activity.

We started the show in 2012 with an investigation of Waverly Hills Sanatorium in Louisville, Kentucky, which aired on Halloween night. It premièred to good ratings, so SyFi, the network that aired the show, ordered eleven more episodes for the season. We were currently working on our third season and still going strong.

Life has a funny way of working out in expected ways. I met my best friend the first week in my new school, got the zoo job I wasn't expecting, then I landed a syndicated TV series, which I *definitely* wasn't expecting, and I happened to reunite with my childhood best friend from Minnesota.

I was working at the zoo, doing my usual chores of making sure the animals had enough food and water and a clean enclosure. Texas is really hot, and that day was no exception. After I refilled the water troughs for the African elephants, I dumped the excess water over myself to cool off.

"Oh, my God! Ben? Is that really you?"

I turned to see a girl waving frantically at me. She had bleached-blonde hair with cobalt-blue and magenta highlights, a medium purple tank top, bright white shorts, and what looked like cork wedge shoes.

I held my hand over my eyes to shield them from the sun, forgetting I wore sunglasses. "That depends on who's asking," I said, half-joking.

She pointed at herself. "Don't you recognize me? It's Callie from Minnesota!"

It took a few seconds for my brain to register. Once it did, I was super excited. "Callie? It *is* you!"

I ran out of the elephant enclosure, made sure the gate was latched behind me, and sprinted to her, picking her up and spinning her around in a huge hug. "It's great to see you again. Wow, you've changed."

Her natural hair color was dark brown, and she still had a little baby fat, although not enough to be overweight. She changed so dramatically, I thought she was a stranger at first. She bleached her hair, added highlights, and was super toned. She was very different from the last time I saw her in Minnesota.

"Yeah, well," she said, shrugging, "this is what happens when one spends a semester in California."

After graduating at the top of her class in Bemidji, Minnesota, she went to UCLA to work on a degree in screen writing. She quickly realized it was insanely expensive to live alone out there unless she was super rich, so she transferred her credits to Texas State and moved in with her older sister, Sierra, and her brother-in-law, Calvin Harrison.

Callie squinted at me. "You look different, too."

I chuckled. "No, I don't. I'm one of those people who never changes."

"Oh, come on. Sure they do." She grabbed my left arm and held it straight out. "This looks super toned." She squinted at my chest. "Is that a tattoo above your right pec?"

I got a star of the champion tattoo on my chest to celebrate graduating from Texas State University. "I reckon it is," I said nonchalantly.

"You swore you'd never get a tattoo. Something about the needles terrified you."

"They did. I figured the best way to get over a fear is to face it."

She crossed her arms. "Did you do the same thing for your fear of spiders?"

I stared at her. "Are you insane? I'll never get over those eight-legged demons."

She smirked. "Interesting."

"You're one to talk. You're afraid of snakes."

"Don't remind me. They're so damn unnatural. Things that don't have legs and smell with their tongues are weird."

"And you think hairy things with eight legs aren't?"

Callie grinned. "Touché."

I glanced at my watch. "My shift ends in a couple hours. What say you come to my place afterward, so we can catch up a little more?"

"I'd love that."

"Very good. Then you can meet my roommates. I'm sure they'd love that."

I told her to meet me at my car after my shift and went back to my assigned tasks.

At five o'clock, I walked to the visitor's center and clocked out in the staff room. Callie was waiting by my orange Mitsubishi Eclipse convertible when I walked into the parking lot.

I grinned. "I didn't think you'd find my car unless I told you which one it was."

She gestured at the vanity plate, which read *BBUSTER*. "It wasn't too hard."

I got in and started the engine. "Follow me to my place."

She nodded and walked to her own car. I drove toward home with Callie following close behind in her powder-blue Chevy Aveo.

Twenty minutes later, I pulled up at the Bromance Bungalow, the nickname Brady and I gave our humble abode. It wasn't a bad-looking place. Cobalt-blue siding covered the outside, a maple wood deck sat along the front, and we had a detached two-car garage. On the inside, it had a very modern kitchen, with stainless-steel appliances, cherry wood cabinets, white marble countertops, an oak dining table with five oak chairs, and black-and-white linoleum.

The living room had maple flooring, a cobblestone fireplace, a 50-inch flat-screen TV above the mantel, a faux tiger fur rug in front of the fireplace, and a forest-green couch, a leather loveseat, and a navy-blue La-Z-Boy recliner facing the fireplace.

My dad helped us buy the furnishings. I didn't ask him to. He offered. I guessed he was proud of me for getting out on my own and learning to support myself. Even though he bought everything we had, we paid all the bills—electricity, Internet, the mortgage, water, and everything else. He told me I could always go to him if we needed help for a month, but we managed to cover the bills ourselves.

I unlocked the door and stepped inside. Callie followed and froze. "Wow. This place looks amazing."

"Well, thank you." I hung my keys on a hook near the door. "I try to keep things that way."

Sitting on the couch, I turned on the TV. "Anything you want to watch while we wait for the others?"

"Sure." She sat in the recliner. "Find out if *American Dad* or *That 70's Show* is on."

I flipped to the guide and found a rerun of *American Dad.* We watched ten minutes of the episode before the front door opened and closed.

Two minutes later, my roommate, Calvin Brewster, walked in thumbing through the mail.

"Dude, we really need to do something about these credit card applications," he complained. "I'm really getting sick of receiving them when we can't use them."

He was twenty-four and lived with Brady and me. We met in an unorthodox way. I dated a girl named Leona Heinemann for six months. She slept with at least sixty-three different guys, and I started getting calls and Facebook messages telling me they slept with her.

Then one day, Calvin arrived on my doorstep with a hand-written note from Leona saying how much fun she had with him the previous night. After confirming he didn't know I existed beforehand, and then he apologized, I blocked her from my life and built a friendship with Calvin. Last I heard, Leona found work as a prostitute in a brothel in Mexico. I wasn't surprised.

"I hear you, Bro," I said, "but what else can we do if the companies won't listen?"

"Ugh." He groaned. "Then we have to keep shredding them, or...." He stopped and stared at the unfamiliar girl on the couch. Walking over, he gave her a once-over. "Well, hello there. Who are you?"

Callie giggled and held out her hand. "I'm Callie, Ben's best friend from Minnesota. Charmed to make your acquaintance."

Calvin shook her hand. "The pleasure is all mine. My name's Calvin."

"That's funny. That's my brother-in-law's name."

"Neat. It's a pretty studly name." He glanced at me. "What's for dinner, Man?"

"I thought we'd have a cookout. We could use those hamburgers and hot dogs we have in the freezer."

"Oooh," Callie said. "That sounds tasty."

I went to the basement to get the packages of hamburger and hot dogs, brought them to the kitchen, and let them thaw on the counter. When my phone buzzed in my pocket, I pulled it out to see who it was.

It was a text from Giovanni Polanski with something completely spontaneous, and I was in the middle of responding in the same sarcastic manner when someone grabbed me from behind and squeezed the air from my lungs.

I turned and saw my best friend, Brady, smirking at me. "Hey, Bud. Did I scare you?"

"Of course you did, Bro." I punched his shoulder. "You scared the shit out of me."

"Maybe you should be more alert."

"You'd think so when I'm living with you."

He was my best friend of eight years. He was twenty-six, and I met him in my first week at New Braunfels Township when he offered to show me around the school. We bonded quickly. He was really popular, because he was nice to everybody and stood up for anyone who couldn't do it for himself.

I had to admit that in Minnesota, I never spoke out against people who were disrespectful to others. Dealing with people who were rude to me, along with Brady teaching me how to stand up for myself, brought me to a new level. I ended up helping out a few people who couldn't defend themselves.

One memorable example was an idiot kid named Austin Kratos. He and his posse catcalled a female classmate and wouldn't leave her alone even when she demanded they back off. I stepped in when Austin touched her and told him to back off. His response was swift—eight magic words that made me snap.

"What are you going to do about it?"

I shoved him hard enough to knock him on his ass. He jumped up and lunged at me, so I punched his face repeatedly. He got in only one or two hits. Justice was served that day.

Since it happened after school hours, the administration couldn't do anything about it, but he and I were called to the office the next day. When I explained I was defending a girl from sexual harassment, I was given a light sentence of only a two-day suspension. Austin got two weeks. The girl's parents sued him and his family for sexual harassment.

I felt ashamed to admit I was in a fight, but it was for a good reason. My dad took me out for an expensive dinner that night and said he was proud of me for standing up for a female classmate.

If people didn't know any better and were super close-minded, they might misconstrue my relationship with Brady as gay, because we're so touchy-feely with each other. We give each other real hugs with both arms, not a "bro" hug with one hand, random shoulder rubs occasionally, and non-sexual cuddling when we watched movies or TV together. We're both straight guys who enjoy hanging out together.

"We've known each other for eight years," Brady said. "You knew what you were getting into living with me." He laughed and saw the packages thawing on the counter. "What's this for?"

I adjusted my glasses. "I thought we'd have a cookout tonight. My best friend from childhood showed up at the zoo unexpectedly, and, since he's here to stay, I thought it would be fun for you and Calvin to meet him."

"Sounds good. Where is this dude?" he asked, looking around. "I can't wait to meet him."

Callie came through the doorway. "I don't know where this dude is, but I'm right here."

Brady's jaw dropped. "My God, you're hot."

She laughed. "I haven't heard that one before."

She walked over and held out her hand. "I'm Callie, Ben's OG bestie from Minnesota."

Brady shook her hand confidently. "I'm Brady. It's nice to meet a part of Ben's past."

"It's also nice to be part of his present." She glanced at me. "When will you start the grill?"

I picked up the packages off the counter. "I could do that now."

"Oooh, how fun!" Brady said. "I'll come with."

We walked to the grill together, and I fired it up. Brady offered to take over the cooking. Since he was our resident grill master, I let him.

Meanwhile, I walked back inside to chill with Callie and Calvin. They were on the couch, watching something on Callie's phone and laughing.

Calvin looked up when I came in. "Dude, there's no way this is you. You're so hot now."

I gave him a confused look. "Thanks, I guess. What are you talking about?"

"This pic of you from Minnesota."

Callie handed me the phone. It was a picture from my freshman year at high school. I had rimmed glasses, a black-and-blue Polo shirt, shaggy black hair to my ears, and a really weird smile.

Freshman year was rough. The only thing that remained the same was that I wore glasses. I sometimes wore actual T-shirts with sleeves, but, given the Texas heat, I preferred tank tops or sleeveless shirts. When I moved to a new state and new school, I had the chance to reinvent myself, so I cut my hair, spiked it, and frosted the tips. Surprisingly, it looked good, even though my hair was black.

I worked out with a friend, Spike Ramirez, before he was deployed to Iraq, which gave me a toned body and six-pack abs. I also grew a goatee, some facial stubble, and got the star of a champion tattoo on my chest above my right pec.

The tattoo was a dare, but it worked. I got over my fear of needles, and it made me look sexy.

"Yeah, that wasn't one of my prouder moments." I handed the phone back to Callie. "I actually thought about skipping the whole 'picture thing' day."

"Oh, come on," Callie said. "You didn't look that bad."

"True, dat," Calvin agreed, "but you look sexier now."

I laughed. "That's new."

Brady called us out to the patio, saying the burgers and hot dogs were ready. I grabbed a package of Styrofoam plates and red Solo cups from the cabinet beside the sink. Once we loaded up on hamburgers, hot dogs, chips, and pistachio salad—also made by Brady—we set up the umbrella table on the patio to protect us from the Texas sun. It helped me get a super fast tan, but I sometimes preferred shade, especially when it was disgustingly hot.

Callie took a bite of her burger and said, "Oh, my! This is good!" She looked at me. "Now that I met your roommates, you should tell me how you met them."

"It's an interesting story," I began. "I met Brady in high school the first week I was there. I was lost. He noticed and offered to show me around. It took off from there."

Callie stared at me blankly. "That's not interesting. That's average."

"That makes me feel wonderful," Brady joked.

I drank from my Mountain Dew. "Calvin and I have an unorthodox story."

"It's hilarious," Calvin said. "I slept with his then-girlfriend."

Callie stared in shock. "That doesn't sound hilarious. That sounds terrible."

"It was funny," I interjected. "She slept with sixty-three different guys in six months, including him. Since he was the only one who came with any kind of proof and apology, I decided to befriend him and turn lemons into lemonade."

I thought about that for a moment. "It wasn't funny at the time, but now it's a story to look back on and laugh at, especially now that she's stuck where she is."

"Where is that?" Callie asked.

"Last I heard, she's working at a bordello in Mexico. That kind of thing is right up her alley."

"Right in it, too," Brady added.

Of all my friends who knew about the situation, Brady hated Leona the most. He was an outsider looking in on something he went through himself, feeling like there was nothing he could say or do to help, and that broke his heart. When I finally realized what was going on and dumped her, he was the first one to celebrate. He took me to All the King's Women, an amazing strip club, and gave me fifty single-dollar bills from his wallet to help me celebrate with the ladies and blow off some steam. I had to admit it worked.

Callie popped a few Doritos into her mouth. "So this Leona chick was something of a hussy?"

Brady laughed. "That's one way to see it."

In the middle of the ensuing laughter, my phone rang. I glanced at the caller ID and saw the word *Restricted*. I could either hang up or screw with someone before he screwed with me. I decided for the latter.

I slid the keypad to answer and put on a horrible fake Indian accent. "Curry Club," I said.

"There's a present on your doorstep," the caller said.

"Geh?"

"You should open your door, for there's a present on your doorstep."

I was a little creeped out. I slowly got up from my patio chair, telling the others I'd be right back. Seeing a banana cream pie on the kitchen counter, I carried it with me as a protective measure to toss into someone's face.

I crept to the front door with the cream pie in hand, said a silent prayer when I arrived, took a deep breath, and threw open the door. No one was outside. When I glanced down, I saw an eighteen-bottle case of Budweiser.

"How nice," I said, balancing the cream pie in one hand and picking up the beer case in the other.

Suddenly, a crazy woman popped out from behind the huge rose bushes by the stoop, screaming, "Oogly boogly!"

Startled, I screamed like a little girl, dropped the beer, and shoved the banana cream pie in her face.

"Aack!" she sputtered, followed by both of us laughing. She wiped cream off her face with her bare hands and glared at me.

"Ben, what on Earth was that for?" she demanded.

"Angela? Why on Earth did you think scaring me was a good idea?"

"I thought it would be funny."

I grinned. "It was...to me."

Angela rolled her eyes. "Well, whoop-dee-do."

Brady was my best male friend. Angela Gordon was my best female friend and another member of the Ben Should Dump Leona bandwagon. She came very close to beating up Leona before we separated. It was good that Leona left the country when she did.

Angela, like Brady, was in the popular clique at New Braunfels Township, but for her it was because of her athletic ability. She was the star of every girl's sport at the school, including softball, basketball, soccer, track and field, and anything else. The only thing she didn't like to compete in was swimming, which she said she didn't want to do unless it was purely recreational.

Angela inherited a townhouse from her uncle when she was twenty-one. After a few months living alone, she decided to rent the other two rooms. She met Katie Leland and invited her to move in. A little later, the two of them met Vanna Steinman randomly at a bar and hit it off. They invited her to move in, too, so all three lived together in what I imagined was a crazy environment.

Brady, Calvin, and I went insane on guys' nights, but I couldn't begin to imagine what those three girls got into.

"Do you like the beer?" Angela asked.

I looked down at the case. "I do. I just hope you got one with cans, not bottles."

"She got cans," Katie said. "No worries."

Katie, twenty-three, was an Asian-American. Her father, Lucas, met her mother, Sue-Li, when he was on a mission trip in South Korea. They fell in love. Two years later, Lucas had all the paperwork finished to bring Sue-Li to the States so they could be married. They settled in a small town in Maryland and welcomed Katie three years later. She grew up there and stayed until she was nineteen, when she received a scholarship to Texas State and decided to go. She met Angela in a college-level math class one day, and they hit it off.

"Oh, good," I said. "Then nothing broke." I picked it up again. "I'll give the first one to Brady."

She grinned back. "Good choice."

Opening the door, I let the ladies in first. I found Brady, Calvin, and Callie in the living room watching reruns of *The Banshee Busters*.

"I'm back," I announced, "and I found beer."

Brady looked over and saw Angela had the remnants of banana cream on her face, making him snicker. "You look like you just gave a blow job."

Angela narrowed her eyes. "Maybe I did. He had a bunch of cream, and it tasted like bananas."

"What?" Vanna asked. "I thought it never changed taste. At least, the ones I knew didn't taste anything like bananas."

The others stared at her blankly, then she realized Angela meant the pie on her face and turned bright red. "Oh, my. Forget I said that."

Vanna Steinman was twenty-four and not a promiscuous woman. She'd been dating Brady for seven months.

They started the relationship without being virgins. Brady lost his when he was seventeen in a Port-a-Potty at the Texas State Fair. From my understanding, Vanna lost hers at the age of sixteen in a cemetery mausoleum. When Brady officially offered God his heart and his life at twenty-one, he promised himself and God not to have sex until he married. As far as I knew, he kept that promise, but if he backslid, all he had to do was ask God's forgiveness.

Vanna was a huge sweetheart. I was glad she was dating my best friend, especially after his ex, who'd been a total bitch.

"Oh, Honey, that made you sound like such a ho," Brady said. "I love you, anyway."

Vanna stared daggers at him. "Watch yourself, Mister."

The three girls noticed the new girl in the room.

"Who's the blonde hottie?" Angela asked.

Callie laughed. "I'm Callie, one of Ben's best friends from Minnesota."

"How curious." Katie studied Callie, then me. "You two would make an amazing couple, since you're both so incredibly hot."

"Funny you should say that." Callie walked over to me. "There's actually something I've wanted to say to him since we reunited earlier, but I've been a bit too afraid to say it until now."

She took my hands in hers and got down on one knee.

Calvin squealed with excitement. "Oh, my God! She's going to propose!"

Callie looked into my eyes. "You've been my best friend since we met at summer camp when we were eight-years old. When you turned thirteen, and the whole 'boys have cooties' thing wore off, I started seeing you in a different light. My feelings for you came to a head at fourteen, and I haven't stopped thinking about you since you moved."

She took a deep breath and dropped the bomb on me. "Now that we're reunited after all this time, I want to ask...will you take our friendship to the next level and be my boyfriend?"

I was so shocked, I couldn't speak for a few seconds. I wasn't expecting anyone to reveal feelings for me, let alone Callie. I quickly went through the list of pros and cons before replying.

The pros were:

I'd known her for years

I knew she wouldn't turn into another Leona

We'd been out of contact for a while, so things wouldn't be too awkward if it didn't work out

Regardless of how it worked out, I'd either have a great girlfriend or be reunited with my best friend after ten years.

I couldn't think of any cons.

"Yes," I said.

Callie's eyes lit up, and she jumped into my arms. The others acted like we'd just become engaged.

"Our baby boy got himself a girl," Brady joked to Calvin.

I chuckled when I heard that. Callie eventually released me, and Brady gave me a bear hug.

If that was how my friends reacted to my having a girlfriend, I was interested to see what they'd do whenever I got engaged. Knowing them, it would be that times a hundred thousand.

"I have some news for you."

I went to Gold's gym to work out with my personal trainer and good friend Randy Uno. We didn't get much chance to talk when we went through our workout, so I waited until we were unwinding in the sauna afterward to tell him about Callie.

He glanced at me. "What's up?"

I met Randy when I needed a workout partner. For a while, I worked out with Spike Ramirez doing P90X and Insanity videos at his place until he was deployed for the Army. He still wrote to me occasionally to update me on his situation, but that was another story.

Brady's preferred workout method was jogging, which we sometimes did as our bro time. I needed a partner who could do more than jog, which was where Randy came in. I went to Gold's Gym one day looking for a personal trainer, and he was the only one available at the time. I explained my situation, and he agreed to help. We became close enough that we sometimes had sessions at his house, but that was on his days off.

I took a deep breath. "Well, I got a girlfriend."

"Shut the front door! Really?" He grinned. "That's awesome, Bro. What's her name?"

"Callie. She's my best childhood friend from back in Minnesota. I ran into her yesterday at the zoo."

"Good deal. At least you know she won't be another Leona."

"That's one of the main reasons I agreed to take the next step."

Randy looked at me. "You mean you agreed to go out with her?"

I nodded.

"Baller, Dude." He raised his fist, and we bumped fists with a grin.

When our time was up, we tied towels around our waists and headed to the locker room to dress. While I was pulling on my shorts, my phone rang inside my locker. I opened it and checked the caller ID, then I grinned and decided to mess with the person.

I slid out the keypad to answer and spoke in Mrs. Doubtfire's voice, "Helllooooo?"

"Hello? Who's this?"

"Mrs. Doubtfire. Hooo, did I miss anything?"

"Uh...."

"I'm sorry, Dear. I'm melting like a Sno-Cone in Phoenix. Would you like me to get Danny for you?"

Randy gave me a weird look. I winked to let him know I was messing with the caller.

"You're so weird, Mrs. Doubtfire."

"Thank you, Dear." I couldn't keep up the charade and broke up laughing. "I'm just messing with you. What's up?"

"My sister heard we're dating," Callie said. "She's planning a small party to celebrate. Can you come over?"

"Sure thing. See you soon."

I hung up.

"Who was it?" Randy asked.

"It was Callie. Her sister heard about us taking the next step and is so excited, she's throwing a tiny party for us."

"How exciting."

We dressed and walked to our cars, where I held out my hand. "Thanks for the workout, Bro. It really kicked my ass, but I needed it."

Randy, grinning, gave me a bro shake. "No prob, Man. See you next week at my place for our next workout."

"It might actually be sooner. If you're down for hanging this weekend with Calvin and me, that'd be fun."

"I'd like that." He climbed into his Honda Civic. "I'll keep you updated."

"Sounds great." I got into my Mitsubishi Eclipse, rolled down the top, and drove toward Callie's place for our impromptu party.

2

Callie lived with her older sister Sierra and her brother-in-law, Calvin Harrison. I met Sierra a couple of times in Minnesota, but she moved to Austin, Texas, two years before I moved to New Braunfels. She met Calvin during a night out with her girlfriends. They started dating, and three years later, they married. Having children wasn't high on their priority list at the moment, but they were open to the idea later.

Their house was a quaint, two-story ranch with canary-yellow siding and sky-blue window shutters. A cobblestone walkway led to the wooden porch, which had an off-white wraparound rail. A porch swing sat on the left, and two rocking chairs occupied the right. Various rose bushes lined the walkway, planted by Sierra to make the place look and feel more like home.

I pulled up to the house, got out of my car, went to the door, and rang the bell. A thin guy who wasn't very ripped answered. He looked in his late twenties or early thirties, with short, light-brown hair, a small beard, dark-blue eyes, and bright-green pajama pants.

He gave me a once-over and stared at me, waiting.

"Hi," I said. "I'm looking for Callie."

"Boy, state your name and occupation!" He put me in a headlock.

"Uhhh.... Ben Becker, zookeeper and paranormal investigator."

Callie walked into the living room. "Calvin, what on Earth are you doing? Let my boyfriend go."

He took another look at me. "Oh, so you're the boyfriend." He released me and brushed me off a bit. "Sorry about that. I'm a bit protective of my baby sister-in-law."

When he offered his hand, he said, "Calvin Harrison. Hope I didn't rough you up too badly."

I grinned and shook his hand. "No worries. I'll just assume it was all in good fun."

"It was. Come and take a load off, why don't you?"

I kicked off my sandals, went to the sofa, and sat beside Callie. Calvin sat on a maroon recliner.

Five minutes later, a woman walked in from the kitchen, wiping her hands on a towel. She wore a pink sports bra, gray sweatpants, glasses, and had her black hair in a low ponytail.

When she saw me, she looked me over and asked, "Ben? Wow, is that really you?"

"It is." I chuckled. "You're Sierra?"

"Nice to know you remember me, but damn, you look different now."

"Is that good or bad?"

"Obviously good. You're so ripped." She paused for a second. "All right, what say we get this party underway?"

We agreed that was a good idea, so we followed her into the kitchen to get the food she prepared. I saw hamburgers, hot dogs, brats, and assortment of chips, fruit salad, Jell-O with fruit in it, pistachio salad, and a variety of sodas and beers. I decided to start light and got a burger, a small bag of Sun Chips, a spoonful of Jell-O, and a can of Mountain Dew.

I sat at their dining room table when my phone vibrated in my pocket. Checking the ID, I saw it was my cousin, Lindsey Carmichael, so I slid the keypad to answer.

"Hey, Cuz," I said.

"Hey, you. How goes it?"

Lindsey, better known by her stage name of Liberty Belle, was my cousin. Born in Nebraska, she decided to take a shot at stardom right after graduating from high school. She moved to LA and lived with our grandmother while working as a waitress until she landed a role.

After a couple failed auditions and a few promises with no callbacks, she landed the lead role of Sidney Ramirez in the romantic comedy, *Ain't No Mountain High* when she was twenty. Her strong suit was romantic comedies, but she also appeared in different genres, most recently in a psychological horror film called *Paranoia.*

She was in the middle of a production of a slasher film called *Coulrophobia.* All I knew about it was it was set in an abandoned carnival, where seven strangers had to learn to work together to outrun and outwit an unknown killer clown hell-bent on murdering them all.

Even though I was related to a celebrity, it didn't mean I got Hollywood insider information. Many times, I didn't particularly want it. I would rather see a movie in the theater when it was finished like a normal person. If it was insider info on celebrity gossip or drama, I was all for it, as was Katie. She was the group's celebrity gossip queen.

"It goes well. How about you?" I asked.

"About the same. We're taking five on the set of *Coulrophobia,* so I thought I'd call and see how my favorite cousin is doing."

"Neat. Now that I have you, I have some news."

"Oooh, I love news! Dish."

"Well, I have a girlfriend now."

"Aaah!" she said. "Congratulations. I'm so excited for you. Give me the details. What's her name?"

"Callie. She was my best friend back in Minnesota, but I ran into her in Texas yesterday after not seeing her for ten years."

"Oh, my God, I'm so happy for you. I have to know what she looks like."

Callie sat beside me, and that gave me an idea.

"How much time do you have before you go back to the set?"

"About ten minutes. Why?"

"It just so happens that the new lady is right here." I poked Callie's arm playfully. "If I could FaceTime you, you can meet her and see what she looks like."

"That sounds wonderful. I'll talk to you again in a bit."

I hung up and pulled up FaceTime.

"Who is it?" Callie asked.

I glanced at her and grinned. "You'll see."

I connected with Liberty on FaceTime and made sure Callie couldn't see the screen to keep it a surprise.

Liberty answered right away. "Yoo-hoo."

"Hey, again. I have the girl right here."

I turned the phone around, so Callie could see. The color drained from her face, and she began babbling.

"Buh...buh...you...you're...."

Liberty grinned. "Nice to see you're a fan. So you're the new girlfriend Ben's talking about?"

Callie nodded slowly.

"Let me tell you, you're gorgeous." She pointed at Callie through the phone. "Be sure to treat my cousin right."

"No worries there." Callie chuckled.

"Good to hear." Liberty smiled. "It's very nice to meet you."

"You, too."

"Yo, Cuz? Let me see your face."

I turned the phone back to me. "What's up?"

"The director's calling for me to get back on the set. I have to be going. It was nice to hear from you again, and your girlfriend is beautiful. Come see me sometime."

"I'd love that. I'll talk to Dad and figure that out." I waved to her. "Have fun filming."

"I will." She laughed.

I disconnected and started eating my burger like it was no big deal. Callie was still in shock.

"You're eating like nothing huge just happened."

"Yeah?"

"You just talked to Liberty Bell, the actress. She's in movies!"

"She's also my cousin. I was close with her before she blew up in Hollywood."

"Wait. Liberty's your cousin? How come you didn't tell me before?"

"I didn't think it was super relevant. She got famous when she was twenty. By that time, I was here. Plus, before then, she wasn't able to visit often."

"That makes sense."

Calvin rushed into the room a few seconds later. "Did I just hear someone mention Liberty Belle?"

"Maybe." Callie sipped her Diet Coke. "Ben was talking to her over FaceTime."

Calvin's jaw dropped. "Son of a whore! And you didn't tell me?"

"Why does it matter so much?" Callie asked.

"I'm her number-one fan. You should have gotten me, so I could say something to her."

"She had only ten minutes," I said. "She's filming *Coulrophobia,* and the director called her back to the set."

"Lame." He sat across from me and Callie, taking a bite from his brat and wearing a really confused expression. "Dude, how do you know the hottest actress in Hollywood?" he asked.

I shrugged. "She's my cousin."

"How curious."

.

The party continued until 11:00 and consisted of a couple games of Corn Hole, with guys against girls, a couple drinks, and more sitting around and chatting, letting Calvin get to know me better. I went home and noticed the driveway was devoid of cars when I arrived. Brady must be at work, and Calvin was probably out with friends, so I could get straight to bed easier.

I unlocked the door, stepped inside, turned on the lights, and locked the door behind me. I saw a note on the dry erase board beside the door, so I kicked off my sandals, as I read the message.

Hey, Ben,

I'm going out with some friends. If I don't come back tonight, I'll be sleeping off the drinks at one of their places. Either way, I'll see you in the morning.

Love you, Bro,
Calvin

That answered that question. I noticed Brady's work schedule beside the board and read it. He was working that night and wouldn't get off until two o'clock the next morning.

As long as they weren't being scandalous, I was good with that, but even if they were, I wouldn't have cared. I would still love them if they slept with every girl in the greater San Antonio area. It would guarantee they'd be stuck with certain diseases for the rest of their lives, but if that was what they wanted to do, who was I to judge?

I went to my room, put on my favorite pair of Pittsburgh Pirates pajama bottoms, and climbed into bed. I was asleep in five minutes, probably due to the beer I drank at Calvin and Sierra's.

I didn't wake up until my alarm went off at 9:15 the following morning. I sat up slowly, stretched, and got out of bed, walking to the kitchen. Brady was at the stove making something for breakfast. Seeing me walk in, he winked.

"Morning, Bro. Good to see you awake."

I took a bowl down from a cupboard. "Same to you, Man. How was work last night?"

"It was to be expected." He flipped his eggs over. "Most of the customers acted like decent human beings and left fair tips.

Throughout the night, I always get that one special customer I'd love to impale through a fence post."

I took my box of Crispix and a half gallon of whole milk from the fridge. "Oh, dear God. What happened this time?"

"This one woman came in with her hopefully-by-now ex-boyfriend. She complained about everything, from the fact that we didn't have an entire bar's selection of drinks to choose from to how we weren't a vegetarian restaurant." He flipped the eggs again. "I pointed out that we have a veggie burger on the menu, and she said it wasn't good enough for her."

"Wow." I added milk to my bowl. "She sounds super high maintenance."

"Tell me about it. Not only that, but it was deadly obvious the guy with her was super embarrassed by her horrible behavior. The only good thing was, he left me a $100 tip and a note of apology."

He flipped his eggs once more. "I appreciated what he did, but it didn't change the fact that I still wanted to impale her on a fence post."

I wasn't a supporter of violence against females and would never physically lash out at one, but I would be lying if I said I never considered it, even as bad as it sounded. I dealt with a ton of disrespect from women in my life, and I was only human. My patience ran thin sometimes.

Brady slid his eggs onto a plate and brought them to the dining table. After adding salt, he scooped up a forkful and ate. "You talk to Calvin lately?"

"Yeah. He said he was going out last night with some friends." I took a bite of my Crispix. "If he didn't come home last night, he said he'd be sleeping off the alcohol at someone else's place."

Two minutes later, Calvin walked in the door wearing a black undershirt, red-and-black basketball shorts, and he looked a mess. He was missing a shoe, the left strap of his undershirt was torn, and there were huge bags under his eyes, as if he hadn't slept.

Brady and I stared at him for a few minutes before I spoke.

"Dude, what happened?" I asked. "You look like you've been through hell and back."

He sighed. "Last night was rough."

"I can see that. Want to talk about it?"

"Yeah, if you've got the time." He motioned me to follow him into the other room.

I quickly washed out my bowl and went to Calvin's bedroom. He closed the door and indicated I should sit on his gaming chair.

"What's going on?" I asked.

He took a deep breath. "I screwed up badly. I had too much to drink, and I don't remember anything about last night. It's like one minute I was at All the King's Women with my buddies, having a good time, and the next, I woke up in bed with my best friend's girlfriend."

I stared blankly at him. "Dude, you didn't."

Calvin nodded slowly. "According to her, I did."

"So that's why your shirts are torn and you have bags under your eyes?"

"Yeah, except those aren't bags. Garrett and I got into a bad fist fight. He gave me two black eyes."

"It's safe to assume you two aren't friends anymore?"

"I guess. He wouldn't hear what I had to say or accept my apologies. He doesn't care that I regret what happened." He looked into my eyes. "I know you're good at Godly advice, so how should I go forward from here?"

I leaned back and folded my hands on my chest. "Honestly, there isn't much you can do about sleeping with Garrett's girlfriend. It happened. It's in the past, and I believe you regret it. All I can say is that even though Garrett won't forgive you, God will. That's what matters in the long run."

I thought for a minute. "You're guaranteed to get into Heaven, because you choose to believe. You've accepted God and Jesus into your heart, and you live by Their Word and law. The fact that your ex-best friend won't forgive you won't bar you from eternal happiness. God loves you regardless of the bad choices you make. If you ask for forgiveness, He'll give it to you.

"The other thing is that Garrett will hold onto this for a while. If he doesn't let it go, it'll end up hurting him. Let that be his drama and his problem. You tried explaining your side. He doesn't want to listen, so that's on him. All you have to do now is ask God for mercy and move on, plain and simple."

Calvin smiled. "Thanks, Man. It really helps to hear you say that."

"Absolutely, Bud. That's not biased advice just because we're close. That's what my mentor, Zach, taught me. I figured it was a good time to share his wisdom with you."

Zach Kinsinger, thirty-three, was the mentor I met with every Thursday night. We first met when I was twenty-one and on the verge of suicide. God saved me from making a life-ending mistake and led me to Zach. We talked a little bit after church one day, and he asked if I'd be interested in meeting again for coffee. I agree, and we set up a time for the following Thursday. We'd been meeting ever since.

I struggled to get out of Calvin's chair. It sat lower than I expected, and I realized I couldn't do it, so I held out my hand. "Help me up?"

Calvin, chuckling, pulled me to my feet and gave me a big hug, something I loved. Hugs were one of my top love languages, along with quality time and words of affirmation.

"Thanks again for being there for me, Man," he said.

"You got it, Bro." I held him for a moment. "You can come to me with anything."

I released him, patted his back, and walked into the kitchen.

Brady washed his plate in the sink and looked up at me. "Everything good?"

"Yeah. Seems to be. Calvin needed a little advice on a huge issue he's dealing with."

"Ah. Well, that's good."

I'd known Brady for eight years, and I knew when something was bothering him. Even the slightest change in his voice gave it away. The way he just replied made it clear something was up.

"What's going on?" I asked.

"It's nothing, really."

"Bro, we've been best friends for eight years. I know when something's bothering you."

He sighed. "All right. Fine. I'm feeling a little left out. That's all. It seems like Calvin always asks you for advice. No one ever asks me, and I guess that bothers me."

"That's what it is? All right. Let me be honest with you."

I sat at the table and motioned him to sit across from me. "Calvin asks me for advice, because I've been a Christ-follower my entire life. I give him spiritual, Godly advice. You know I love you, but you've admitted you aren't the best with advice. If you're worried about our friendship falling apart, let me be the first to say you shouldn't."

I showed him the scar on my palm. "See this? That's from the day we did that ritual. I don't do that with anyone I don't care deeply about."

The day we moved in together, Brady and I thought it would be neat to become blood brothers. He took a steak knife from our cutlery drawer, made a small slit in his palm, and handed the knife to me. I did the same, then we held hands, letting our blood mingle.

It might sound weird and gross, but it brought us to a level that surpassed friendship. Given that neither of us had STDs to worry about, I felt it was a success.

Brady smiled. "I know, Man. I just want to be some kind of help."

"You are. Just being there for us helps me more than you can imagine."

"That actually makes me feel better."

His phone buzzed on the table, and a quick glance showed Vanna's picture on it.

"Oooh," he said. "My girlfriend is calling." He stood and walked toward the next room. "Thanks again for your help, Bro."

Job well done, I thought.

My watch showed 11:30. There was nothing to do but go for a jog. I went to my room, changed out of my Pirates PJ bottoms, slipped on a pair of dark-blue running shorts, a black runner's top, and my white Nikes.

Walking back out through the living room, I saw Calvin on the couch, watching Jerry Springer. I grabbed my sunglasses from the ceramic bowl I kept on a shelf near the front door and put them on over my glasses. "I'll be back, Bro. I'm heading for a jog."

"Sounds good. Maybe we can hang this afternoon if you don't have anything going on."

"I'd like that. See you soon." I closed the door, scrolled to my jogging playlist on my iPhone, and took off.

"I've got the eye of the tiger, a fighter, dancin' through the fire, 'cause I'm a champion, and you're going to hear me roar...."

Katy Perry serenaded me during my jog. I loved jogging to upbeat music, because I could match my strides to the beat in her songs.

She needed to write more music. That would give me more songs to run with, plus I loved her stuff. She was incredibly hot, too, but that was another story.

At the halfway mark was a park bench by a lake two miles from my house. I walked to the bench and decided to people watch for a bit and catch my breath.

My attention went to a couple walking by with a yellow lab. The dog pulled, trying to reach me, but the girl kept pulling it back. The dog persisted, and she finally had to let it go. It ran over to me and jumped up, licking my face. I laughed and stroked its back.

"What a silly pooch," I gasped. "Is it a boy or a girl?"

"It's a girl," the guy said. "Her name is Honeydew."

"That's a cute name. I have a black lab named Rocketeer. She's my whole world," I said.

"That's awesome, Dude. Labs are the best."

"They sure are."

"We have to get going." He coaxed Honeydew away, and she went with them. The couple waved as they left.

"Have a good one," he said, jogging away.

"You, too, Man." I leaned back on the bench and resumed watching people.

Carson, a friend, came up and said, "Hey, Bro. Anyone sitting here?"

"Nope. You want it, go for it."

He sat down and started people watching with me. After a bit, his glance went toward me.

"What do you have going on tonight?" he asked.

Carson Wright was twenty-four. I met him three years earlier when he was dating McKensie Mallard, a friend of mine, before she moved to San Diego to get into the entertainment industry. She had a thing for Black guys, and they were pretty strong for a year and a half, then she moved. They tried to keep a long-distance thing going, but four months along, Carson found out she slept with a guy she met at a vocal audition for a record company.

He decided stepping out once was one time too many and broke off the relationship. Along with McKensie, he cut out many of her friends, but thankfully kept me around. Our friendship grew stronger ever since.

"I was planning on hanging out with Calvin," I said. "Don't know exactly what we're doing, but maybe we can make it a guy's night if you want to come along."

"I'd love that."

"Very good." I glanced at my phone and saw it was 12:45, time to get moving. I stood up. "I'm heading back home. You want to come along? We can start our guy's night a little early."

"Sounds good to me. Let's do it."

We jogged back to the Bromance Bungalow with Carson talking about different things along the way. When we came up the driveway, I saw Calvin's white Ford Escape was there, but Brady's maroon Mazda 6 wasn't. Either he was cavorting with Vanna, or he was called in to work early.

I stepped inside with Carson, put my sunglasses in the bowl on the shelf, and walked into the living room. Calvin was on the couch, playing Grand Theft Auto 5, running around and shooting random people, trying to steal cars.

"Having fun?" I asked.

He glanced back at me. "Yeah, Man. I'm pretending every person I kill is Garrett." He zoomed in with his pistol and shot a man in the face. "Helps me get over what happened faster, and it's legal."

Carson glanced at me. "What's he talking about?"

"Very long story." I looked at Calvin. "How does day-drinking sound?"

"Oh, God, Bro. I thought you'd never ask." He turned off the Xbox One. "I need it after the shit I've been through."

I grabbed the eighteen-bottle case of Bud from the fridge and set it on the counter. All three of us took a bottle and walked to the patio to chill under the umbrella table. We talked about life. While Calvin explained to Carson what happened with him and Garrett, my phone buzzed.

I checked the caller ID and saw it was Jason. Standing, I said, "I'll be right back."

I walked into the house. "Hey, Brotato Chip."

"Yo, Brofessor. What's new?"

Jason Lancaster was a singer-songwriter best known for his country/pop crossover *California Cruisin'*. He also was dating Liberty Belle, which was how I met and became close with him.

A year earlier, my dad, sisters, and I flew to LA to be with Liberty for a week, and Jason took me out for a guy's getaway for a day. We went to Inside-Out Burger, Sea World San Diego, and to the Hollywood sign, among other places, and we talked about guy things. He also laid out his plans to propose to Liberty within two years and asked me to be the best man at his wedding. Naturally, I agreed, and I promised not to tell Liberty.

"Just doing some day-drinking with my buddies," I said. "My roommate's going through a rough time, and we decided to start our guy's night a little early."

"Sounds like fun."

"It can be. What's going on with you?"

"Not a whole lot. Liberty's on set for a new movie, so I'm at the beach house, bored out of my mind."

I knew Jason and Liberty shared a beach house in Malibu.

"You're bored? How can you be bored? You have half of Hollywood on speed dial. I'm sure you can find someone to do fun things with."

"I'm not sure it's that many." He laughed. "Besides, I'm content doing what I'm doing."

"What's that?"

"Watching some of her previous movies. I swear, she should've at least gotten an Oscar nomination for *Paranoia*. Her performance was incredible."

That was the first psychological horror film Liberty did. She played Kristin Lansing, a woman who was stalked by her obsessed therapist. It did better than expected at the box office, and the critics praised her performance as truly believable, as if she'd been in that situation in real life.

It was released too late in the year to be considered for an Oscar nomination. That sucked, but Liberty had plenty of other opportunities to snag a nomination, and, hopefully, an Oscar.

"I'm on the highway to hell!" Calvin shouted on the patio.

"Oh, geez," I said. "My roommate's drunk already. I have to make sure he doesn't do anything stupid."

"Sounds good, Brotein. Hit me up sometime when you're free again."

"You got it, Man. Tell Liberty I said hi when you see her next."

"Will do."

I hung up and walked back onto the patio. Carson sat in his chair looking shocked, and Calvin's shirt lay on the lawn. When I glanced toward the fence, I saw the gate slightly ajar and frowned.

"Carson, what happened? Where's Calvin?"

"He got really drunk and decided to go find Garrett. Something about how he was going to kick his ass for the last time."

Great, I thought. That presented several problems. I didn't want Calvin to do that, but calling him wouldn't help. He probably didn't have his phone, anyway. If and when the cops caught him, he'd be charged with assault and public intoxication, and I'd have to bail him out of jail.

It was shaping up to be a fun day. There was nothing to do but wait for a phone call or a visit by a cop.

Carson and I went inside, started the Xbox, and played Halo online.

Two-and-a-half hours later, the doorbell rang. I went to answer and saw a police officer outside. His badge had the name Officer Persimmons on it.

"Can I help you?" I asked.

"Yes. Are you Benjamin Becker?"

"Yes, Sir. What's this about?"

"Your roommate, Mr. Calvin Brewster, listed you as an emergency contact should something happen to him. We need you to come to the station to bail him out."

I sighed. "All right. Give me a second." I stepped back to slip on my sandals and called my dad. "Hey, Dad, can you meet me at the police station downtown? I'll explain when you get there."

"Are you in trouble?"

"Not me. It's Calvin."

"That's still not good. I'll be there in twenty."

I hung up. "OK," I told the officer. "I'm ready to go."

Carson came to the doorway. "What's going on? Did they find Calvin?"

"Seems like it," I said. "I'll be back in an hour or so. Do me a huge favor and hold down the fort until I'm back."

"You got it, Dude." He gave me a thumbs-up.

I grinned. "Nice use of the Full House reference."

He was confused. "The fuck is Full House?"

I rode to the station in the patrol car. Dad met us there two minutes after the officer parked.

"What's going on, Son?" Dad asked.

"If I had to guess, I'd say Calvin got drunk, went looking for his ex-best friend Garrett, and tried to fight him in retaliation for what happened the other night."

The cop had a stunned expression. "That's exactly right. How on Earth did you know?"

I shrugged. "Lucky guess."

He clearly didn't believe that, but he must have felt I wasn't associated with the mistake Calvin made. He opened the station door for us. "Please follow me to the holding cells."

We walked down to the place where they held minor offenders awaiting quick bail.

Calvin saw me walk in with Dad and ran to the bars. "Dude, thank God you're here. Please help me."

"Don't worry, Man. We have it covered."

"How much is his bail?" Dad asked.

The officer studied a sheet of paper. "According to his arresting officer, he's charged with public intoxication, which carries a fine of $500 in Texas."

Dad wrote a check for $500, and the guard opened the cell.

"Mr. Brewster, you're free to go," the guard said.

Calvin walked slowly toward me, probably fearing I was mad. I wasn't. I'd never bailed anyone out before, but my dad did it for me several times when I was younger and was used to it.

We got into Dad's BMW, and he drove us home. Talk in the car was minimal, but, when Calvin and I got inside the house, he started talking like he couldn't stop.

"Dude, I'm so sorry. I hope you don't hate me. I didn't mean to drag you into that. I promise it'll never happen again. Please forgive me. I feel so awful...."

I raised my hand. "Bro, you're fine. We're fine. Everything's fine."

Carson walked into the room. "Hey, Dudes. Everything OK?"

"Yeah," I said, "everything's good. We got Calvin bailed out, and now we can resume the fun."

I looked at Calvin. "Good thing I didn't tell the cops about your threat to kick Garrett's ass again."

Texas law was screwed up. I could understand a felony if someone actually beat up another person, but apparently, even *threatening* to do it could be treated as a felony. Someone's life could be screwed up forever over a few words.

That was why it was better to beat up somebody than just threaten him. At least then, the consequences would be worth it. I didn't condone violence, so if anyone wanted to go through with a beating, he shouldn't complain to me.

"Let's get the guy time back on track," Carson said, walking to the couch. "There are people on Halo just waiting to lose."

I laughed. "How arrogant of you."

"Arrogant, my big black ass. Half those people suck. Almost like they never played Halo before."

"Oooh! Easy targets," Calvin said. "Count me in."

I set up the game for three of us and was ready to kick ass when my phone vibrated. I pulled it out and saw it was Brady. He texted to say he was with Vanna and then had to work from 5:00 to 1:30 and would spend the night with her.

Apparently, Angela and Katie were with Angela's visiting cousin, Faith Collins, and planned to sleep over at the Air B & B Faith rented.

I texted back, *Sounds good, Bro. don't do anything too scandalous.*

I'll try not to, he replied with a wink emoji, which meant he would definitely be doing something scandalous.

I just hoped it wouldn't end the way Calvin's failed night did.

The zoo has a fun thing for employee birthdays. We shut down the place early and had a party of the person's choice to celebrate. My birthday was May 1, which fell on a Sunday that year. Since we were already closed on weekends, we decided to hold it on April 29, a Friday. I thought a costume party sounded fun, so I chose that. All the employees were allowed to bring two guests if they wished. I would have loved to bring Brady, but Chili's always scheduled him on weekends.

The Earth was round, the sky was blue, and Brady always worked weekends. Despite that, he took the 30th and the 1st off to spend my actual birthday with me. He was a thoughtful friend.

Since Brady had to work, I asked Callie and Randy if they were down to go, and they agreed. I dressed as Calvin from *Calvin and Hobbes.* It wasn't easy. I dyed my hair golden blond with some temporary dye that would wash out in the shower, and I did the same to my facial hair, planning to be an older version of Calvin. I bought a red T-shirt, which was his signature shirt, put on black jean shorts, and borrowed Bianca's stuffed tiger that resembled Hobbes. One look in the mirror proved I looked damned good.

I posted a selfie on my personal Facebook page as well as my verified *Banshee Busters* fan page. I looked too good not to share it with the world.

I drove to Callie's house to pick her up an hour before the party, because she always took forever to get ready. I walked up the sidewalk and was ready to ring the bell when the door opened, and Sierra appeared.

She gave me a once-over. "Calvin and Hobbes. Nice."

"Why, thank you," I said with a grin. "Is Callie ready?"

"Almost. You can come in and wait for her if you like."

"Funky." I stepped inside and sat on the couch with Sierra.

Calvin walked into the room eating a slice of bacon pizza. "Yo, Bro." He looked at me quizzically. "Is that some kind of costume? What are you supposed to be, and where are your glasses?"

I grinned at him. "I'm Calvin from the Calvin and Hobbes comic, and I'm wearing contacts. I want to look the part."

"Looking good, Bro. I saw your post on Facebook. That picture has upward of 2,000 reactions, most of them *love* and *wow.*"

Banshee Busters had over 2,000,000 likes, so it wasn't surprising that one post could gather that many reactions in half an hour.

"OK," Callie called from the top of the stairs. "Who's ready to see me?"

That was fast.

"Let's see what you got," Sierra called back.

Two minutes later, Callie came into view wearing a dark-blue wig, white booty shorts, clear five-inch heels with pastel-pink trim, and a bra made to look like peppermints. She twirled once for us at the bottom of the stairs.

"Damn, Girl," Calvin said. "You look like Ben's one lucky son of a bitch."

We laughed, then she looked at me.

"Do you like it? I'm Katy Perry in that *California Gurls* video."

I promised myself and God to keep my virginity until I was married, but I sure was thinking about breaking it right then. Katy Perry was my favorite celebrity crush, and seeing my already hot girlfriend dress up as a famous woman I had a crush on made things very hard.

"I love it," I said. "If I wasn't holding onto my virginity until we're married, I'd plow you on the couch right now."

"Ben you're so silly." She giggled. "What are you dressed as?"

"I'm Calvin from my favorite comic strip."

"Oh, *Calvin and Hobbes!* I have to say, blond looks good on you."

"Why, thank you." I offered my hand. "Ready to go?"

"I think so." She clasped my hand, and I escorted her to my waiting Mitsubishi Eclipse.

Before Calvin closed the door behind us, he shouted, "Have fun, but not too much fun!"

I gave him a thumbs-up, as we climbed into the car, then I started the engine and drove to the party.

We reached the zoo twenty minutes before it was to start. Callie and I climbed out of the car and went to the entrance, where I flashed my badge to the security guard, explained Callie was one of my two guests, and that the second was probably on his way.

"Keep an eye out for a guy named Randy Uno," I said. "He's with me."

The guard nodded, and we walked into the visitor's HQ, where the main party would be held. The entire zoo was open for us, with different things in different areas. There was corn hole in the African Safari section near the giraffe enclosure, and different shops and food or drink stands were open, too.

My coworker and friend, Giovanni Polanski, walked up and hugged me. "Happy early birthday, Bro."

I laughed and returned the hug. "Thanks, Man. How'd you know I wasn't someone else?"

"You're the only one who would dress as a beloved comic strip character." He looked me up and down. "I must admit, the costume threw me off for a few seconds. You look like a completely different person."

"That's the point." I studied his costume. He wore a medium-length silver wig, silver muscle sleeveless vest, black-and-silver wrist bands, black stretch pants, silver boots, and a black mask over his mouth. He was Smoke from Mortal Kombat.

"You make one sexy Smoke."

I assumed he grinned, but I couldn't see his mouth.

"Thanks. You're the first person, besides my own guests, who know who I am."

A girl walked up who I assumed was one of his guests. She wore a one-piece emerald-green bathing suit partially split down the center and held together by lace, along with matching knee-high boots with three-inch heels, matching green gloves, and emerald-green cloth mask over her mouth, and a bright purple staff. Her back-length black hair was tied in a ponytail.

"What's up, Calvin?" she asked.

"Not much, Jade." I grinned at her, calling her by her character name, too.

Giovanni put his arm around her. "This is my sister, Traci. She's one of my guests."

Randy eventually arrived in a Scorpion costume, and soon, the party began.

After a couple hours, my phone vibrated. I checked and saw it was Dad. *How strange,* thought. *It must be important. I'd better see what's going on.*

I slid the keypad and asked, "What's going on, Dad?"

"Are you in the middle of anything right now?"

"Uh...a party for my birthday. Why?"

"You need to get on the Internet and check a credible news site. Something happened to Liberty."

Oh, dear. This could go one of two ways—either tragedy struck, or she finally got the Oscar nomination she deserved, I thought. "I'll check it out."

I hung up and quickly opened the browser on my phone. When I googled Liberty's name, I saw a headline on the first site that popped up that read, *Actress Liberty Belle Dead at 29*.

All I remembered after that was darkness.

4 █

I woke in my own bed. Looking around, I saw the time was 9:30 AM. The date was April 30.

What the hell? I wondered. *That was one messed-up dream, or was it? Did I black out from shock after hearing about Liberty's death?*

The only way to find out was to call my dad.

When he answered, I said, "Hey, Dad. I've got a question for you."

"Sure thing, Son. What's up?"

"What were you doing last night?"

"Um...I was having relations with a nice lady from my workplace."

"Ugh, Dad! I don't want to hear about that."

"Sorry. I was pulling your leg. I was playing poker with the guys. Why?"

"You didn't call to say Liberty died?"

"She died? What? Where'd you hear that?"

"You called to tell me to check a credible news source and said something happened to her."

"Son, I'd know if I did that. I assure you I didn't."

"All right. That's reassuring. I have to call Jason."

"OK. Just don't say anything about Liberty dying."

"I wasn't planning on it. Love you."

"Love you, too."

I hung up and dialed Jason.

"Hey, Brotein Shake," he said. "What's new?"

"Hey, not a lot. How are you and Liberty?"

"We're doing well. Just eating some breakfast before she heads off to wrap up filming on *Coulrophobia.* "

"Hi, Cuz," Liberty said.

"Hey, you. I just wanted to see how things are."

"They're good. Like Jason said, we're finally wrapping *Coulrophobia* today."

"Fun. I expect tickets to the première."

"For sure." She laughed. "I'll save some for you and the family."

"Yay, I'm special. I have to get going. I'll talk to you again soon."

"Sounds good, Man," Jason said. "Love you."

"I also love you," Liberty said.

"I love both of you. Talk to you soon."

I hung up and remained in bed for a few minutes, feeling totally confused. If Dad hadn't called to say Liberty died, and she was still alive, that meant it was a very screwed-up realistic dream. I never had a dream like that before.

Granted, I had some fucked-up dreams, like the one where I woke up on an operating table after a sex change. That one was so realistic, I had to make sure I was still a man when I woke.

I never had a dream about someone dying before. It shook me up. I got out of bed wearing only my favorite Pirates pajama bottoms and shuffled to the kitchen, where I found Brady making pancakes and bacon.

He smiled when he saw me. "Hey, Bro, how you doing?"

"I'm all right." I sat at the table. "I'm a little shaken up, though."

"Oh?" He flipped the pancakes and looked at me. "What happened?"

"I had a screwed-up dream about Liberty."

"Your actress cousin?"

"No, the Statue of Liberty. Seriously, it was my cousin."

"Hmmm. Was it screwed up the way your dream about the sex change was, or is it like the one where you were randomly shot by some female snipers in trees?"

"It's more like the second one, except it wasn't me who died."

"Who did?"

I gave him an *are you insane?* look and said, "Angela."

"No way." He moved bacon on the griddle. "That's kind of funny."

"Dude!"

"What?"

"You should not wish death on Angela. She's my best friend."

Brady shot me a weird look.

"My best *female* friend."

"That's what I thought you said."

"Anyway, I had a dream where I was at a costume party with Callie and Randy when my dad called. He said to check a credible news site, that something bad happened to Liberty. I got on my phone, googled her name, and saw a headline that said she was dead. I blacked out and woke up in bed."

"Hold up. A costume party? Where the hell was I?"

"Probably working, but that isn't the point. The point is, it was super realistic and scary."

"Because it was so realistic?"

I nodded. "I've had dreams that came true before, but they were unmemorable things, like when you and I were at Sweetie Pie's and you said something about Gina being a semen demon."

Gina Yates was one of his ex-girlfriends. She cheated on him with a random guy she met at a bar one night, so he dumped her the next day.

"She was, though," Brady said.

"Yes, I know, but now I'm scared this one might also come true. That would be a nightmare."

Brady slid pancakes onto a serving platter. "I don't know what to say. This is one of those situations where I really wish I could help. Now I feel bad."

"What are you talking about? You're helping by listening. That's what I need right now."

"That's refreshing. How do you feel about pancakes?"

"That sounds tasty. Maybe they'll get me past that horrid dream." I took a plate from the cabinet, grabbed some silverware from the drawer, and took the syrup from the fridge. I carried all that to the table, while Brady brought over pancakes and bacon.

I took two to start with and bit into the first one. "The fortunate thing right now is that Liberty's still alive. I talked to her and Jason this morning, and they said she'd be wrapping up *Coulrophobia* today."

"That's exciting." He bit into his first bacon strip. "I want tickets to the première."

I laughed. "She said she'd work on it."

"Very good. I look forward to it. Would you believe I've never been to a movie première like that in Los Angeles before?"

"I would, because I haven't, either. There's always a first time for everything. It's a wonderful place to visit, but not to live unless you're super rich."

I picked up my plate, took it to the sink to wash off, and placed it back in the cabinet. "I'm going for another jog. I need something to clear my mind."

"All right, Man. Love you. See you when you're back."

"Love you, Bro. Thanks for breakfast."

I changed out of my PJ bottoms into my neon-green basketball shorts, Pirates tank top, and blue Nikes. I set my playlist on the phone and headed out.

Thoughts flooded my mind, while the singers on my playlist flooded my ears with music. The main question was, what if? What if I had a *déjà vu* moment like before, and Liberty died? Should I say anything or let it go? If I didn't speak up, and it was true, how would I live with myself?

I didn't know what to do, so I looked at the heavens and asked God what He thought I should do. I asked for a sign.

I was lost in my thoughts and asking God for a favor when I stumbled over a pen. I walked back to pick it up and saw an inscription on the side that read *Matthew 6:34.* That was too ironic to brush off as a coincidence. I took the pen and continued my jog.

As soon as I got home, I pulled out my Bible and flipped it to Matthew 6:34. *Therefore do not worry about tomorrow, for tomorrow will worry about itself. Each day has enough trouble of its own.*

I smiled. That was God's way of telling me to let Him take care of it. Whatever happens would happen, and He had a plan either way.

Brady walked into the dining room while I was reading the Word. "Hey, Man, how you feeling?"

"A little better. I asked God for a sign in dealing with the whole dream debacle while I was jogging, and I got this." I took the pen from my pocket and showed it to him.

"Matthew 6:34? I wonder what that means?"

I showed him the Bible verse. "This."

He skimmed it and grinned. "Nice. There's your answer."

"I'd say so." I closed the Bible. "I have to say, it's rather comforting to get such an obvious sign so quickly."

My phone rang. I checked and saw it was a restricted number. It was my chance to mess with whoever was behind the call.

I slid out the keypad and asked, "Yes, would you like to purchase a pair of inflatable underpants?" using my best British accent.

The caller laughed too hard to say much. "Damn it, Ben, you messed up my prank!"

"You slut! You should have kept up with it."

"Hold on a second," I said. "Angela? Katie? Am I on speaker?"

"Tee-hee," Callie said. "Yes."

"Callie, what are you doing there?"

"Planning your birthday surprise for Sunday."

"How fun. Why are you calling?"

"We were wondering what you and the boys are doing tonight," Angela said.

"Well, let's see…. As far as I know, we're free. Why? What's up?"

"You should gather the boys and meet us at the Confetti Condo," Katie said.

"We thought it would be fun to make a weekend out of your birthday."

That was their nickname for their townhouse. We enjoyed naming things.

"OK. Let me get this straight. You're throwing me two different parties for the same occasion?"

After a few seconds of silence, I said, "That sounds like fun. We'll be there."

"Funky fresh," Angela said. "Be here at five-thirty."

I hung up, went to my room to change, and bumped into Calvin.

"Sorry, Bro." He picked up the gamer manual for GTA 5 he was reading. "I should have been more aware."

"It's all good, Dude. What are you doing tonight?"

"Nothing. Why?"

"The girls are having a weekend bash for my birthday, and they asked I gather you, Brady, Randy, and Carson to meet them at the Confetti Condo at five-thirty."

Calvin gave me a weird look. "The Confetti Condo?"

"It's what Angela, Katie, and Vanna named their place."

"Don't they live in a townhouse?"

"I don't know why they gave it that name. They just did."

"Girls are weird."

Some might argue that guys who called their house the Bromance Bungalow shouldn't talk about weird names for one's home, but that wasn't my problem.

"I'm going to dress," I said. "Try to get hold of Randy and Carson and tell them to get here as soon as possible."

"I'm on it." He pulled out his phone.

I went to my room and closed the door. I looked into my closet for a nice shirt, settling on a hot-pink tank top after two minutes. I put it on with a pair of stonewashed blue jeans, black sandals, and my bright white visor fitted backward. After debating about putting my contacts in or stick with my glasses, I chose the latter. They'd be easier to handle if I got drunk.

I knew I wouldn't lose my contacts easily, but I might forget I had them in and pass out, then I'd be taken to the hospital to have them surgically removed. That happened to my mother when I was younger. She didn't drink much, but she had contacts that got stuck once. It sounded like a terrible thing I didn't want to deal with.

I stepped out of the room and sat on the couch to wait for the others.

Brady came in carrying the mail. "What's going on, Man?"

"I'm waiting for Calvin to dress and for Randy and Carson to get here. We're going to Angela's place at five-thirty for my birthday weekend. Apparently, they're throwing the Saturday celebration."

"Sounds like fun. Whose car we taking?"

"Obviously not mine. I'm becoming an old man tomorrow, and I intend to drink until I can't feel feelings anymore."

"You're turning twenty-six."

"Thanks for the reminder."

The doorbell rang two minutes later. I walked over to open it and found Randy and Carson outside, both holding gifts. Randy's was in a light-blue bag, and Carson had a medium-sized box in neon-green wrapping paper.

"Happy birthday, Bro," Carson said.

I grinned. "Thanks, Guys. Come in."

They stepped inside and were ready to remove their shoes when I stopped them. "Calvin's supposed to be ready in a few minutes. As soon as he comes down, we're heading to the Confetti Condo."

"Confetti Condo?" Randy asked. "Is that a bar?"

"No. That's the nickname Angela, Katie, and Vanna gave their humble abode."

"Like you, Brady, and Calvin naming this place the Bromance Bungalow?"

"Yup."

"Don't they live in a townhouse?"

"They do. That's the confusing part."

Calvin came downstairs in a neon-yellow tank top, black basketball shorts, and white flip-flops. "I'm ready. Let's get this show on the road."

"Neat." I looked around. "Where's Brady?"

He walked into the room wearing nothing but forest-green boxers. When he saw the rest of us, he turned red. "Oops. pardon me, Fellas." He speed-walked to his room and shut the door.

Five minutes later, he joined us wearing a cobalt-blue Polo shirt, white slacks, and black sneakers. "That's more like it," he said.

"All right," I said, grinning. "We ready?"

The others nodded.

"Let's do this. Calvin, you're driving."

"Why me?"

"Because your car has the most room, and I sure as hell ain't driving. I'm planning to drink my liver into oblivion."

"Why?"

"I turn into an old man tomorrow."

"Since when is twenty-six old?" Randy asked. "You should drink yourself into oblivion when you turn thirty."

"I plan to." I grinned.

"All right," Calvin said. "Who's ready? Ben, you'll have to direct me. I've never been there before."

"You got it, Bro." I adjusted my visor. "Let's do it."

The Confetti Condo was a two-story townhouse in a nice neighborhood in San Antonio. Angela's great-uncle owned it at first, but, when he came down with terminal kidney cancer, he put in his will that Angela would get the townhouse, because she was his only niece. It was in poor shape when she inherited it, so her family hired a crew to do some renovations. The siding was painted crimson red, the sidewalk leading to the door was redone, the steps were rebuilt, and new carpeting was added to suit Angela's tastes.

We arrived at 5:20 and saw all the girls' cars were there. Callie's Chevy Aveo and Katelyn's silver Mazda 3 were parked on the street, while Angela's black Mustang, Katie's dark-blue Toyota Corolla, and Vanna's lime-green Ford Focus were in the driveway. After parking behind Callie's car, we walked to the door.

I knocked four times, and the latch clicked open. Angela peered at us through the slit.

"Password."

"Beg pardon?" I asked.

"Password."

"Slut," Brady said.

"Incorrect."

"Obviously." I elbowed his ribs.

"Angela, stop being a whore and let them in," a voice inside said.

"Bitch." She closed the latch, unlocked the door, and opened it. "Come in, Boys. Put your gifts on the table in the kitchen."

The five of us walked in, left our shoes at the front door, and made ourselves comfortable. Katie and Vanna brought out various beers for the occasion, and Callie set up a shots table. We each got a bottle of beer, and Brady gave a toast.

"To my best friend on his special day. Here's to eight years of friendship and a lifetime longer. Love you, Man."

They all drank to that.

"Let's do some shots," Angela suggested.

That quickly turned into body shots. I lost count of how many I did after I had five beers, two shots of straight vodka, and a shot of moonshine.

I was *not* a lightweight, but moonshine was very strong shit, and one shot could knock a guy on his ass.

According to everyone else, along with pictures Angela posted on Facebook and Twitter, I did a body shot off Callie first, then Calvin. Then Brady took one off me, as did Randy and Carson. Everyone did at least one body shot from me for my birthday.

It was kind of weird, since I was the one turning twenty-six, and everyone else benefited from it. One would think I should do body shots off them, which would have felt more like it was celebrating me, but my friends and I were oddballs. As long as they were having fun, that was what mattered.

They weren't normal body shots, either. Instead of pouring liquor into my belly button like usual, they decided I should take off my shirt and place a shot glass on my chest between my pecs. The others had to take a body shot with only their mouths.

They were weirdos, but that made them more endearing to me.

I woke up the following morning in a backyard flowerbed without my shirt and with a terrible hangover. If that was what twenty-six felt like, it sucked.

I stood up slowly, holding my head in pain. It pounded like a bass drum, and there was no way to relieve that without a ton of water and some aspirin. I had to look on the bright side. Brady ended up in a tree. At least when I woke up, I was on the ground.

I staggered into the kitchen and found Katie passed out on the floor before the dishwasher. I slowly opened the cabinet door, took out a big glass, and filled it with water.

"Hey, Bro," someone said behind me.

I choked on my water and turned to see Calvin standing there.

"Hangover?" he asked.

I nodded slowly. "You'd think I'd learn not to overdo it with the shots. This is what it gets me every fucking time."

I stared at him. He didn't seem hung over at all. "What gives? You don't have it as bad as the rest of us."

He grinned. "I've been drinking hardcore since I was eighteen. My body has a tolerance for alcohol."

He pulled out his phone. "Apparently, someone online gave you a birthday shout out."

"Really? Who?"

"A ton of your fans, for one. Your birthday is trending on Facebook, and TMZ wrote an article about you."

He gave me his phone. Pics from the party, mostly body shots, were posted on the site, and the article basically said, *Happy Birthday, Banshee Buster.*

That was nice, except for the fact it was a shot of Brady getting a body shot off me. People would think I was gay.

They included one of Callie doing the same thing, so maybe that would offset it. I decided I didn't give a shit either way.

I appreciated the birthday wishes from my online fans, but I had to turn off my phone after a while, because it was blowing up with Facebook notifications and tweets from people tagging me in birthday greetings.

That was why I missed my dad's urgent call.

The rest of the birthday played out nicely. I got a five-pack of shot glasses from Randy, a pack of sweatbands from Brady, and gift cards to various places from the others. I decided to use Callie's gift card to the Cheesecake Factory for a birthday double date with her, Brady, and Vanna to end the day.

While we were waiting for our cheesecake to be served, I turned on my phone again to see what happened. I had 150 notifications from Facebook, 200 tags on Twitter, and a voicemail from Dad. Maybe he wanted to wish me happy birthday, and, since the cheesecake hadn't arrived, I listened to it.

"Son, call me back as soon as you get this. It's Godzilla-level urgent."

That was a family code. Instead of saying something was important or rating it from 1-10, we rated things on a mythical creature scale. One was Chupacabra (most believable) to ten being Godzilla (no chance in hell it would happen in real life).

I immediately called him back.

"Ben. Thank God you called."

"Dad? What on Earth?"

"I can't tell you over the phone. Can you come to the house?"

"I guess. I'm with Callie, Brady, and Vanna."

"Bring them along. You'll need all the support you can get."

That didn't sound good. "All right. I'll be there soon."

Hanging up, I stared out the window in confusion. The only thing that snapped me out of it was when Callie said, "The cheesecake is here."

She tapped my shoulder and watched as I stared at my cheese-cake. "Are you all right?"

I looked at her. "Not really."

"I figured." She cut a chunk of her blueberry cheesecake with her fork. "You wouldn't ignore a slice of strawberry cheesecake unless something was bothering you, or something was physically preventing you from eating it."

I once sprained my ankle playing basketball in high school with Brady and two of our friends, Andreas Renner and Giovanni Samuels. That was the time when Christina Wilken, Dad's girlfriend, told us she made cheesecake for us. I put off going to the hospital to eat the cheesecake first. I was obsessed with it.

"What's the matter?" Brady asked.

"My dad called. He wants me to come to the house right away. He wouldn't say what it was, but he said it was extremely urgent and sounded worried and upset."

"Maybe we should get boxes for this and see what the deal is," Vanna suggested.

"That sounds like a good idea," Brady said.

He flagged down our waitress and asked for four to-go boxes. Once we boxed up the cheesecake and paid our bill, we left.

When we arrived, we found a bunch of cars parked on the side of the street beside my house, most of which I recognized as family. I thought it must be a surprise for my birthday, so I tried to get into the right mindset for being surprised.

The four of us came to the door. My Uncle Jon opened it before I could.

"Hey, Guys," he said. "Thanks for coming. Take a seat."

My sister, Bianca, and Cousin Rob scooted over to make room on the couch for me, so I sat there. Brady found a chair in the dining room and brought it to the living room. Vanna sat on the floor near our feet, and Callie stood behind me, her hands on my shoulders.

I looked around. "What's going on here?"

"Would you rather hear it from me, or do you want to hear it from the news?" Dad asked.

I shot him a quizzical look. "The news? What would I hear from the news that...?" *Dear God. Tell me something didn't happen to Liberty.*

Dad nodded to Cousin Reese, who turned on the TV. It was paused on a news segment featuring a brunette woman with brown eyes, an unbuttoned powder-blue blazer, and a maroon tank top sitting behind a desk.

"Good evening, America," she said. "This is a breaking news report. Actress Lindsey Carmichael, better known by her stage name Liberty Belle and best known for her breakout role in the romantic comedy *Ain't No Mountain High*, as well as her upcoming slasher film *Coulrophobia*, was found dead in the Malibu Beach house she shared with her boyfriend, singer/songwriter Jason Lancaster."

5

I put my head in my hands. "God, this can't be real."

"According to authorities, Lancaster discovered Belle's body the next morning and immediately alerted the police," the anchorwoman continued. "At the moment, it's being ruled as an accidental death. This is a developing story, and we'll keep viewers informed, as more details in the case arise."

Reese turned off the TV "There you have it."

Happy fucking birthday to me, I thought.

I was speechless for what felt like forever. I finally said, "This is a nightmare."

"I know," Dad said. "That's how it feels for all of us."

"No, literally." I looked into his eyes. "I had a nightmare that this happened last week. Don't you remember?"

"Oh, yes. I thought it wouldn't happen in real life, though."

"Neither did I."

Once my tears started, they wouldn't stop. Callie wrapped her arms around me from behind to comfort me. The rest of the night was spent with my family and Callie, Vanna, and Brady, all comforting each other and helping us through this unexpected tragedy.

I spent the next week in a fog. I couldn't concentrate on anything, and my depression was so bad, I called in to work twice to say I wouldn't be coming in. I gave them a not-feeling-well excuse, because I didn't want them to know the real reason.

Somehow, the animals knew how to make me feel better when I went through a rough spot, like when I first learned Leona was a whore. I dumped her as soon as I understood, held my head high, and went to work the following day. Every animal I tended that day sensed something was wrong and broke their routine of eating, sleeping, and going to the bathroom to make sure I felt better. Hobbes and Suzie, the zoo's Bengal tigers, turned into giant kitty cats and let me give them belly rubs while they purred with delight.

For some reason, petting an animal or spending time with one always made things better. The following Monday, I confronted my feelings head-on, put them aside, and went to work.

I went to the visitor's HQ to clock in, and our receptionist, Kari Clarkson, smiled warmly at me when I walked through the door.

"Hey, Ben. You feeling better?"

"As good as I ever will, I guess. Sorry about the last two days."

"No worries. You're one of our top zookeepers. As far as I know, you rarely miss a day. I'm just glad you're feeling good again."

"Me, too." I managed a smile, then I walked into the staff room, clocked in with my badge, and checked the day's schedule.

I didn't know how other zoos operated, but we had a whiteboard with all the animal exhibits on it. Each exhibit had a box beside it, and the zookeepers got to choose which animals they took care of each day. We switched things around, so the animals became accustomed to all of us, not just one specific person.

I studied the board for a minute and saw the crocodiles and lions were unaccounted for, among others. I checked the boxes beside those with a dry-erase marker and went to the exhibits to see what was needed.

The crocs were low on meat, while the lions needed more water. I made a mental note and went to the storage shed to pick up meat when I ran into Giovanni Polanski.

He grinned when he saw me. "Hey, Bro. we missed you last week. Everything OK?"

He wasn't just a coworker. He was a friend. We were close enough to see each other every day at work and still want to hang out together on weekends. Sometimes when I wasn't scheduled to work out with Randy at Gold's, I worked out with Giovanni.

We picked up where Spike left off when he was deployed to the Middle East. Gio, as I called him, preferred to keep his midnight-black hair buzzed short and his goatee neatly trimmed. Our workouts gave him an insanely chiseled chest and abs, and girls got lost in his dark-blue eyes. On top of that, he was a really nice guy, so it was hard to believe he was still single.

"On the outside I'm trying to make it all seem good, but in reality, my world is falling apart."

"That's no good. What's going on?"

I looked around to make sure we were alone. "I'll tell you, but you have to keep it quiet until I can tell everyone. It's too hard to face right now."

"Dude, you have my word."

"All right." I nodded. "Here it is." I took a deep breath. "You've heard the news by now, I'm sure."

"You mean about Liberty Belle's death?"

"Yeah."

"You're being hit hard by that?"

"You could say that."

"Was she an actress you loved?"

"Yes, but she was more than an actress to me."

"A friend?"

"My cousin."

He was silent for a moment. "Oh, my God, Bro. I'm so sorry. I really had no idea."

"It's all good, Man. That's why I don't want word getting around right now. If people find out I'm related to Hollywood royalty, they might view me differently. I want to keep things unaffected."

"Got it."

We worked in silence for a few beats.

"What are you up to after work?" he asked.

"Nothing. One roommate's working, and another has pre-planned sexy fun with his girlfriend. My lady isn't feeling well."

"Awesome. Then we're going to have fun."

"That sounds great. Meet me at my place around five-forty-five. We can figure out things then."

As I loaded a wheelbarrow with meat for the crocodiles, I thought over what happened. Liberty's death shook the nation, and it hit me especially hard, because she was my cousin. Jason was her would-be fiancé, and, if I was that torn up over her death, I couldn't imagine how he must be taking it.

I called him on my break. He answered on the fourth ring, obviously reeling from the news.

"Hello?" he asked in a shaky voice.

"Hey, Bro. It's Ben."

"Oh. Hey, Bud. How are you?"

"Heartbroken. The news is hitting me pretty hard. I just wanted to see how you're doing."

"Not good. I don't know what happened. Last thing I remember was saying good night to her. She said, 'I love you,' gave me a kiss, and went straight to sleep. Next thing I know, I walk into the bathroom and find her dead on the floor."

"That's what the reports said."

"It feels like someone stabbed me in the heart several times. Thanks for checking on me, Man. It means more than words can describe."

"Absolutely, Bro. You know I'm here for you."

"If you get some time off work, maybe you can come out to see me soon. Maybe spending time together in person can jump-start healing for both of us."

"I'd love that."

"Me, too, Bro. I have to get going. Thanks for checking on me. Seriously, it means a hell of a lot. I love you, Man."

"I love you, Bro. Take care. I'll see you sooner than later."

I hung up and sat in the break room for a couple more minutes, trying to process everything. While I was there, my boss, Rick Morrison, walked in.

"Hey, Ben," he said. "You OK?"

Rick, thirty-four, was the supervisor of the zookeepers. Our zoo had three types of employees: zookeepers, tour guides, and maintenance workers. Each group had its own boss, who were all under the orders of Chuck McAlister, the owner. Zoe McCarthy was the tour guides' boss, while Kevin Wright was in charge of the maintenance workers. I didn't know about Zoe or Kevin's managerial styles, but Rick was flexible. He was tough as nails when things needed to get done, but otherwise, he was more like a friend than a supervisor.

I glanced up at him. "Honestly, not really. I was hit with some unexpected news recently."

"Is that the news that your actress cousin died?"

I stared blankly at him. "Uh, yes. How'd you know?"

"It's on TMZ." He handed me his phone.

I studied the article. It shared the news that Liberty was found dead in her beach house, which I knew, but part of the story featured me. I was cofounder of the fairly popular syndicated TV series, *The Banshee Busters,* and someone at TMZ explained I was related to Liberty and added the news must be hitting me hard. They included a message to me, saying, "Our prayers are with Ben and his family in this difficult time." The story ended with the words, "RIP Liberty."

At least they used a good photo of me. The shout-out helped a bit.

"Why didn't you tell me about this?" Rick sat beside me.

I looked into his eyes. "How am I supposed to tell someone something like this? 'Hey, Everyone, here's some news. My famous cousin you didn't know I was related to just died.'" I shook my head. "That isn't happening."

"I'm sorry, Bud." He placed a hand on my shoulder. "If you need to take time off to grieve, don't be afraid to let me know."

"Thanks, Rick." I nodded.

"You got it. If you want, I can give you some paid vacation time. It's hard enough losing a loved one in any circumstances, but when it's someone famous like Liberty, the coverage will haunt you for weeks."

"Will it affect the paid time off I saved?"

"In most cases it would, but, since you rarely missed a day in the last eight years, and because this tragedy is especially difficult, I'll make an exception."

I stood slowly. "That'd actually help a lot. Thanks again, Man."

He offered his hand. "Take all the time you need. When you're ready to come back, we'll welcome you with open arms."

I smiled and shook his hand. "That means a lot to me. Thanks."

I clocked out and walked out of the visitor's HQ after saying good-bye to Kari. I got into my car and started the engine before texting Giovanni.

Hey, Bro,

Rick gave me extended time off to deal with the Liberty tragedy, so I'm headed out. Meet me at my place at the time we agreed, and we can still hang then.

I got home, parked in the garage, and went to the front door. When I put my key in the lock, I noticed two boxes and a bouquet of flowers beside the door. A nametag on the boxes showed they were addressed to me. A closer examination failed to find a return address.

I picked up both boxes and the flowers and brought them inside. My birthday hadn't been that long ago, so maybe they were late presents from a family member. Maybe it was a gift from a fan of my show. People sometimes sent gifts to us. I set the boxes on the coffee table and sat on the couch to open the first box.

"Bro, what are you doing home already?"

I turned to see Brady looking very confused.

"I thought you worked until five," he said.

"Normally, I do, but Rick gave me extended time off to deal with the death."

"Ah. That's nice of him. I can't imagine how hard it must be to face the news every day." He glanced at the packages. "What are those?"

"I don't know. They were sitting by the door, addressed to me."

I opened the first and found a framed poster inside with a letter. It was a promotional poster for *Coulrophobia*, Liberty's last movie before she died. The letter was from a fan of the series saying how sorry he was to hear about the tragedy my family faced and to remember the good times with Liberty while she was alive.

The flowers came from another fan and had a card that read, *Stay strong, Dude. Liberty's watching over you with love.*

The second box contained a steel sign I could hang in the house with the phrase, *Always on your mind, in your heart, and in your soul* engraved on it. Under it was a press photo of me with Liberty when she invited me to the première of *Paranoia*.

"That's sweet," Brady said. "The fans care enough to send you gifts to comfort you."

"That's nice of them, but how'd they get my address?"

I called my dad. "Dad, I have a question for you. I found two packages and a bouquet of flowers on my front porch a few minutes ago from fans of *The Banshee Busters*. I was wondering if you know how they got my home address."

"Of course, Son. They didn't get your address specifically. They knew you lived in San Antonio, and they sent the gifts to the Post Office. The postal workers did the rest."

"They can do that?" I asked, surprised.

"Apparently so."

"How weird." I stared at the gifts on the table. "I have to figure out where to put them."

"All right. Have fun with that."

I hung up and examined the steel sign. "Maybe this can go in my room. It would look nice above the headboard of my bed, almost like Liberty's watching over me."

"That's a nice thought." Brady lifted the vase of flowers. "Are these real?"

"Yes. Plastic blue roses with glitter actually grow in the wild. Real or not, it's the thought that counts."

"Good point. You mind if I put these on the dining room table? They'd make a good centerpiece and conversation starter."

I found a thumbtack in the kitchen's junk drawer. The sign came with a wire on the back for hanging. I walked to my room and held it to the wall to see if it looked good. Since it did, I put the tack in place and hung up the sign.

It comforted me, like a Native American dream catcher. My Native American side believed that dreams, good or bad, floated around at night. The dream catcher allowed good ones to fly past, but it caught the bad ones to keep them from bothering anyone.

Liberty's death was a nightmare, but having her picture in my room reminded me she was watching over me from Heaven.

I went to the kitchen to get some orange juice.

Brady sat at the table eating a BLT. "What do you have going on tonight?"

"Giovanni's coming by after he gets off." I took my carton of OJ from the fridge. "Don't know what we'll do yet, but I hope it involves drinking."

"Or strippers. They always make me feel better."

I grinned. "That would be fun."

Brady finished his sandwich and set his plate in the dishwasher. "I have to get ready for work."

"Already?" I looked at my watch. "It's barely past three."

"Yeah." Brady left the room. "I go in at four today."

I washed my glass and set it back in the cupboard, then I sat on the couch to play some Halo online while waiting for Giovanni to show up.

Brady came up behind me and wrapped his arms around my neck in a weird hug. "I'm off, Bro. Love you. Stay strong. Promise me you won't do anything dumb."

I grinned and patted his arm. "I promise. Love you, Man. Have fun at work."

He walked out the front door. Once I heard it click and lock in place, I turned on the Xbox to have some fun "pwning noobs," as it was called.

Around 5:15, my phone rang. I picked it up, expecting Giovanni to tell me he was on his way, but instead I got someone with a caller ID I didn't recognize.

My first thought was it was a prank or some advertising bullshit, so I let it ring. Two minutes later, my phone rang again with the same number. The person wasn't willing to give up, so I decided to be respectful until someone was rude to me. Then I'd unleash my alter ego, Kilabenjaro, on him.

That was a fun nickname I got from some coworkers at the zoo. It was a play off the name Kilimanjaro, the mountain in Tanzania. If someone pissed me off enough, they'd get to see me being an asshole, and I could guarantee he wouldn't like it

"Hello?" I asked cautiously.

"Oh, Ben. Thank God you answered."

I sat up quickly. "Jason?"

"The one and only."

"What's going on?" I was suddenly worried. "Why don't I know the number you're using? Are you all right?"

"No, I'm not all right. You don't recognize the number, because I'm using an LAPD phone, and you have to promise me you're sitting down before I tell you what's going on."

"I am. What's happening?"

He took a deep breath. "Well, there's been a break in the Liberty case."

"There was? Good!" I jumped up, excited. "Did they figure out her cause of death?"

"They did."

I was excited that I might get some closure. "What did they find?"

"You're still sitting down?"

"I sure am."

"All right." He sighed. "Her death wasn't an accident. It was murder, and I'm the prime suspect."

6

It was a good thing I was sitting down, because my legs turned to jelly. "You're kidding, right?"

"I wish I was, Bro. They found stab wounds on Liberty and snips of my hair at the scene of the crime." His voice cracked. "I don't know what to do. It was bad enough losing her. I can't believe they think I killed her."

"This is fucking ridiculous. I know you. You wouldn't hurt a damn fly, let alone my cousin."

"The cops are saying the only way I can get out of jail is if someone can testify about my character. No one in my family can come out and help."

His mother was at a work retreat in Belize, and his brother, Justin, was backpacking through the Andes Mountains. His sister, Kelsey, was studying abroad in Japan as part of a foreign-exchange program.

This is idiotic, I thought. *I can't let him rot in jail for a crime he didn't commit.*

I remembered that Rick gave me extended vacation time. I could fly to LA to help Jason. I might not be immediate family, but I knew him well enough to be able to testify that he wasn't capable of murder, especially against someone he loved.

"What about me?"

"What?"

"What about me? You're like a brother I never had, and we're close enough I can testify for you."

"That's a good idea. I pray you do it soon, though. Being in custody is a nightmare."

"I'll get a flight out of San Antonio as soon as possible. We'll get you out of there."

"Thanks, Bro. Hey, they're signaling for me to wrap this up. Please hurry."

"For sure, Man. I'll see you soon."

"I love you, Bro."

"I love *you*, Bro. Stay strong in there."

I hung up and sat on the couch in disbelief. It was bad enough I lost a cousin forever, but knowing someone had it out for her badly enough to kill her made me sick to my stomach.

The door clicked open five minutes later, and Giovanni walked in.

"Hey, Ben. You ready to have fun?"

He stopped short when he saw my expression. "Everything OK?"

I shook my head slowly. "There's been a break in Liberty's case."

"My God, that's awesome!" He sat beside me. "Must be nice to have some closure."

I sighed heavily. "I wish. The new development involves Jason being a prime suspect."

Gio was confused. "Prime suspect? I thought her death was accidental?"

"They thought so at first. New evidence came in showing she was murdered."

He was quiet for a few seconds. "Oh, my God, Dude. I'm so sorry. I had no idea."

I teared up. "I don't understand why someone would want to do that to her. It makes me sick."

He rubbed my back gently. "I wish I could say something to help, Bro."

"You're good, Man. Just being here helps a lot."

"We'll make you feel better. How does a visit to Wimbledon sound?"

Wimbledon wasn't just the biggest tennis tournament in the world. It also was the name of a kickass bar and grill in downtown San Antonio.

"It's worth a shot. If getting plastered won't cheer me up, I don't know what will."

He smiled. "That's the spirit."

Wimbledon really took after its namesake. The place was decked out in a tennis theme. The bar area had a marble floor made to resemble a clay tennis court, the dining room had green carpet like a regular court, the wait staff dressed like referees, the stools looked like tennis balls, and the bartenders dressed like tennis superstars.

They really went overboard with the layout, but, since the food was amazing and the drinks were great, I was able to let it slide.

Gio and I took two seats at the bar. As we were deciding what to order, a bartender who looked like Serena Williams came over.

"Hey, Guys," she said. "What can I get you?"

"I'll take a strawberry daiquiri to start," Gio said. "Give my friend here whatever will get him drunk the fastest. He's dealing with an unexpected tragedy."

"Oh? That's no fun." Her nametag read *Keyona*. She flipped the towel she held over her right shoulder. "It's a bartender's job to be a listening ear, so if you need, fire away."

I looked at her. "All right. I guess I could."

She gave me three separate shots of tequila, as I tried to figure out how to tell her what happened.

"I assume you heard about the whole Liberty Belle thing," I began.

"I sure did. It's impossible to avoid with all the coverage it's been getting."

I downed the first shot with the lime. "Yeah, well, that's the tragedy I'm dealing with."

"I see. Were you a huge fan of hers, and you're sad to see her dead?"

"Actually, I'm her cousin."

That brought silence for a few seconds. Few people outside my family knew how to react when they heard I was related to a murdered Hollywood actress.

"Wow. I'm so sorry to hear about that," Keyona said, setting up three more shots for me. "All these are on the house."

A second bartender, dressed like Maria Sharapova, came over and handed me a bottle of Coors. "This is from the man down the bar." She pointed toward him. "He recognized you from your TV show, *The Banshee Busters,* and wanted to buy his favorite ghost hunter a drink."

"You're the guy from the *Banshee Busters?*" Keyona asked. "I *love* that show. The time you and the gang explored that ax murder house is probably my favorite episode of all time."

The Villisca Ax Murder house in Villisca, Iowa, was one of the scariest investigations we did, apart from the live Halloween episode at Alcatraz and the time we went to Eastern State in Pennsylvania. We were rarely physically assaulted by the ghosts, but nearly all of us had at least one encounter in Villisca, with the only exception being Randy.

Something shoved Brady and me in separate occasions, Katie had her hair pulled, and Angela was dragged across the floor for three seconds. Why the ghosts targeted us specifically, I never knew. Some fans speculated online that I might have resembled the man suspected of committing the murders or that the girls resembled some of the victims, but it was all conjecture. We never figured out why it happened to us.

"Thank you," I said. "It's always nice to meet fans of our work."

Apparently, word spread fast. Once the guy at the end of the bar recognized me, the drinks kept coming. I wasn't complaining. The less I had to spend getting drunk, the better it would be for my finances.

It was one of the perks of being somewhat famous. Having a syndicated TV show with a dedicated fan base constituted at least a bit of fame.

The night ended at 2:30 the following morning, when Gio helped me into the car and then into the house once we got back. I stumbled into the kitchen with him and saw Brady at the dining room table, reading the latest issue of *People*.

"Look, Gio," I said, laughing drunkenly. "A kitchen person!"

Brady grinned. "This looks fun. He's hammered again."

"Does this happen often?" Giovanni asked.

"Not really. He doesn't drink all the time."

I wasn't paying attention and tried to fit a pot on my head. Grabbing a spatula from the drawer, I looked at it. "I'm a robot." I pointed it at him and said, "Bzzzrp!"

He grinned again. "Did you just shoot me with a spatula?"

"Yes," I slurred. "You shouldn't be able to walk anymore, on account of you're now a pile of human dust."

I blinked a few times, then burst out laughing. "Oh, my God! Bradley Cooper is in my kitchen!" I held out the spatula. "Will you sign my laser gun?"

I passed out on the kitchen floor.

I woke the following morning with my alarm going off at 9:30. There was no hangover, but I couldn't remember a damn thing from the previous night.

Either I was building a greater tolerance for alcohol, or I couldn't retain those memories for another reason. Maybe Brady could help jog my memory.

I found him at the kitchen table, eating an omelet and reading the newspaper. He looked up when I walked into the dining room.

"Good morning, Bro," he said. "Nice to see you sober."

That answered one question. "Dude, what happened last night? I don't feel hung over like I usually do after drinking."

"Good. That means you're building a tolerance to alcohol. As far as what happened, let's review the facts."

He pulled a scroll out from under the table. It looked like something people used in ancient times. That was going to be fun.

"You got super drunk at Wimbledon's due to people buying you a bunch of drinks, then you came back here with Giovanni at two-thirty in the morning." He studied the scroll. "You saw me sitting at the table, called me a 'kitchen person,' put a pot on your head, grabbed a spatula, and claimed you were a robot before you zapped me."

"Oh, dear. This sounds embarrassing."

"It gets better." He chuckled. "After blinking rapidly a couple times, you burst out laughing, claimed I was Bradley Cooper, asked me to sign your laser gun, and passed out on the floor."

It was humiliating, but at least it wasn't on video.

Brady helped up his phone. "I have it all on video."

Fuck me, I thought. "So I made an ass of myself?"

"You might see it that way. I found it hilarious."

"Well, whoop-de-doo." I sat across from him. "What do you have going on today?"

"Not a lot. I'll probably chill here for a while. Vanna got food poisoning after eating at Taco Bell, so I don't think she's up for much except vomiting and complaining she's dying."

"How interesting. I was thinking of calling a meeting this afternoon."

"For the Banshee Busters?"

"No, for something more important."

He narrowed his eyes. "What's more important than the Banshee Busters?"

I pulled out my phone. "You'll see this afternoon at one."

"Thank you all for coming on such short notice," I began.

Everyone gathered in the living room for the meeting I called, except for Vanna and Katie, although they were connected via FaceTime on our Smart TV. Vanna was still vomiting, and Katie stayed behind to care for her.

"What's up?" Katelyn asked. "It sounded urgent."

Katelyn Abraham was a girl Calvin was currently talking with. They weren't yet boyfriend and girlfriend, but they were on the way. I joked she was his "pre-girlfriend," which he seemed to dislike, given that he always replied, "Shut up, Dude" before tackling me. I felt he secretly liked it.

After the incident with Garrett and his girlfriend, Calvin started talking with Katelyn, so at least he wasn't considered to be cheating on her.

"I'm sure you've heard about Liberty's untimely death," I said.

"Yeah," Angela said. "It's impossible to ignore given all the press it's received."

"I heard the case has escalated from accidental death to murder," Katie said over FaceTime.

The room fell silent. She looked at us.

"The rest of you didn't know?" Katie asked.

"They do now," I said. "That's what this meeting is about."

I closed my eyes to regain my composure, and Brady went to the kitchen for a beer to calm my nerves. "Thanks, Bro. You're a good friend."

I popped the top and took a few swigs, then said, "I talked to Jason a few days ago. He was the first to tell me Liberty was murdered, and now he's the prime suspect."

"I heard that, too," Katie said.

"Dude!" Angela said from the couch. "Let Ben tell it."

"Anyway," I continued, "he's being held in police custody, because nobody can give a character testimony on his behalf."

"Why not?" Callie asked. "Doesn't he have a family?"

"Yes, but they aren't available," Katie said.

"Did you talk with Jason?" Angela asked, slowly getting annoyed.

"No, but I keep up with celebrity gossip," Katie said. "His mom's in Belize, his brother's somewhere in the Andes Mountains, and his sister's in Japan."

"Where's his dad?" Randy asked.

"He disappeared before Jason was born," Vanna said.

The rest of us stared at her.

"What?" she asked, shrugging. "Katie's not the only one who knows the private lives of celebrities."

"If everyone is done interrupting," I said, "I can get to the point of this meeting. I told Jason I won't let him stay in that horrid cell for another minute. The only way he can get out is if I give character testimony."

I took another swig of beer. "I'm flying out there within the month to help him out. He obviously didn't murder my cousin, and I plan to find out who did."

"If you go out there, I'm coming with you," Brady said. "I won't take no for an answer."

"Same here," Callie said. "If I didn't, I'd spend all my time worrying about you."

"I'd love to, but PNC won't give me time off on such short notice," Calvin said. "Besides, someone has to watch the house."

I hadn't planned to go alone. I doubted I could handle it without the emotional support of my friends. Once I knew who wanted to come with me, the only thing left was to talk to my dad and get the tickets. Maybe we could put the whole business to rest at last.

7 |

"I guess you know why we're here."

I visited my dad with Brady and Callie to discuss his buying tickets to get us to LA. The four of us sat in his living room, talking about how to get what we needed.

"I actually don't," Dad replied. "What's going on?"

"We need tickets to Los Angeles," Callie said. "We're going out to clear Jason's name from the murder charge."

"Hold on a second! What does Jason have to do with Liberty's death?"

"The fucking cops think he killed her," I said bluntly, "even though it's painfully obvious he'd never do anything like that to someone he loves."

Dad's face drained of all color. "That's terrible."

"I know. Apparently, he's in a holding cell, and those pigs won't release him until someone gives testimony about his character on his behalf."

"Doesn't he have family? Why can't they do it?"

"They're all out of the country for different reasons," Brady said. "At this point, Ben's the only shot Jason has at walking out as a free man."

Dad thought for a moment, then his expression lit up. He pulled out his phone and dialed a number. "I know how you kids can get there cheap."

He waited until someone answered. "Dave? It's Nick. It's time to cash in some of those favors you owe me." He listened for a few seconds. "As you probably know, Lindsey's boyfriend, Jason, is being held in police custody for her murder."

Another pause came. "Uh-huh. It's hard to miss given all the coverage the news networks have dedicated to the case. Anyway, there's no way he'll get out unless someone close to him gives a character testimony on his behalf. Ben's the only chance for that, so I need three plane tickets to LA for him and two of his friends."

I held up seven fingers.

Dad nodded. "Actually, make it ten. Can we give back the ones we don't need? Awesome. Thanks, Bro."

He hung up. "It's taken care of. You can go in and pick up as many tickets as you need at any time. He'll hold them for you."

"Very good. Thanks, Dad."

"Hold on a second," Callie said. "I'm confused. Are those tickets free?"

"How'd you swing that?" Brady asked. "I hear they're super expensive."

"Yeah," Callie added. "It was close to two thousand bucks round trip when we went there the last time."

In addition to the live Halloween special in Alcatraz, the six of us involved in the Banshee Busters investigated a couple other places in California, most notably a former reform school for boys in Ione, known to locals as Preston Castle. The flights were expensive. Fortunately, SyFy, our network, paid for our flight and hotel, so it all worked out.

"That was Ben's Uncle Dave," Dad explained. "Hence my calling him Bro." He leaned back in his recliner. "Dave was a wild child when we grew up. He went to a lot of parties, lost his virginity in the weirdest place, and had plenty of run-ins with the law. I was the one who always got him out of trouble and hid the things he did from our parents. He always said he owed me a favor for having his back. It seemed like now would be time to cash in."

"Now I have to ask," Brady said. "Where'd he lose his virginity?"

"Dude," I said, "that's an awkward question."

Dad grinned. "It's a funny story. When we were eighteen, Dave slept with his then girlfriend in an abandoned grain silo. My first time was with Ben's mother on a weight bench in a public gym after hours, God bless her soul."

I was mortified. My best friend was discussing lost virginities with my dad, for God's sake! I didn't want to hear about it.

The next day was my weekly workout with Randy. I went to his place, as we planned to do the Insanity workout video, which always kicked my ass. I wouldn't have the abs I did, though, without it.

"You ready to do this, Bro?" Randy asked, putting the DVD into his video player.

"Yeah, Man. Let's get it on." I stripped off my shirt and got psyched.

An hour later, I was in one of the two showers in Randy's house, washing off the sweat I created during Insanity. I walked upstairs and collapsed into an overstuffed chair in the living room, waiting for him.

I must've fallen asleep, because he woke me with an ice-cold bottle of Gatorade against my neck. I shot up and took the bottle away.

"You pass out again?" he asked, laughing.

"Yeah. Those workouts kick my ass." I grinned.

"True, but look at the bright side." He lifted his tank top to show off his eight-pack abs. "I got these by doing Insanity."

"That's a good point. Female visitors at the zoo find mine very sexy."

"So do females everywhere. Remember that time in Arizona?"

One of the first cases for the *Banshee Busters* as a new team with its current members was the Bird Cage Theater in Arizona. The day of the investigations, we liked to go around town, taking in the sights and mentally preparing ourselves for the walkthrough. It was common to be recognized and have people ask for our picture or autograph.

"I want to eat your spicy Italian sausage!" a girl shouted from across the street, making it one of the weirdest things that happened.

Admittedly, I had three Native American tribes in my background—Blackfoot, Cherokee, and Iroquois. As ashamed as I was to admit it, it took me a moment to realize she wasn't talking about food.

"Any updates on how we're getting to LA?" Randy asked.

"Yeah. My dad scored us free tickets to fly out in two weeks. All we have to do is pick them up at Twin Pines Travel Agency."

"Free?" He swigged from his PowerAde. "How'd your dad swing that?"

"My Uncle Dave. Apparently, Dad bailed him out a lot when they were kids. He felt it was the perfect opportunity to cash in on the favors he was promised."

"Nice. When do we pick them up?"

"First we have to see who's going. I know Brady and Callie are coming. I assumed you would come, too, but Calvin can't. Everyone else is up in the air."

My phone beeped with a text alert from Angela. *Dude, tell me when you're planning on going to LA. I know we're going to clear Jason of murder, but I need a vacation.*

I looked at Randy. "I guess Angela's in."

Two seconds later, my text tone played again. It was from Katie, though her message wasn't quite as desperate.

"That's Katie," I said.

Randy looked around. "Where?"

Confused, I looked at him.

"You said Katie's here."

"No, I meant she also wants to come to California with us."

"Oh." He leaned back in his chair. "You could've said that."

I always wondered if Katie and Angela had a psychic ability to know when someone was talking about them.

The next day, I took an informal census to find out who was going to LA and who would stay behind. Calvin wouldn't be able to get time off from PNC. Vanna opted to watch the house and tend the two cats the girls had. Katelyn had a family reunion in North Carolina she wanted to attend. Carson's ex, McKensie, lived in LA, and he worried he might run into her, even though it was a huge city and the chances were a couple million to one.

He didn't want to risk it, and I wasn't going to force him to do something he didn't want to do regardless how weird it seemed.

I went to the Twin Pines Agency with Brady and Callie to pick up our six tickets. We walked in, and I assumed I'd have to explain the situation to the lady up front I guessed was the secretary. I started telling her why we were there when a middle-aged guy with a blond buzz cut and Dad's overall physique walked up.

"Ben," he said, offering his hand. "Good to see you again."

I shook his hand. "You, too, Uncle Dave."

He noticed my friends standing behind me. "These are your friends?"

"Sure are. We're here for the tickets."

"Oh, yes. Your father called about those. Follow me to my desk, and I'll get them for you."

We walked back to Dave's cubicle, and he motioned us to sit in the three chairs before his desk. He typed on his computer and asked, "You're going for two weeks?"

"Yeah, give or take a few days. If it takes longer, we'll figure out a way to get home."

"How fun." He finished typing, then pulled six tickets from a desk drawer. "Here you are." He handed them to me. "Good luck on clearing Jason's name and solving Liberty's murder."

"Thanks. We'll need it."

"I have to say, Bro, that abandoned grain silo sounds like a hot place to do it," Brady said.

Uncle Dave looked confused. "What are you talking about?"

He blinked when it hit him, then he glanced at me. "Did your father tell him about my first time?"

"Yes. It was very awkward listening to my best friend talk about sex with my dad, especially when I haven't had it myself."

"I'll have to talk with him soon," Uncle Dave said.

I stood from the chair. "Have fun with that."

He shook our hands before we left. "Good luck with the case. All of America will be rooting for you."

"Thanks," Callie said. "We'll need all the support we can get."

We walked out to my car and got in. "So, we've got this planned out, right?" I asked, starting the engine.

"I think so," Brady said. "We leave in two weeks. When we get there, we'll clear Jason of Liberty's murder."

"It'll be nice to get that mess situated," Callie said from the back seat. "I can't imagine how stressful it must be for him to deal with this."

"He won't be soon," I said. "Then it'll be my problem."

"What do you mean?" Brady asked.

I glanced at him. "If the LAPD doesn't have a lead on who the hell killed my cousin by the time we get there, I plan to take matters into my own hands."

"You'll be arrested for interfering with a police investigation," Callie said.

I laughed. "What investigation? They're probably sitting around, not doing a damn thing, letting the dumbass who did it get free."

The rest of the car ride passed in silence. Brady made a couple jokes to lighten the mood, which was nice. I needed all the laughs I could get. The trip to California wouldn't be all fun and games. I expected some fun, a few games, and a lot of stress and heartache.

The week and a half leading up to our departure to LA I spent packing, mentally preparing for stress and heartache, and spending time with the family and friends who weren't going. The day before our flight, Calvin surprised me by waking me at 8:30 to tell me the other Banshee Busters were outside, waiting for me and Brady.

"What?" I sat up slowly. "Where are they going?"

"You mean where are *you* going," Calvin corrected me. "It's out to breakfast, on me."

He handed me a roll of twenties, which I accepted. "Thanks." Then I had a thought. "Please don't tell me you stole this."

He laughed. "Of course not, Dude. It's a $500 loan from the PNC I work at."

I got out of bed and walked to my dresser. "What's the catch?" I pulled out a neon-green tank top." "You seem to be pushing Brady and me out of the house pretty quick. It's awful suspicious."

He grinned. "Do you want me to ruin it, or should I lie?"

I chuckled and slipped on the shirt. "Lie."

"All right. You know I love you, Bro, but I need a little time to myself this morning. I haven't had sex in a couple weeks, and I need to release some tension, if you know what I mean."

"I see." I pulled out a pair of jeans and looked at him. "Maybe Katelyn can help you when we're in California. Just be sure you stay off things other people might use, like the couches or the dining room table."

"No worries there." He laughed.

He closed the door to give me time to pull on my jeans. I did that and grabbed my Pittsburgh Pirates hat from the hook above my bed and got my sandals on at the front door.

Brady came up behind me to give me a quick shoulder rub. "Morning, Dude. You ready?"

"I suppose, but I have no idea what's going on."

"I already told you," Calvin said, escorting me out the door. "I need time to myself to complete a special project."

"I thought you said you needed to release some sexual frustration."

"That's the special project."

Brady followed me out, and Calvin locked the door behind us. I checked my belt loop for my keys and muttered, "Shit. Calvin forgot to give me my keys."

The door clicked open, and Calvin handed me a house key. "I just realized you guys might need this to get back in." He closed and locked the door again.

Brady and I exchanged glances at Calvin's odd behavior, then we noticed Randy's charcoal-colored Dodge Dakota parked at the curb. Angela and Katie were in the truck bed, motioning us to join them, while Angela called, "Get your fat asses in this truck so we can go have fun!"

"Isn't it illegal to ride in a truck bed?" Brady asked.

"Not if you're properly restrained," she shot back, holding up the bungee cords wrapped around herself as proof. "See?"

"Bungee cords aren't proper restraining tools for humans, you whore."

"Whatever. I'm getting cheese fries."

We went to IHOP for breakfast, then to the mall for some last-minute items for the trip. We ended up at the park for an hour and a half. At 2:30, we got back to the house only to find all the lights off inside, but I didn't care. It was the middle of the day and really bright out. Maybe Calvin was finally being responsible and conserving electricity.

Brady, Callie, Randy, and I got to the front door and looked back at the truck to see Angela and Katie still in the truck bed.

"What the hell do you think you're doing?" she asked.

I put my key in the lock. "What?"

"Help me out of this truck."

I wore a shit-eating grin. "You have such muscular legs, though. It shouldn't be a problem getting yourself out."

Some would call that a back-handed compliment, because some girls equated muscular legs with fat legs. Thank goodness she didn't.

I opened the door and stepped inside, with the others following closely. It wasn't just dark in the house. It was pitch black. I could barely see two feet ahead. Had Calvin blown out the breakers? That would suck for all of us.

Then I realized the windows were covered in cardboard. "It's dark in here. Where's the light switch?"

"Here, Bro. I got it," Randy said.

He moved to the wall, found the switch, and flipped it on. The moment the lights were on, Calvin, Katelyn, Vanna, Carson, and some of my coworkers from the zoo jumped out and shouted, "Surprise!" so loudly, I fell over in shock.

Calvin laughed and came to help me up. "Didn't mean to scare you, Man."

I dusted myself off. "It's all good, Dude."

The living room was decorated with balloons and streamers in cobalt blue, maroon red, and metallic silver, my favorite colors.

A banner hung over the entryway to the kitchen with the words, *Good Luck in LA!* The counters were stocked with sodas, a table was set up with different liquors, including Fireball whiskey, Jose Cuervo and straight tequila with a stack of disposable shot glasses. Calvin must've fired up the grill outside, too. A volleyball net hung in the backyard.

"This is why I needed to get you two out of the house this morning," Calvin said. "I wanted to throw you a good luck going-away party, so you could have even more fun before you deal with the stress of the next two weeks."

"Wow." I looked around, taking it in. "I don't know what to say."

He grinned and opened his arms. "How about thanking me with a hug?"

I gave him a bear hug, lifting him off the ground. "Thanks, Bro. You don't know how much this means to me."

"You know I love you, Man. I want you to have a clear mind before you leave. This seemed like the best way to get there."

We released each other.

"Well, that was nice," Angela said. "Who wants to lose a game of volleyball?"

Apparently, she did. She lost badly, then bitched about it the rest of the time. Actually, she bitched for five minutes before getting over it.

Once we started drinking, things got a little wild. I made sure to be prepared ahead of time, knowing we had to be at the airport at 5:30 AM the following morning to catch our flight to LA. I already set my alarm for 4:00 AM and had three large glasses of water on the nightstand to help me deal with any hangover I might have.

Before things got too insane, they all clamored for me to make a speech. I grabbed a bottle of Bud from the cooler, and Brady escorted me to a stepstool I could stand on.

"All right. I got this. Calm down." I drank from my Bud. "Now that I'm here, I have a few things to say, starting with thanks to all of you. Losing Liberty was severely heartbreaking, second only to losing my mother to breast cancer."

I downed another mouthful of beer. "I may not have known any of you, except for Callie, when I lost my mom, but I feel very fortunate and blessed to have you here to help me navigate the tragedy of my cousin's murder. I couldn't have asked for a better support system."

I took a deep breath to calm my nerves, and Giovanni put his arm around my shoulders to comfort me. "These next few weeks won't be easy, but I'm confident with your thoughts and prayers, and with God with us every step of the way, we'll pull through this in one piece."

I raised my bottle of Budweiser. "Here's to my cousin. May we help her rest in peace soon enough."

"Cheers!"

We all drank to Liberty.

I didn't remember much after that, probably because I was too drunk, though some events stood out. I remembered Katie using a floor lamp for a stripper's pole, which went about as well as anyone could expect. Ashley LeCrae, a coworker from the zoo, accidentally knocked Carson out demonstrating how high she could kick. She clocked him good in the head, and he was out cold. That was impressive. We got him to a spare bed to sleep it off, and he was fine the following day.

My alarm went off at 4:00 AM that morning. I felt walking around in public wearing my Pittsburgh Pirates pajama bottoms with a blank tank top would be fine. I got out of bed and slipped on my black shirt, grabbed my suitcase, and took my carry-on from the closet. Some guests were still passed out around the house, so I tried to be quiet and avoid waking them.

I took my sunglasses from the shelf by the key ring and opened the front door to see a black stretch limo parked at the curb.

That's odd, I thought. *I wonder whose limousine broke down here.*

Angela's head popped out of the sunroof. "Come on, Ben! Get in so we can catch our flight!"

"Shut the hell up, you crazy skank!" someone yelled from a neighboring house.

Angela looked around. "Who said that?"

"You're mother's ass!" a second person shouted.

The trunk popped open, and I set my luggage inside. I opened the limo door and got in while Angela remained standing through the sunroof. Two minutes later, she finally sat down, "People irritate me."

"What were you doing up there for the extra two minutes?" Callie asked.

Angela looked her in the eye and reached for a mini bottle of Fireball. "Flipping off the arrogant assholes who called me a crazy skank and commented on my mother."

"Jesus, Angela," Katie asked, "couldn't you leave well enough alone? If they're going to be asshats, let them. Don't egg them on."

Angela downed her bottle in ten seconds. "Ouch. That shit burns."

"Of course it does," Brady said, getting in. "It's called Fireball, not Snowball."

Angela glared at him. "Don't sass me, Boy."

"I guess we're ready to go to the airport," Randy said, turning to the driver up front. "Sir, all ready and accounted for."

"Roger that." He tipped his hat and pulled into the street.

We arrived at the airport at ten minutes before five. Our flight would take off at 7:15, but we needed time to get through airport security and to our gate. It all went smoothly, thank the Lord, but it took a long time. Callie had a ton of bags that needed to be scanned.

I began to wonder if she was moving to California. She had a separate bag for everything. There was one for her everyday clothes, one for formal clothes (as if we needed any), a bag for shoes, a bag for makeup and toiletries, and a bag for socks and undergarments.

We were staying for only two, maybe three, weeks. Depending on how our investigation went, it might be only one. Everything I needed fit into two bags.

I don't understand women.

We finally got to our gate, and Angela collapsed into a chair. "Ugh. Now the fatigue is hitting me." She turned to Katie. "Why'd we have to get here so early?"

"Don't ask me. Ask Ben. He booked this trip."

Angela looked at me.

"We need to get to LA as soon as possible," I explained, "and this was the earliest flight."

"Ick." She pulled sunglasses out of her bag and put them on. "I'll take a nap. Let me know when it's boarding time."

I decided to visit a Starbucks and get coffee to help me stay awake. After I ordered, someone put his arm around my shoulders. When I glanced to the right, I saw Brady beside me.

"You OK, Bro?" he asked.

I nodded slowly. "I guess. I just want the nightmare to be over."

"I get that. We all do." He rubbed my back. "Just remember all of us are here with you. Everyone at home is rooting for you, too, along with our fans."

He looked into my eyes. "Most importantly, God is here with us every step of the way."

I smiled. "Thanks, Man. That really helps."

The barista gave me the venti pumpkin spice latte I ordered. Thanking her, I returned to our gate.

I spent the rest of the time preparing a plan with Brady and Randy, chatting with Callie and Katie, and laughing at Brady when he drew a mustache on Angela, who was sound asleep.

At 7:15, a woman stepped up to the desk near the jetway entrance. "Good morning, Ladies and Gentlemen, the flight from San Antonio to Denver is ready to board."

Uncle Dave couldn't find us a direct flight to LA, so the next best option was a layover in Denver.

"We'd like to begin by preboarding elderly passengers or those with small children."

Katie tapped Angela's shoulder to wake her, but she was out like a rock.

"Step aside." Brady cracked his knuckles. "I got this."

He sneaked up behind her and tickled her. She shot up and smacked his face.

"Ouch, you whore!" he said. "Why'd you do that?"

"Boy, you should know better than to tickle me." She dusted herself off. "I have a natural reaction to that."

"And that is to punch me?"

"Sure seems like it. Is it time to board?"

"Yup," I said. "They haven't called our section yet, though."

"Now we'd like to welcome first-class and Gold-Card Members," the lady at the podium said.

"Ohhh, first class!" I grabbed my carry-on. "That's us."

We boarded and waited for everyone else to get on. We took off on time at 7:45 AM, got to Denver at 9:00, and left on our connecting flight to LA at 10:30, arriving at 9:15 with the time change.

When we planned the trip, I initially talked to my cousin, Jeremy Whalen, who lived in LA, about the possibility of staying with him. He agreed. He managed a frat house, and the guys were away for the summer, so that worked, as long as he disinfected the place first.

Callie needed assistance with her many bags. A nice lady driving one of the carts around the airport stopped to help. Callie stacked her bags in the back and hopped in the front seat.

Reaching the waiting area, we looked for Jeremy. It was years since I last saw him, and I expected a guy with dark-red hair and a matching beard who was slightly overweight, but I didn't see him.

I began to assume he wasn't there yet when someone called, "Ben!"

I looked and saw a guy waving. His black hair was shaved, he wore a black goatee, and he had a maroon tank top with black wind pants. I didn't know him and approached cautiously.

"Hi," I said. "Who are you?"

He laughed. "Apparently, it's been longer than I thought since we saw each other. I'm Jeremy."

"My cousin Jeremy?" I squinted at him.

He nodded. "That's me." He opened his arms and added, "Now give me a hug, Bro."

I did, and he lifted me a few inches off the ground.

When he set me down, I said, "Whoa, Dude. You look different."

"Yeah?" He grinned. "So do you."

"How'd you recognize me?"

"Dude, we're family. I can pick you out of a crowd." He playfully punched my arm. "Plus, I follow *The Banshee Busters* religiously on Facebook and Twitter."

That explained it.

The rest of the gang followed shortly after, and I introduced Jeremy to them.

"My God, you're hot," Angela said.

Katie hit her on the back of the head. "I apologize for my idiot friend. She needs to think before she speaks."

Jeremy laughed. "It's all good. I get that a lot now."

"Seriously," I asked, "what the hell happened to you? I mean in the best possible way, of course."

"Well, a bitch cheated on me." He picked up one of my bags and carried it toward his van. "I dumped her ass and hit the gym hardcore for a year and a half to make her regret stepping out on me."

"Did she?" Callie asked.

"Did she what?"

"Regret it?"

"Actually, she did. After I dumped her, she started dating the asshole she cheated with. I ran into her after I started looking like this, and she wanted to have nasty hate sex for old time's sake."

He grinned. "She was still going out with the douche at the time, so I slept with her and videotaped it. I made her believe we were making a private porn video. I mailed an anonymous copy to her boy-friend, who dumped her for cheating on him."

"Karma hit her full force," Randy said. "I like it."

"Yeah. I should've thought of flaunting my new hot body when Leona cheated on me," I said.

"You could have, but karma hit her in the whore ass in its own way. Look what's going on now."

He had a point. I was a semifamous ghost hunter with a solid fan base and, according to the fans, a hot body, while she was a worn-out ho having breakfast for dinner with an abusive Persian, or so I assumed.

We got into the van and tossed our bags in the back.

"You have one of the highest-rated ghost-themed TV series on SyFy," Brady said, "right after *Ghost Hunters* and *Ghost Hunters International*. Plus, you have a hot body. Leona's a prostitute in some Mexican brothel."

"She's probably super fat, too," Callie said. "I don't even know her, but she sounds like a huge bitch."

We had all our luggage, so Jeremy drove us toward the frat house we'd live in during our time in LA. He made sure the girls, par-ticularly Callie, knew the house was almost soaked in bleach, so nobody would catch anything. I'd heard Betas were animals, so it was always wise to clean and disinfect after them.

We arrived at the house twenty minutes later. It wasn't much on the outside, made of red brick with a porch of poured concrete, four bright ivory pillars out front, and a wraparound wood railing. Three strange Greek letters hung over the entrance.

Jeremy explained it was the Beta Thi Beta House, but I didn't know how anybody could tell that from the characters written in an alien script. I took his word for it.

He gave me a key to unlock the house. I took my bags, unlocked the door, and stepped inside to look around. It was a three-story build-ing, with basement, main floor, and upper floor with bedrooms. The kitchen was great—stainless steel almost everything, including fridge, stove, sink, dishwasher, and fan over the stove. The cabinets were varnished pine, with an island counter with a bright white marble top, a bay window on the wall opposite the stove, and a cherry table with ten cherry chairs, all nicely varnished.

The living room had a seventy-inch TV with surround-sound stereo, an Xbox One, PS4, and a Wii U game system in front of the TV. There was a gold coffee table with Egyptian artwork stained glass, two couches—one black leather, one dark red—and a snow white loveseat and two La-Z-Boy recliners, one dark blue, the other black. The entire downstairs, including the bathroom, had maple flooring.

There were eleven rooms upstairs, one for each frat brother and Jeremy. Four of them had waterbeds, while the other seven had standard but comfortable king-sized beds. I wanted a water bed, so I claimed one first. That felt like a perk for being related to the house manager. Besides, I unlocked the door, so I had first dibs.

I wasn't the only one who wanted a water bed. Everyone besides Katie did, too. She chose a regular mattress, because she had a fear of popping a water bed in her sleep and waking up on a wet floor. Callie and Randy got water beds, but Brady and Angela argued over the last one.

Once they realized only one waterbed was left, both ran for it. They arrived at the same time and dumped their stuff on the bed simultaneously. Neither could say who got there first. They squabbled over it for five minutes before I got irritated and decided to stop them.

I walked into the room and stood in the doorway with my hands on either side of the frame. "Hey, Dumbasses."

They stopped bickering and looked at me.

"Both of you want the bed, right?"

They nodded vigorously.

"Why not have a contest to see who gets it?"

"That's a wonderful idea," Angela said, looking at Brady. "Are you down?"

He narrowed his eyes. "Oh, yes. I'm down."

They went downstairs, and I walked to my room, thinking I kept the peace. I unpacked my suitcase and moved in, then I realized neither Brady nor Angela had said a word in ten minutes. Peace and quiet were good, but knowing those two, I felt something was wrong.

I walked downstairs to find them sitting at the kitchen table with a bottle of silver Captain Morgan rum and two shot glasses. I closed my eyes and took a deep breath. I knew the answer, but I didn't really want to ask.

"Guys, what the hell are you doing?" I finally asked.

"Having a contest like you said," Brady replied.

"With Captain Morgan?"

"Yup," Angela responded. "We're going shot for shot. Whoever takes the most without blacking out gets the bed."

I held my head in my hands. "When I said to make a contest out of it, I didn't mean something that would kill you."

"Oh, really?" Brady sat back and crossed his arms. "What do you propose?"

I shook my head. "I don't know. Both of you are athletic. Why not have a race?"

"Oooh," Angela said. "A race sounds good." She stood and pushed her chair against the table.

"Don't be so sure, Ho," Brady shot back. "I've gotten faster recently."

"Yeah, well, put up or shut up." She took off her blouse and knee-length skirt to reveal a magenta runner's top and black shorts. "Let's go right now."

He stared at her for five seconds. "I see how it is." He smirked. "Give me a bit to get dressed in an outfit appropriate for kicking your ass."

He jogged upstairs to get his running clothes.

"Don't use all your energy now," she called. "I want to beat you, but I don't want you to hand it to me."

"Shut the hell up."

Five minutes later, he was back wearing a bright blue tank top, a black sweatband, and black knee-length shorts.

"All right," I said, looking outside for a potential mile marker. A huge maple tree stood a mile-and-a-half away. "You see that maple tree down there?"

They both nodded.

"You start and end here. The turnaround point is that tree. Whoever gets back first wins the water bed. All clear?"

"Yup." Angela settled into a runner's stance. "I'm ready to feel like I'm sleeping on an ocean."

"That's right. Get cocky." He took the same position. "It'll make this more hilarious when you lose."

I counted them down and made an air horn with my hands. "On your mark, get set, take off!"

I blew my air horn, and off they went.

Katie stepped outside a minute later holding a half-full wineglass. "What be going on?"

"Brady and Angela are running."

"Really." She sipped her wine. "What did he do this time?"

I gave her an are-you-insane look. "What do you mean?"

"Usually, the only time they run together is if she's chasing him. If she is, he must have done something to warrant it."

"Maybe they're competing to see who gets the waterbed."

Katie stared at me for a moment. "Huh." She took another sip of wine. "I never would've considered that."

Six minutes later, according to my stopwatch, a blur of pink ran past, and Angela stopped, bending down to catch her breath. She looked around and became excited. "I win!" She raised her arms in celebration. "Ha!"

She bounded up the steps. "I'm moving Brady's stuff out of my new room."

A minute-and-a-half later, according to my stopwatch, Brady arrived.

"Where's Angela? Did I win?"

"I'd say yes, but I'd be lying. She's moving your things out of the last waterbed room."

Brady glared up at the house. "That whore."

8

We got everything settled in. The next day, we went to the police station to find out when I could give character testimony on Jason's behalf. There was no way I'd let him stay in a cell for something most of America knew he didn't do.

We got inside the waiting area to find a woman behind a counter lined with what I assumed was bulletproof glass. I walked up and waited for her to notice me. She didn't look up from her computer for five minutes, and I felt a bit irritated.

"Ahem!" I said loudly.

She sighed. "Yes, how may I help you?"

"My name is Ben Becker. I'm here to give a character witness for Jason Lancaster."

She grunted. "Does it look like I care?"

My I'm-putting-up-with-you grin vanished. "Excuse you?"

"Did I stutter?"

"As a matter of fact, you did, you fat bitch. Get someone out here who can talk to me like an adult."

I could go from 0 to 100 in three seconds if I was disrespected. That land whale was pushing me seriously close to asshole territory.

Then she said the magic words. "Go to hell, you dick."

She was damn lucky she sat behind bulletproof glass. That was the only thing keeping her alive.

Before I could consider doing something I might regret, an older man who kind of resembled Tom Hanks when he played Captain Sullenberger in the movie *Sully* came out.

"Good morning," he said, extending his hand to me. "I'm Police Chief Alexander J. Boone. How may I help you?"

"Hello, Sir." I shook his hand. "My name is Benjamin Becker. I was trying to figure out when the court hearing for Jason Lancaster is."

"It's in a few hours. Why?"

"I don't know if anyone informed you ahead of time, but I was called to provide a character testimony in his defense."

"I see." He crossed his arms. "How are you related to Mr. Lancaster?"

"The murdered woman was my cousin. I'm not directly related to him by blood, but he's like the brother I never had. I'm not the only one who could vouch for him."

"Wow. I'm sorry for your loss. I didn't know the victim was related to you."

"It's hard to deal with, and it's even more difficult thinking Jason has to suffer for something I don't believe he did."

"Hmmm. The trial starts at one. If you want to come back, we'll escort you to the courthouse, and you can give your testimony there."

"Thank you, Sir. I appreciate the opportunity."

"No problem. We'll see you in a few hours."

To kill time, all six of us decided to visit IN-N-OUT Burger for a bite to eat and to show Brady, Angela, and Katie what it was like, because they'd never been to one.

Around 12:40 PM, we decided it was time to head back to the police station for the court hearing, but Callie suggested we stop at the frat house and let me change into something more formal.

Given how little time I had, I kept my jeans and changed from my dark-blue muscle shirt to a black Polo shirt.

We got back in enough time for Chief Boone to escort us to the trial. At 1:00, Jason was led into the courtroom by two security guards.

We listened to the standard things, like "All rise, Judge such-and-such presiding," the swearing of the litigants, and more.

Finally, they called for character testimony. That was my time. I hadn't prepared anything beforehand, but I knew what I wanted to say.

The defense for Jason called me to the stand. I was sworn in and sat down. The defense attorneys questioned me first, and I answered truthfully. Things were going smoothly.

Then came the prosecution's turn. The first question was, "Do you believe Mr. Lancaster is capable of murder?"

"Absolutely not. He's one of the greatest men I've had the pleasure to know. I don't believe any part of him would even think of murdering someone, let alone the woman he wanted to spend the rest of his life with."

"Oh-ho! He was going to be engaged to Miss Belle?"

"Yes. He told me the entire plan. He wanted to take her to Sea World in San Diego, take her to the Sky Tower, and pop the question at the top of the ride. He even asked me to be his best man at the wedding."

"Interesting. If Mr. Lancaster loved Miss Belle as much as you claim, why did he murder her?"

"Haven't you heard a word I've said during this trial?" I became frustrated. "He didn't have any motive to murder Liberty. He isn't capable of murdering *anyone.* He isn't that kind of man. He's on the brink of international success with the release of his third solo album and world tour next year. I've known him for four years. I don't believe he'd be so stupid as to screw all that up by killing his would-be fiancée."

"No more questions."

After the testimony, the jury deliberated for two hours. When they returned, the foreman said they took my testimony seriously, but they wanted physical proof that Jason didn't murder Liberty.

The judge took that into account and decided the next-best course of action was to place Jason under house arrest until further evidence could prove he wasn't involved in any way.

It seemed unorthodox, but I was OK with the ruling. I hated the fact that Jason was still a suspect, but at least he wouldn't be stuck in jail any longer.

Outside the courthouse, the paparazzi swarmed us. Boone gave a statement to the press and escorted us back to the station afterward. "There you go," he told me. "You did well."

"Thank you, Sir, but Liberty's death is still haunting me. I need closure as soon as possible. I'd like to offer my help in finding who did it. Maybe if more of us were investigating, we'd solve it faster."

"Hmmm." He rubbed his chin for a few seconds. "Anyone else might consider that interfering with a police investigation, but, given the circumstances and the fact that you'd be assisting us, I give you my blessing."

"Thank you, Sir! I swear you won't regret it."

"Absolutely." He shook my hand and gave me his business card. "Be sure to call me directly if you find any new developments in the case."

I slid the card into my wallet. "I will."

We left the police station with Jason, and he hugged me pretty hard once we got into the van. "Thanks for coming to my rescue, Bro," he said emotionally. "You don't know how much I need time with someone who cares."

"You got it, Man." I rubbed his back with one hand. "We're all here with you and for you."

Since the judge hadn't specified which house Jason had to stay in, we offered to take him to the frat house unless he really wanted to be at his manor. It seemed best if he stayed at his own home. We planned to visit him regularly.

We returned to the frat house, and Jeremy gave me the keys to his Ford Mustang, so I could drive Jason home and also spend more one-on-one time with him.

I pulled into Jason's driveway and set the transmission to Park. "You all right?"

He nodded slowly. "I guess I will be. Losing Liberty destroyed my world, but if you guys can help me find closure with what really happened, that would be the next best thing."

Placing a hand on his shoulder, I said, "Trust me, Bud, we will. I won't rest until then. Losing her destroyed me, too."

Jason got out, and I followed. He came to my side of the car and gave me another hug. "I love you, Man." He held onto me for a second.

"I love you, Bro. Things will get better, I promise."

I released him and checked his appearance. He looked pretty bad. His normally short dark-brown hair reached past his ears, his typically trimmed facial hair was out of control, and his clothes were stained. "Dude, you look a sight."

He chuckled. "Yeah, I'll bet I do. I'll contact Sherylena tomorrow. She can make a house call and spruce me up a bit."

"Is she your stylist?"

He nodded. "She's the one who helps me prepare for red carpets and award shows."

I slid into the Mustang. "When you see her, tell her I think she's doing a great job."

Jason chuckled. "You got it, Bro."

I started the engine. "I'll be back to check on you soon enough." After I backed from the driveway, I drove toward the frat house.

"What doesn't kill you, makes you stronger, stand a little taller, doesn't mean I'm lonely when I'm alone...."

Kelly Clarkson's song woke me at 7:30 the following morning. I deliberately set my alarm to play an empowering song to motivate me to kick ass on the investigation. It really worked.

I sat up slowly, rubbed my eyes, and crawled out of bed. Once I had my glasses, I went downstairs for breakfast and to write a list of potential people to interview about Liberty. Maybe if we found someone in her circle with a motive to want her dead, we could get started. It would be a hell of a lot easier if someone just confessed, but no one seemed inclined to be that stupid.

I looked up the main cast from all her movies, from *Ain't No Mountain High,* her breakout role, to *Coulrophobia,* the latest movie.

I narrowed it down to three people to start: Mikaela "Micki" Parsons, an actress who portrayed Olivia Wright in *Coulrophobia;* Brian Judea, who portrayed Kevin Lloyd in *Paranoia*; and Dinah Masterson, who played the part of Lori Burkins in *Christmastime Is Fear.*

Throughout the investigation, I planned to assume people were innocent until proven guilty. I would start by interviewing those three actors and seeing what I might learn from them.

I made pancakes and sat at the table to eat them when Brady strolled in wearing his favorite black robe.

"Morning, Bro," he said, grabbing a box of Corn Flakes from the cabinet over the stove. "Any idea how we should start the investigation?"

"I figured we would interview three of Liberty's costars and see if any could shed light on the case." I sipped some orange juice. "We'll start with Micki Parsons this morning, then we'll split into two groups to get the others. You, Randy, and I will talk to Brian Judeah, while Callie, Angela, and Katie get Dinah Masterson."

"Sounds like a good start." He poured coffee from the pot Jeremy made before he left for his girlfriend's house. Holding up the pot, he asked, "Want some?"

"Sure. That sounds good." I took a bite of my pancakes. "I also talked to Jason. He gave me a list of people of interest we can start on after the first three today."

"Sounds like a plan." Brady sat across from me with his Corn Flakes and coffee. "Who's on the list?"

I slid a piece of paper closer and read from it. "Harley Crank, Liberty's personal trainer; Alicia Carbanaro, her chiropractor; Brooklynne Grace, another personal trainer; and this guy, Travis Cain, with a skull and crossbones and the words *Very Important* written beside his name." I looked up at Brady. "Maybe that's a hint to start with him."

"You think?"

Callie sauntered in a bit later wearing a pastel-pink robe and matching slippers. "Morning, Boys." She looked around. "Everyone else asleep?"

"Seems like it." Glancing at my watch, I saw it was 9:00. I got up and walked to a weird rope hanging from the ceiling near the fridge. I picked up a pair of ear protectors like those people wear at firing ranges and glanced at Brady and Callie. "Cover your ears."

They did, and I pulled the rope, blasting an air-raid siren throughout the house. Jeremy told me they used that to wake up the frat brothers who were going to be late for class.

Once the siren stopped, screaming started.

Angela and Randy came down first, followed by Katie.

"The hell was that for?" Katie demanded. 'Scared me half to death and almost made me break my damn neck!"

"You were out like a rock," Brady said. "We couldn't think of any other way to get y'all up."

"Ugh. I'm awake now, so thank you for that."

"You're welcome," Callie said in a bright, bubbly tone.

Katie glared at her. "That was sarcasm."

"Now that we're all awake," I said, "I have a rough game plan for today. We should start by interviewing the three costars from

Liberty's last three movies and see if they have any insight into who would want her dead."

"Jason gave Ben a list of people to talk to as well," Brady added. "We can start on them tomorrow."

"Sounds legit to me," Angela said. "Who do we get first?"

"Micki Parsons," I said. "I think she'll be very helpful and cooperative."

"What makes you say that?" Katie asked.

I stood from my chair and walked to the front door, where Jeremy hung the keys to the minivan I planned to drive. "Just a hunch."

Mikaela "Micki" Parsons had been acting since she was fifteen. She started in TV commercials and small spots on shows, then landed her first movie *Holy Hell* at the age of eighteen. That was a found-footage horror film about five teenagers who explored an abandoned Catholic cathedral only to end up the victims of the demons haunting it, similar to *Paranormal Activity*. It had mixed reviews, but I liked it.

Micki lived alone in a four-bedroom, three-bath manor in a gated Hollywood Hills community. On the way there, I called Jason and asked him to tell her we were on our way to talk to her, so she would let us in.

I pulled up to the gate, and a security guard came to the van. "Good morning, Sir. Do you have an appointment with some-one here?"

"Yes, Sir. We're here to talk to Micki Parsons. I'm working with the LAPD to solve the murder of Liberty Belle, because she was my cousin. I thought Micki would be a good person to give us some possible insight."

After a few seconds of sizing me up to see if I was lying, he nodded to his associate still in the shack. She pressed a button to open the gate, and the guard tipped his hat to me.

"Good luck on the case," he said.

"Thanks." I drove forward.

According to Chief Boone, Micki's manor was a mile off on our right. We pulled up to a red-brick house with neatly cut lawn, five ivory Romanesque pillars, a porch made of bright-white marble, and huge cherry double doors with a bright-blue M designed in the stained glass. Something told me we had the right place.

We climbed out of the van and walked to the front door. "We can go either of two ways with this," I told the others. "Either I let her know I'm directly related to Liberty right off, or we could ease her into it."

"How would we do that?" Brady asked.

I turned my Pirates hat backward on my head. "I could pretend to be a reporter for some pop culture magazine and say I'm trying to get multiple reactions from different people who were close to Liberty."

"Oooh!" Callie said. "Like *People* magazine?"

I stared blankly at her. "Sure, Hon. Like *People.*"

"I vote to see how she answers the door and decide at that point," Katie said. "If her first impression is pleasant, maybe we can let her in on why we're really here."

"That sounds decent. Let's go with that."

I took a deep breath and rang the bell. Two minutes later, the door opened, and a woman with dark-brown hair and what looked like faux fire-engine-red hair extensions stood before us in a leopard print halter top and black sweatpants. "Hi."

"You're Micki Parsons?" I asked.

"The one and only...as far as I know. How can I help you?"

"We were hoping you had a few minutest to talk to us about Liberty Belle."

Her smile vanished. "You aren't the cops, are you?"

"No. I'm Liberty's cousin, Benjamin Becker."

The smile returned. "Oh, my God! You're the star of *Banshee Busters!* I love that show."

Micki looked at the rest of the group and gasped. "Oh, my God. You're *all* the stars of that show!" She stepped aside. "Please come in. I'll tell you anything you need to know."

We walked in and looked around. It was nicer on the inside than the outside. I saw a large open front hall, a stairway to the second floor covered in purple velvet with a bright-white handrail, a bunch of statues and plants around the room, and black-and-white checkered linoleum on the floor.

Micki led us to what I assumed was her living room, furnished with a hanging plasma screen TV, two black leather couches, a zebra-print loveseat, two blue recliners, a fireplace with a cobblestone mantel, and a fake tiger skin rug.

I sat on one couch with Brady, while Callie and Angela sat on the other. Randy and Katie each took a recliner. I opened my notepad. "Why don't you start by telling us a little about your relationship with Liberty?"

Micki crossed her legs. "I first met her when casting for *Coulrophobia* started. My first impression was that she seemed like a really cool person. We started talking after we had our roles and started hanging out. We took lunch breaks together on set and started hanging together outside of work, too. We went on double dates. She was with Jason, and I was with my ex-boyfriend Nicholas Morrison."

Her eyes welled with tears. "She was one of my best friends. I still can't believe she's gone." Taking a tissue from a box on the end table, she dabbed tears from her eyes. "I still catch myself trying to call her and hoping this is a huge nightmare I'll wake up from. It's hitting me hard."

"I get that," I said. "Same here."

"So you were close to Liberty," Callie said. "Do you know anyone she might have had a beef with?"

Micki thought for a second. "Now that I think of it, Julie Capp comes to mind."

"Who's that?" Brady asked.

"She's a whore who claims to be an actress."

"How did Liberty know her?" Angela asked.

"Julie was *supposed* to be in *Coulrophobia* with us, but rumor on the set was she only got the job because she blew one of the head producers."

She sipped from the cranberry cocktail a maid gave her. "Ugh. That bitch was a nightmare. Every day she showed up late *and* high. She tried to claim she was smoking medical marijuana for premature arthritis or some bullshit. We all got fed up with her bitch diva attitude and wanted her gone. Liberty was the one who spoke up for us. The director agreed and booted Julie out the next day. He hired a different girl, Naomi Steele, to fill the role. She was much better, and we got everything wrapped before the deadline."

I wrote Julie's name under *List of Possible Suspects*. "All right. We've got what we need for now," I said, standing. "Thanks for your time, Micki."

"No problem. I loved Liberty, and I'll do anything to see whoever murdered her is behind bars."

"In that case," I said, pulling out my wallet, "would you mind calling me if you think of anything else that might help the case?"

She took it. "Absolutely. You'll be the first to know."

"Awesome. Stay safe."

"Thanks. You, too. Talk to you again soon."

The six of us went to the van and got in.

"That was helpful," I said, starting the engine.

"Yeah," Angela said. "Maybe this is a lead we can follow through on."

"Or maybe she was throwing us off with crocodile tears," Randy said. "Maybe she doesn't like Julie for some reason and is trying to pin the blame on her."

"Oh, come on," Callie scoffed. "Micki may be an actress, but I don't think that emotion was faked."

"Yeah," Brady said. "That much emotion seems really difficult to make up that quickly."

"True dat," Katie said. "It's a hell of a lot easier to fake an orgasm."

The entire car fell silent.

"Or so I've been told," she added quickly.

Angela chuckled. "Nice save."

9 |

We broke for lunch after meeting Micki. Instead of going out to a restaurant, we decided to visit Jason and eat lunch with him.

I pulled the minivan into the driveway, and we piled out. When I rang the doorbell, a voluptuous Hispanic woman answered the door wearing a low-cut black sweater and a shiny black spandex miniskirt.

"Brady, you might want to dry your chin," Angela said. "You're drooling."

"Hush, ho," he shot back.

"Uh, hi," I said to the woman, trying to maintain eye contact. "Is Jason available?"

"Yes. Come in. I'll let him know you're here."

We stepped in and slipped off our shoes. The woman went to a back room, and Jason came out to greet us five minutes later. "Hey, Guys." He gave Brady and Randy high-fives, hugged me, then hugged the women. "What a nice surprise."

"We thought we'd check on you and see how you're doing," I said. "I also wanted to ask some questions about these persons of interest on the list you gave me."

"Sure thing. Let's go talk in the dining room while Nina gets lunch going."

"Who's Nina?" Callie asked.

"My personal chef. She's the woman who answered the door."

"She turned Brady on with that outfit," Angela said.

Brady smacked the back of Angela's head.

"Ouch, you douche nozzle! You can't hit me, I'm a girl!" She punched his shoulder.

"That's enough, Ladies," Katie hissed.

Jason laughed. "I'm a nice boss in the sense that I let her wear what she wants. If she wanted to show up naked, I couldn't care as long as the food tastes as amazing as always."

"Well, naturally, because you're a man," Angela said.

Katie elbowed her in the ribs.

"The fuck is this, Beat on Angela Day?" Angela demanded.

"Hush," Katie replied. "You'll forget all about this when we get drunk tonight."

Jason led us to the dining room, where we sat around the table. I pulled out his list and skimmed it again.

"So this guy is the one who stands out the most," I said, pointing at Travis Cain's name. "Who is he and why is he so important?"

Jason closed his eyes and took a deep breath. "Travis Cain is Liberty's obsessive ex-boyfriend. His only claim to fame was dating her, and he fucked it up by letting the paparazzi catch him cheating on her with a twenty-year-old blonde bimbo. Naturally, Liberty dumped his ass when the truth came out."

"My friend Dinah introduced me to Liberty at a party a few months later. We hit it off and started dating after just talking for two weeks."

"Dinah?" Brady asked. "Dinah Masterson?"

Jason nodded. "Yup. She's a very sweet girl."

Nina brought out a tray with glasses of what looked like strawberry lemonade for us. Jason thanked her and sipped from his glass.

"After Liberty and I started dating," Jason continued, "Travis started stalking both of us. He called and texted her nonstop, demanding she dump me and go back to him. He left me messages threatening me for stealing his woman. He even rented out a bunch of carnival rides and elephants for her."

Katie snapped her fingers. "That's where I know that name. That stunt made headlines for being so absurd."

"Yeah, it did," Jason said. "He's a pathetic excuse for a man." He sipped more lemonade. "The last thing he said to Liberty before she died was, 'If I can't have you, no one can.'"

"That's a serious red flag," I said. "I see why he's so important."

Nina brought out a tray of cheeseburgers. We ate in silence, enjoying the flavor.

After we finished eating, I stood. "That was very good. Compliments to Nina."

She smiled. "Thank you, *Señor* Becker."

I smiled and glanced back at Jason. "I got a favor to ask now that I thought about it."

He swallowed the last bit of burger in his mouth. "Sure thing, Bro. What's up?"

"We're going to talk to two more people this afternoon. The guys and I will try to catch Brian Judeah, while the girls will see Dinah. To cover more ground simultaneously, I thought we could conduct those interviews today, so I was wondering if it would be OK for me to borrow a car and talk to Brian. I'll give the girls the van to see Dinah."

Jason thought for a moment. "Yeah, that should be fine. The keys are hanging on the key ring near the door."

"Thanks, Man."

"Absolutely. It's just sitting in the driveway, since I can't leave the house. I might as well loan her to you, so she can stretch."

We said good-bye to Jason, thanked Nina again for the food, and walked out to the driveway, where I gave Callie the keys to the minivan.

"Take Angela and Katie to talk to Dinah. Brady, Randy, and I will take Jason's car and see Brian."

Callie took the keys. "What about Jeremy?"

"What about him?"

"Won't he be mad if someone else drives the van?"

"No. He's very laid back. If you don't crash it, everything will be fine."

"All right." She got behind the wheel. "Keep in touch."

"Same to you." I opened Jason's garage door and backed out his Mazda 6 convertible, so Brady and Randy could get in. After I backed onto the street, we took off for Brian's place.

Brian Judeah was an actor who hadn't been in the game as long as the others, but he was steadily climbing Hollywood's ladder of fame. He was more of a TV star than a movie star, holding the title role in the sitcom *Carrigan.* He also acted in some movies, like in *Paranoia* with Liberty, but he preferred television acting with its lower stress level, according to him.

We pulled up to the address Chief Boone gave us and surveyed the place. It was modest compared to what most famous people lived in—a two-story bright-white house with a trimmed lawn and dark-red shutters. It seemed more suitable for an average family than a nationally recognized TV actor. Different people have different tastes, and if he wanted to live relatively modestly, I couldn't argue with that.

Brady, Randy, and I walked to the door. Before I could ring the bell, it opened to reveal a guy wearing red-and-black-striped pajama bottoms. "Hey. How can I help you guys?"

"You're Brian Judeah, right?" I asked.

"I sure am."

"Awesome. I'm Ben Becker, and I was hoping we could talk to you about the Liberty Belle case."

"Oh, of course. Please come in." He stepped aside.

Once inside, he led us to his dining room table, and we sat down. I pulled out my notepad. "Why don't you start by telling us a bit about your relationship with Liberty?"

Brian ran his hand through his ear-length midnight-black hair. "I met her about a year before we were cast together in *Paranoia.* She was a beautiful woman, but I never saw her as more than a good friend.

"When we found out we'd be making a movie together, we were both excited and celebrated with some drinks. That was a fun night."

I wrote down some notes. "So you never had any romantic feelings for her?"

"Absolutely not. She was one of my best friends, and I had no intention of taking things any further."

He drank from a bottle of water. "I was the first one she confided in when she became official with Jason, and I was so excited for her. He seems like a great guy, and I hoped they would last forever, then this tragedy struck."

My phone rang. At first, I thought to let it go to voicemail, but I saw an unlisted number on caller ID, and something told me to answer. "Hello?"

"I know what you're doing," a distorted voice said.

I was confused. "What the hell? Who is this?"

"The person who murdered the bitch."

My heart started pounding. "Who the fuck are you?" I shouted, startling the others at the table.

"You'll have to catch me to find out." The person hung up.

I slammed my fist on the table.

"Whoa, Dude," Brady said. "You all right?"

I shook my head. "That was the person who supposedly killed my cousin." I crossed Brian's name off the list of suspects. "That obviously means you didn't do it, not that we suspected you."

"I get it, but now I'm angry," Brian said. "I want to see this person brought to justice more than ever. Murdering someone is horrible enough, but taunting the victim's family is infinitely worse."

I immediately called Chief Boone. "Chief, I've got something. I just received a call from an unlisted number. The person claimed he was the one who killed Liberty."

"A possible lead? Meet me at the station as soon as possible. I'll get my best investigator to try to trace that call."

I hung up. "I have to go to the station." We stood. "Boone said he'd try to help me trace the call and figure out who the hell the asshole is who killed my cousin."

"That's good news," Brady said. "Hopefully something will come from it. I hate seeing you suffer like this."

"So do I, Bro," Randy said. "We want this nightmare over as badly as you do."

I thanked Brian for his time, gave him a business card, and asked him to call if something showed up that would help the investigation. He promised he would.

Brady, Randy, and I got into Jason's car and drove to the station as fast as we could.

10

We reached the station in record time. I walked quickly inside, and a pleasant-looking woman behind the bulletproof glass, not Bertha the Land Whale, looked at me. I walked over.

She smiled. "Hi. How may I help you?"

"I'm here to see Chief Boone. I have a possible break in my cousin's case."

"You must be Ben Becker." She picked up a phone. "I'll let him know you're here."

"Thank you."

The three of us took seats, but Boone came out to greet us only a minute later.

"Ben, good to see you." He offered his hand.

I shook it. "Good to see you, Sir. Do you need my phone to trace that call?"

"Yes, but only for a few minutes. I promise it'll be returned in the same condition you gave it to us."

I gave him my iPhone 6S.

"I'll be back in a bit." He walked down a hallway. The girls arrived at the station a minute later.

"We heard what happened." Callie struggled to catch her breath. "Are you all right?"

"I'm sure I will be. Boone's having his top investigator trace the call."

"Good." Katie bent over to catch her breath. "Hopefully he or she can find something to solve this case faster."

Angela, looking at the other two women, tried not to laugh.

Katie glared at her. "What's so funny?"

"You two." Angela's hands went to her hips.

"Because I don't run marathons...or not at all?" Katie asked between gasps.

"That's why it's so funny."

Katie gasped some more. "You...bitch."

Boone came back out. "We got it traced." He handed the phone to me.

"Great," I said. "What did you find?"

"Unfortunately, nothing. Whoever it was called from a pay phone and use a voice-distortion mechanism."

Fuck, I thought. *Back to square one.*

At least I knew who it wasn't. I was with Brian when the call came through, and the girls were with Dinah. Micki didn't seem like she would do anything that cruel.

Next on the list was Harley, one of Liberty's personal trainers. Jason said he had reason to believe Harley also had a thing for Liberty. Maybe he had the same idea Travis did, that if he couldn't have her, no one could.

We went to the Red Lobster to eat and relaxed for an hour and a half. I took the Mazda back to Jason, since we would conduct the next interview together. He said not to hesitate if I needed to borrow the car again.

We got into the minivan and drove toward the private gym where Harley worked.

Harley Crank was a thirty-four-year-old personal trainer to the stars. Most of the time, he conducted his workouts in a gym he owned called the Crank Dat, which I thought was a stupid name. He was also known to have one-on-one sessions at his manor.

I felt the best place to start was the gym. If he wasn't there, we'd go to his home. I had an idea how to keep him from becoming suspicious about my intentions.

We stopped at the frat house, and I changed into workout clothes—a white top, white sweatpants, my dark-blue Nikes, and a black sweatband. Jason loaned me a couple of wigs from his stylist, so I could go undercover. I chose a bald cap, contacts to change my eye color from brown to dark blue, a dark red men's short-haired wig, and a matching fake red goatee. I had Callie do the same thing to make things more convincing. She came out wearing a dark brown straight-haired wig she tied in a ponytail, a neon-green sports bra, gray yoga pants, and sunglasses.

We did that to be unnoticed. We weren't superstars, but our TV series had a decent fan base, so we were often recognized on the street. While we appreciated our fans and loved meeting them, we wanted to work on Liberty's case without being spotted.

Callie and I went inside the gym, while the others stayed in the van. I saw a Hispanic guy our age behind the counter and walked toward him. He smiled.

"Hey, Guys," he said. "How can I help you?"

"Hi. My name's Aaron Uchilda, and this is my girlfriend, Christina Cass." I put my arm around Callie. "We're kind of famous and were looking for a personal trainer to keep our hot figures."

"All right," the worker, whose nametag read *Vince,* said.

"We heard that Harley Crank is a great trainer," Callie said. 'We hoped he was in, so we could talk to him about taking us on as clients."

"That'd be great, but unfortunately, he isn't here today. He's holding a one-on-one workout at home." He squinted at us. "I recognize you two from somewhere, but I can't pinpoint it."

"Maybe you've heard my cover of *Midnight in Montgomery* by Alan Jackson. I'm a rising singer, and I was discovered in a karaoke bar performing it," I said.

"I'm a rising actress," Callie said. "Perhaps you've heard of my new movie, *Horror in the Big House,* that'll be in theaters next year."

I gave her a sideways glance.

Vince shook his head. "No, I don't think so. Your voices sound familiar, though...." He snapped his fingers. "*The Banshee Busters!* That's it!"

Shit, I thought.

Vince picked up the phone on the desk and pressed a button. "Attention gym patrons! We have a member of the ghost-hunting documentaries *The Banshee Busters* in our presence! This is so exciting!"

I took the phone from his hand. "No, no. My name's Aaron Uchida, and I'm a singer," I said in a vaguely British accent.

That didn't seem to work, so I took Callie's hand and rushed her to the van. I started the engine, and drove out like a maniac.

"I take it things didn't go as planned?" Brady asked.

I glanced at the rearview mirror. "That's one way to put it."

"The guy saw through our disguises and realized Ben was from *The Banshee Busters,*" Callie added.

"Ugh." Angela took out her phone. "Siri, tell me where Harley Crank's house is."

A minute later, we had the address. Technology is wonderful, but it was kind of scary, too. Harley actually had his personal address on his website. I was never stupid enough to put the Bromance Bungalow address anywhere public. Brady and I would be prone to random stalkers, and Calvin would get dragged in by association.

It was ten minutes from the gym to the house, so that was in our favor. Harley had a manor house, showing he made good money working out with famous people.

We discussed how to extract information from him and decided Callie and I would continue our masquerade, and the others would be themselves. If Harley recognized us from the TV series, Callie and I would remove our disguises and say it was part of a social experiment.

Obviously, that was a lie, but people would believe almost anything given a good reason.

We walked to the door and rang the bell. A bald guy in a black goatee, who looked like he was on steroids, answered, looking me up and down. "Who are you?"

"My name's Aaron Uchida. I'm an up-and-coming singer looking for a personal trainer. Someone referred me to you. I went to your gym, but the guy at the front desk said you were here."

"How fun." Harley shook my hand. "Come in, and I'll answer any questions you have."

I stepped in with Callie. Brady, Angela, Randy, and Katie remained hidden outside as per our plan. Harley led us to his living room and invited us to have seats. He sat across from us and folded his hands on his chest, staring at me intently. "What can I do for you?"

"First, I wanted to ask you about the person who referred me here. Her name was Liberty Belle."

Harley tensed. "Liberty Belle? I don't know anyone by that name."

"According to her fiancé, Jason Lancaster, you worked with her a couple times," Callie said.

"Ugh. That asshole brought me into this?"

"Uh, yeah?" I said. "Is there some animosity?"

"That's one way to look at it. Jason was insanely jealous of the time I spent with Liberty."

"You just said you didn't know her."

"So I lied. Sue me."

An older Hispanic woman handed him a bottle of purple PowerAde. "Thank you, Leona." He drank from it. "I know I just met you two, but if I tell you something, will you promise to keep it among us?"

Callie and I looked at each other, then back at him. "Sure," I said, hoping he would admit to some part in her death.

Harley took another drink. "It doesn't surprise me that Jason tried to drag me into his personal hassles."

"Why's that?" Callie asked.

"Because like I said, he was insanely jealous of the time I spent with Liberty. For God's sake, I was doing my job. It's in my description to help people stretch out when they need it and get a bit closer than usual. That doesn't mean I'm getting fresh with my clients."

"Did you give him any reason to suspect you were trying to sleep with her?" I asked.

"Not any up-front reason. Maybe I developed a thing for her after a couple sessions, though. What's the big deal?"

"He might have caught on to that," Callie said. "Most men don't like the thought of anyone trying to make moves on their women." She placed her hand on my leg. "I don't like the thought of another woman trying to seduce Aaron."

"I guess I get that, but I wasn't going to take it anywhere."

"I see," I said. "One last question. Did you have anything to do with her murder?"

He fell silent. "She's dead?"

"Found murdered in Jason's beach house a couple weeks ago," Callie said.

"Damn. I don't know what to say to that. I may've had a thing for her, but I'm not the kind of guy who would ruin a relationship over that, plus I'm not a murderer."

"So you're saying you didn't kill Liberty," I said.

"Absolutely not."

"All right." I stood. "That's all I need for now. Thanks for your time."

"Hold on a second. You didn't ask me anything about my regimen."

"I'll get in touch with you about that later. My manager needs to see me right now."

Harley seemed skeptical, but he walked us out and shook my hand. "I look forward to hearing from you again."

"You will."

He closed the door, and I looked around. I didn't see anyone, though the van was visible, so they couldn't have left.

I saw Katie walking up the sidewalk a moment later, looking at her phone. She saw me and grinned. "How did things with Harley go?"

"Where on Earth were you? I thought the plan was to bring in the rest of you to see if Harley recognized you from *The Banshee Busters.*"

"I suppose that was the plan, but Vanna called wanting an update, so I gave her one." She looked around. "Brady caught wind that Katy Perry was around somewhere, so he tried to catch her."

"Katy Perry? Where?"

"Calm down, Boy," Callie said. "I haven't seen you this excited since we landed our first international investigation."

The season three finale of *The Banshee Busters* took us to the Leap Castle in Ireland. Since our series began, we made it a point to visit unique, famous places for each finale, with its live Halloween special. Those live specials were so popular, our fans asked for another one.

We were currently looking for a suitable location, but our first choice was Alcatraz Prison off the San Francisco coast. Other possibilities included the Myrtle Plantation in Louisianan and the Lemp Mansion in Missouri, but we had several months left to work out the details.

Brady jumped out of the bushes and shouted, "Oogly boogly!"

I jumped almost a foot in the air. When I caught my breath, I said, "Dude, you know better than to do that."

"Sorry, Bro. It was Katie's idea."

I glared at her. "Is that true?"

She gave me a smug grin. "Sue me."

"Where are Angela and Randy?" Callie asked.

"Dear God, don't tell me they're hiding to scare me, too," I complained.

Angela popped through a shrub and screamed, "Aargh!" and I almost punched her.

"The hell is this, Scare the Shit Out of Ben Day?" I asked. "I only enjoy scares on Halloween or during our investigations."

"It's so fun, though," Brady said. "You're pretty much fearless, so the only way to scare you is get you off guard."

"Where the heck is Randy?"

Randy walked up staring at his phone and looked up at us. "Sorry. There was an Arcanine in the area."

He played Pokemon Go religiously.

I sighed. "If you're all done scaring me, we should get back to the frat house and go over what we know so far."

"Sounds nice to me," Katie said. "Maybe we can get some dinner, too."

We got into the minivan and drove to the house to unwind from the full day we had.

I woke the next morning to Kelly Clarkson's song again. I got up, stretched, and put on my dark-blue robe before walking downstairs, mulling over the facts we had so far.

Micki, Brian, and Dinah had no part in the murder. Harley claimed he had a thing for Liberty but would never do anything to ruin the relationship. Boone's investigator thought he caught the hint of a female voice in the call I received, so I considered focusing on women next.

Something about Harley threw me off. Travis Cain was still a big suspect because of his obsession over Liberty.

I poured a bowl of Crispix when the doorbell rang, jarring me out of my thoughts. I crept to the door, trying to make as little movement as possible, and glanced through the peephole.

No one was outside. I opened the door carefully but saw only a white box with violet bow sitting in front of the door.

How nice, I thought. *A present.*

I carried the box inside, along with an envelope I found under the bow. Setting the box on the counter, I put the envelope aside and opened the lid.

11

Staring up at me was the decapitated head of Harley Crank, his expression frozen in fear.

Screaming, I threw the box to the floor. With shaking hands, I picked up the envelope. It was addressed to me, so I opened it and saw a letter made by cutting and pasting words and letters together.

I know what you're doing, Ben. This is your first warning. Stop trying to avenge Liberty, or the next time, it'll be your head in the box.

I calmly walked to the rope hanging down, put on the ear protectors, and pulled. The others screamed as expected and ran downstairs quickly.

"You know, Ben," Katie said, "Jeremy made it clear that the siren was reserved for emergencies only."

I gestured to the decapitated head on the counter. "What would you call that?"

They looked inside and nodded. "That would do it," Katie said. "We need to get this to the station ASAP."

"There's a letter, too," Angela said. She picked it up and read it, then her face turned pale. "Oh, my God. Yeah, we need to get this to Boone."

"What's it say?" Callie took the letter from Angela and skimmed it, her expression changing to one of rage. "No one threatens my man with death and gets away with it!"

She looked around and saw all of us wearing our robes. "Maybe we should dress before going to the station."

I didn't like putting the head in Jeremy's van, but I had to if I wanted help from the forensics lab. None of us wanted it in our lap, so I put it in the back and floored the gas pedal. I was relieved to see the same nice lady behind the bulletproof glass when I walked in. The plaque on her desk read Mandi.

"Hi," she said. "Welcome back."

I grinned. "Thanks. Is Boone in?"

"He is. Did you get another break in the case?"

I looked at the closed box I carried. "You could say that."

Mandi picked up the phone. "All right. I'll let him know you're here."

"Thanks so much."

She smiled and nodded. "Hi, Chief. Ben and his friends are here with a new piece of evidence." She nodded and hung up. "He'll be out in a few seconds. Have a seat and make yourselves at home."

"We probably should. We'll be in and out a lot over the next week or so."

Mandi laughed. We took seats in the waiting area.

Boone came out a minute later. "Ben, good to see you again. I hear you have a new piece of evidence."

"I do, Sir." I handed him the box. "Be careful opening it."

He took it to the counter where Mandi sat and slowly opened the lid, then grimaced. "Is this what I think it is?"

"If you think it's celebrity trainer Harley Crank's decapitated head, then yes."

"This will be all over the news in a few days," Katie said.

We gave her a look. She shrugged. "Just saying. A person who worked with huge stars just had his head cut off. Something tells me people will find that conversation-worthy."

"This letter came with it." I handed the threatening letter to Boone. "I was hoping you could find fingerprints on it."

"I can try," Boone said. "I'll give this to the forensics team and see what they can do. I have to be honest, though. It'll take over twenty-four hours to get complete results."

"That's fine. If something comes up, that'll help."

"We'll give it our best shot."

"Thank you, Sir. That's all we ask."

"Before I forget, we're taking this threat very seriously. We're sending a bodyguard with you to make sure nothing happens."

He took out a two-way radio and said, "Send Sonja up front."

A minute later, a muscular woman with slick, black hair tied in a ponytail came over.

"This is Sonja," Boone said. "She'll do whatever it takes to make sure you're safe."

"We appreciate that, Sir." I looked at Sonja. "It's very nice to meet you."

"Likewise." She sounded like she had an Austrian accent. "I'll keep you safe."

We walked to the van with Sonja and got in.

"What do you guys think is the next best course of action for today?" I asked the group.

"We should check out that Travis fellow," Randy said. "Jason seemed to really have it in for him. Maybe there's a good reason."

"Or we could look deeper into Julie Capp," Callie suggested. "See if she's as crazy as Micki said."

"That sounds good," I said, starting the engine. "Let's check her out."

I got Julie's address from Micki and drove to her house, a huge mansion in Beverly Hills. I pulled up to the security gate and told the guard, "I'm interning to be a reporter for *People Magazine*, and my first job is getting an interview from Miss Capp about the Liberty Belle murder."

I knew telling the truth would make him refuse to let us in, so I lied.

The guard crossed his arms. "I didn't hear anything about an interview with *People.*"

"Does she tell you every time she has an interview?"

"Well, no."

"That's why I'm here. I won't be long. I promise."

He sized me up like the one who guarded Micki's community. "All right. I'll let her know you're here." He went into the booth and pressed a button to open the gates. "Sorry to hold you up."

"No. I totally get it. You're trying to keep crazies out, so she won't be in harm's way."

"You're the man," the guard said.

I drove past the guard shack to the mansion entrance. "If we're going to pull this off, I need two of you. The other three can chill in here."

"I'll take one for the team and stay behind," Callie said. "I already dealt with Harley, and he ended up dead. Who's to say this won't end the same way?"

"I'm game," Brady said.

"Me, too," Randy said.

"Awesome. I'll be the reporter. Brady's the guy I'm interning for, and Randy is the photographer."

"Sounds like a plan," Brady said. "Let's do it."

I turned my hat backward, and we got out. Brady and Randy followed. Randy took out the camera we used on ghost investigations.

We walked to the door, and I rang the bell. It opened, and a woman wearing denim short shorts and a violet tube top stood there. Part of her crimson hair was mussed, but the rest was well turned out.

She looked at us and asked, "Can I help you?"

"Yes. My name is Gavin DeAngelo, a reporter for *People Magazine*." I gestured to my companions. "This is Davis McCoy, my supervisor, and Mike Reno, my photographer." I looked her in the eye and asked, "You're Julie Capp, right?"

She crossed her arms. "Yes, but I don't remember hearing anything about an interview."

I took a shot in the dark. "I told your assistant about it. They said you'd be notified."

Julie rolled her eyes and sighed. "Ugh. Patricia never tells me anything. She's family, though, so I really can't fire her." She let us in. "Come in."

We walked inside and followed Julie to her dining room, sitting at the table, while she opened a wine cabinet. She took a bottle of white wine and poured a glass for herself. "You want some?" She raised the bottle.

"I'm good. Thanks for offering."

"I'll have some," Brady said.

Julie poured a glass for him. Once she sat down opposite us, Randy took a picture of her for our story, and I turned on the voice recorder we used during ghost hunts. "Gavin DeAngelo interviewing Julie Capp," I said into it.

I set the machine in the middle of the table. "So, Julie, I hear you're working on a new movie. Tell us a little about that."

"I am. It's called *Nightmare in New Orleans,* a slasher horror film with a new take on the Axeman legend. You know about the guy who threatened to kill everyone in every house that wasn't playing jazz music in the 1920s?"

"Neat. Who do you play?"

"I portray a woman in a house who made the mistake of not playing any jazz. Every occupant in the house is slaughtered. It'll be awesome."

"That sounds great. I know this might strike a nerve, but I need to know something else."

She sipped from her wine. "Sure. What?"

"Your last movie was *Coulrophobia*. There's a rumor you were fired, because you constantly showed up late and were high a lot of the time."

She groaned. "That's a smear campaign to try to destroy my career."

"I see. The reason I'm asking is I'd like to hear your side of things."

"Ugh, but thank you. Finally there's someone considerate enough to get my side of the story." She sipped more wine. "While the whole thing about showing up high was bullshit, I admit I smoked a little marijuana occasionally, but it was for medical reasons. My family has a history of arthritis, and my diagnosis came on earlier than usual."

I wrote down a note. "If you don't mind my asking, how old are you?"

"I'm twenty-eight." She pulled her wallet from her purse and slid a card toward me. "This is the card I need to show to prove I have a medical condition that requires me to use medical marijuana."

I studied it. "It seems legit to me. Of course, I don't know what these cards are supposed to look like." I slid it back toward her. "A big part of the rumor is that Liberty Belle had a part in your firing."

Julie chugged half of her wine. "Yeah, that bitch."

I was supposed to be unbiased, but her words made me seethe inside. I closed my eyes to take a deep breath. "She supposedly played some part in your dismissal. Walk me through what happened."

Julie chuckled. "Where to begin?" She finished off her glass and poured another. "I arrived on set one morning, and I was told that Zach needed to see me right away."

Zach Lyons was the director of that movie.

"I got to the office, and he told me to close the door. When I did, he said I should sit down, because it was a very important meeting. He shook his head and said that my 'excessive use of marijuana' was stalling production of the movie. He said something about having a deadline, and my 'smoking habit' was 'disruptive'." She pulled out a pack of cigarettes from her purse. "Y'all don't mind if I smoke, do you?"

We shook our heads.

Julie smiled. "Thanks." She lit up and inhaled deeply. "I tried explaining that my marijuana was medical, and he had the audacity to laugh in my face. He told me I was fired and I had half an hour to gather my belongings and get off the lot."

She took another drag and blew out a mouthful of smoke. "It pisses me off, but I'm working on another movie, so I'm good there. Those people understand that I need the weed for an actual medical condition."

"Let me jump in here," Brady said. "You said Liberty was the one who got you fired?"

Julie nodded. "She did."

"How'd you find out?"

"That's a funny story." She puffed on her cigarette. "I learned the truth from TMZ."

"Oooh," Randy said. "That sounds like a terrible way to find out."

"It is, but when I learned she was found dead, it felt like part of me came back to life."

That made me furious. "Really?" I pushed my acting skills to the ultimate test and continued to pretend to be unbiased. "Why's that?"

"Because I hated her." Julie shrugged. "She led a smear campaign to try to ruin my career, and now karma bit her in the ass."

"Maybe she wasn't the only one who felt that way," I replied calmly. "Maybe the entire cast and crew wanted you gone, but she was the one who vocalized their feelings."

"That may be, but she was the one who said it."

"What the fuck does that have to do with anything?"

"Gavin," Brady said. "You might want to take a deep breath and calm yourself. You're getting stressed."

I closed my eyes and forced myself to calm down. "You're right. I'm sorry. That was unprofessional."

"You're telling me," Julie muttered.

That was too much. I stood. "This interview is over."

I walked over to Julie and leaned in close. "You're a special kind of bitch, and I hope you rot in hell," I said through clenched teeth.

Brady wrapped an arm around my shoulders and led me out. Behind us, I heard Julie say the stupidest thing I ever heard.

"Wow," she said. "You're being an absolute asshole for no reason. I'm the real victim here."

I broke free of Brady's grasp and went back. "You're damn lucky I don't beat your fucking ass right here and now. You aren't a victim. You're a piece of druggie trash who clearly cares only about herself. Have you even considered the family she left behind?"

Julie stared blankly at me.

I shook my head. "Of course not. You're fucking pathetic."

A bark of laughter escaped her lips. "*I'm* pathetic? That's rich talk coming from a nobody like you."

I glanced at Brady who mouthed, *Give her hell, Dude.*

I turned back to Julie and narrowed my eyes. "You happen to be looking at the cofounder of *The Banshee Busters,* the highest-rated TV series on Syfy behind *Ghost Hunters.*"

"It can't be that great if I haven't heard of it."

I clenched my fist. It took all my self-control not to punch the bitch in the face. "We don't broadcast to druggie bitches. Nice try."

Julie slammed her first on the table. "I'm not a druggie bitch!"

I laughed. "Fine. Druggie cunt. Is that better?"

She stood slowly. "You'll pay for that." She rushed me, her fist raised. I easily blocked with one hand and punched her in the face. She fell backward and lay unconscious on the floor.

I looked at Brady and Randy. "You know that was self-defense, right?"

They nodded.

"Do you think Boone will believe that if she calls the cops?"

"I do." Randy held up his camera. "I videoed the whole thing."

I sighed in relief. "I'm really sorry, Guys. I don't know what came over me. I'm usually not that much of a dick."

"I totally get it," Brady said. "We're all under a lot of stress, but you're the one directly affected by this."

We looked at Julie, out cold on the floor.

"Maybe we should get out of here before she wakes up," Randy suggested.

We walked back to the van.

"Finally," Angela said. "What took you so long?"

I started the car. "Let's just say Julie wasn't being very cooperative after a while."

"Ben knocked her the hell out," Brady said, laughing. "It was the funniest thing."

The entire car fell silent. All the women stared at him.

"I mean, the events leading up to it weren't funny," he explained, "and he did it only in self-defense."

"Did that whore threaten you?" Callie asked.

"Yes. She said she was glad Liberty was dead. When I called her a special kind of bitch, she had the audacity to say *she* was the victim."

Everyone burst out laughing.

"She really said that?" Katie said. "That's hilarious."

"For real, though," I said. "I posted a status about it on Facebook. Ninety-nine percent of the comments agree she's a dumb bitch."

"What did the other one percent say?" Brady asked.

"Irrelevant bullshit attempting to defend her. She's stupid, and I won't let her get under my skin anymore."

I focused on the road ahead. "I'm hungry for some reason."

"Apparently," Angela said, "punching out a bitch makes you hungry. I know it does me."

She looked around when the others stared at her. "Yeah, I've had to knock some sense into dumb whores before. Let's get Chinese."

12

We pulled up at a hole-in-the-wall carryout Chinese place to grab lunch to take back to the frat house. Back at the house, we walked in the door and saw Jeremy playing a game on his Xbox.

"What's up, Bro?" I asked. "We're back."

He glanced up at us. "Hey, Guys. How goes it?"

"Ben had to knock a bitch out," Brady said.

"It was self-defense," I added. "She threatened me with physical violence, so I acted first."

"Hold on a second. You knocked someone unconscious? Wow. I never thought you had it in you to do that."

"I got into a couple fights in high school," I replied, "but never with a girl and never to the point where someone lost consciousness."

"Normally, I don't condone violence, but in this case, I can understand it. It sounds hilarious. Tell me the details while you eat whatever you brought back."

"Did you want some?" Callie asked. "If we knew, we would have gotten something for you."

He raised one hand. "No, I'm good. I just had a bite to eat."

We sat at the dining room table and distributed the food.

"Walk me through what happened," Jeremy said.

I took a bite of my General Tsao chicken. "Things started OK. Julie seemed decent and told us about the movie she's filming, which I'm sure will be a steaming pile of garbage with a cretin like her associated with it."

"Then I mentioned the rumor about Liberty being the main reason Julie was fired and asked for her side of things. She seemed relieved someone finally asked and admitted she used marijuana but claimed it was for medical purposes."

"What purpose was that?" he asked.

"A family history of arthritis or some bullshit." I drank from my Mountain Dew bottle. "Then she started after Liberty. She said she was happy to hear that the 'bitch who got me fired' was dead and that 'karma bit her in the ass.' I tried to remain neutral, ended the interview, called her a special kind of bitch, and told her to rot in hell."

I chuckled. "Then she had the audacity to claim I was being an asshole for no reason, and *she* was the victim."

Jeremy burst out laughing. "You're fucking kidding, right? Your cousin, my sister, was murdered, and that stupid bitch is supposedly the victim?"

"My point exactly. That was when I lost it. I told her she was lucky I didn't beat her ass right then and there. I explained what she really was. She insulted our show, and...."

"Wait a fucking second!" Angela said. "What the hell did that wretched bitch say about our show?"

"I pointed out it was the second-highest rated show on Syfy behind *Ghost Hunters*. She claimed it couldn't be that great if she hadn't heard of it." I took another drink. "I said we didn't broadcast to druggie bitches, and she tried to defend herself, saying she wasn't a druggie bitch. I then called her a druggie cunt. She threatened to hit me, stood up, and rushed me. I blocked her fist and punched her square in the nose."

"Good," Katie said. "I hope you broke it."

"He probably did," Randy added. "I heard something crack."

Jeremy got up from his chair. "Sounds like y'all had a rough day." He went to his liquor cabinet, took out two bottles of vodka and tequila, and came back. "What say we unwind with a lot of drinking tonight?"

"Dude, yes," I said. "Maybe this will help me forget the problems for a while."

"And I can have the dark shit," Katie said.

We were reluctant to let Katie have any dark liquor, like bourbon. Some people do crazy things when they drink certain liquor. Katie happened to turn into a stripper. She always pulled off her shirt and used anything she could find for a pole. One time, she ground herself against a pool cue until it broke. Then she complained that her boss would take it out of her pay.

Since we'd been under a lot of stress ever since we landed, we needed a way to unwind. If Katie turned into a stripper for the night, so be it.

My phone vibrated on the table, and I looked and saw it was Calvin. Walking into the living room, I answered. "Hello?"

"Hey, Bro. How's the investigation going?"

I sighed. "It's been stressful. We're getting nowhere fast with the suspects."

"Ugh. That's no fun. What's this I hear about Harley Crank?"

"I'm sure it's all over the news by now. The day after Callie and I talked to him, whoever killed Liberty cut off his head and sent it to me as a warning."

"Wow. So the person involved in your cousin's murder is after you?"

"Not directly, but I wouldn't be surprised if attempts on my life start popping up soon."

"Dude, that scares the hell out of me. I'd go insane without you. Promise to be careful."

"I promise. Boone sent a bodyguard to be with us 24/7. She'll keep us safe."

"Calvin, come back here and plow my field!" Katelyn shouted.

I started laughing. "Dude, are you having sex with Katelyn?"

"I was," he admitted. "We were taking a break."

"Sounds like she's ready for round two."

"Ha. Yeah."

"Just be sure it's not where any other people congregate."

"No worries, Dude. I'm at her place. She can disinfect things easily."

"Have fun with that, Bro. I'll keep you updated on what happens here."

"Sounds good, Man. Love you."

"Love you, too. Have fun playing farmer."

He laughed. "Got it."

I hung up and turned to find Brady with two shots of Fireball in hand.

"Who was that?" Brady asked.

"Calvin. He wanted an update about the investigation."

He handed me one of the shots. "What was that last bit about playing farmer?"

I downed the Fireball. "He was taking a break from sleeping with Katelyn, and she told him to come back and plow her field."

"You mean her lady parts?"

"That's what I assume."

"Fun." Brady took his shot. "How does beer pong sound?"

"It sounds wonderful. Maybe that'll help me forget the bad things that happened over the last couple days."

He grinned. "Then let's do it. Tomorrow, we'll talk to more suspects."

"Ugh. Let's go to Liberty's masseuse, then we'll focus on Travis."

I poured a shot of tequila. "Tonight, let's focus on getting absolutely shitfaced."

"Sounds like a plan. Make me a shot while you're at it."

I made a second shot for him, then he held it up high. "A toast to Liberty getting justice and to tonight. May it be full of fun and laughter."

"I'll drink to that."

We toasted and downed our shots. After that, the evening became a blur.

I woke the following morning on the couch at 9:45. I slowly stood and walked through the house, looking for the others. Katie passed out on the stairs clutching a lamp post. Angela was bent over the rail on the front porch where I assume she fell asleep after puking. Callie sprawled on the beer pong table, and Brady was in a tree in the backyard. I never understood why he did that when he drank. It was like Katie turning into a stripper when she drank.

Randy was the only one who managed to get into his bed like a normal person. I walked into the kitchen and found Jeremy eating breakfast at the table.

"Morning, Dude," he said. "How'd you sleep?"

"Decently, I guess. Did anyone do anything embarrassing last night?"

"I'd say no, but I'd be lying. For starters, Brady's in a tree."

"That happens every time he gets drunk."

Jeremy laughed. "Maybe I should drink with you guys more often." He sipped from his orange juice. "Who do you want to hear about first?"

"You mean more than one of us made an ass of ourselves?"

"Well, yeah. All of you did at least one embarrassing thing."

I thought about it, debating about whether I should ask about myself, Brady, or Angela. I wanted to know about myself for potential damage control. I could blackmail Angela with her story, and I was curious how the hell Brady ended up in the tree.

"Tell me about Brady."

"That's probably the funniest story. We all played beer pong while Katie was stripping. Out of nowhere, Brady announced he was Tarzan."

Jeremy cut into his Belgian waffles. "He tore off his shirt, pounded his chest, and ran outside. He shouted he needed a vine and swung up into the tree only to fall out. He came back inside, then, a few hours later, said he was going to bed. He walked back out, got into the tree, and passed out."

That was classic Brady, always the clown.

I took a deep breath. "All right. Tell me what I did."

"Where to begin?" He smiled. "For a bit, you believed you were an alien. You tried to abduct Katie from her stripper pole and probe her with your spicy Italian sausage."

I stared in mock horror. "Seriously?"

"No. I'm totally kidding. You did try to probe her, but you used a plastic sword one of the brothers had lying around."

I punched his shoulder. "For God's sake, Bro, don't scare me like that. I almost had a fucking heart attack." I looked into his eyes. "Is that it?"

"No. After you probed Katie, you took one look at Angela and started laughing your ass off. Whenever you calmed down enough to tell us what was so funny, you pointed at her and exclaimed that Lea Michele was in the kitchen."

Some of our Tumblr fans pointed out the similarities between ourselves and other famous people. They said Brady resembled Bradley Cooper, which I could understand; Angela looked like Lea Michele, which I could *definitely* see; Katie looked like a young Lucy Liu; and I resembled Danny Gokey, a singer on *American Idol* at one time. I never understood where they got those ideas.

"You asked Angela for her autograph. After you got it, you announced you were going to bed. You walked to the couch and passed out on the floor in front of it. Your alarm went off at seven-thirty, but apparently, you weren't ready for it. You screamed, 'Shut up, Kelly!' and turned it off."

I was surprised I hadn't broken my phone. Kelly Clarkson seemed like a nice, humble woman. I felt bad for yelling at her, even though I was just talking to my phone.

"What do you guys have on your list for today?" Jeremy asked.

I poured a glass of OJ, hoping it would get rid of my hangover. "I thought we'd try to talk to Liberty's masseuse and see if she has any insight into what happened. If there's time, I also want to hit up Travis."

"Travis Cain, her ex-boyfriend? Dude, be careful with him. He's legit psycho."

"Jason said the same thing. That's why he's at the top of our suspect list at the moment." I looked at my watch. "If the others aren't awake by noon, you'll have to help me wake them."

Jeremy grinned. "You got it, Bro."

It was a good thing they woke up by 11:00, because Jeremy was ready to use the air-raid siren. That, combined with six hangovers, would not be good.

I gave them a chance to eat something, then I called Jason, so he could give me more details on Liberty's masseuse. I got addresses for her home and work, input them into my GPS, and we set off.

We checked her workplace first. My initial plan was to pretend to need a massage or adjustment and try to get information out of her during it, but my back was actually aching. I'd be a lot more convincing with that.

It turned out that Alicia Carbanaro did house calls for celebrity clients, but she mostly did massage and non-chiropractic work for regular clients at Dr. Kevin Leland's office. He was no relation to Katie. We saw a bar and grill one block away, so the others went there to wait and have a small bite to eat, while I went to speak with Alicia while she worked on me.

I walked into the office and looked around. It was a standard doctor's office. The front desk was a half-oval against a wall with a polished granite white countertop, the walls were half light-blue and half light-green, the fish tank had many brightly colored tropical fish, and a potted fern sat in one corner with a small fake tree in the opposite one. Framed certificates hung about the room, and two shelves were filled with awards above the fish tank. It was a nice place.

I walked to the front desk, manned by a black guy my age named Wes, identified by the plaque in front of him. He smiled at me. "How can I help you today?"

"Hey, Man. I was wondering if Alicia was in today."

"She is. Do you have an appointment?"

"No. Is that required?"

"It's not. It's easier to handle if people make appointments beforehand, but we do accept walk-ins."

"Neat. Any chance you can squeeze me in?"

He studied his computer screen. "Looks like she'll be free in five minutes. If you could take a seat, I'll let her know she has a new client."

"Awesome. Thanks, Man."

"You got it, Dude."

I walked to the chairs and sat. Five minutes later, a woman walked in from the rear of the building. She looked in her early thirties, with dark-blue eyes. Her light-brown hair was tied in a ponytail. She wore jeans with a pink Polo shirt that had the name *Alicia* embroidered above the right pocket.

"Hi," she said to me. "Are you the new client?"

I stood. "Yes, I am. My back's been really sore since last night, and I heard you're great at getting rid of pain."

"I've been told." She grinned. "Follow me."

She led me through a doorway, down a hall, into the third room on the left. The walls were painted burnt sienna, and some candles sat on different countertops. A radio perched on a nearby shelf. The middle of the room was filled with a massage table.

"I'll give you a few minutes to get settled." She walked out and gently closed the door.

I looked around and found a white towel to cover myself after I stripped off my clothes. I took off everything except my boxers, got the towel, and lay face-down on the table with the towel covering my waist.

I almost dozed off when a gentle knock jarred me awake.

"You ready?" she asked.

"Yup."

The door opened, and she stepped in, closing it behind her. "I'll start with a deep tissue massage on the area of your back that hurts the most. Where is that?"

"Right in the middle. I don't know what happened, but it's killing me."

"I can fix that." She started working.

Once I felt comfortable, I started the conversation. "Out of curiosity, do you know someone named Lindsey Carmichael?"

Alicia worked on the kinks in my back. "That sounds kind of familiar."

"Maybe you'd know her better by her stage name, Liberty Belle."

The massage stopped. After ten seconds, I asked, "Is everything OK?"

She took a deep breath and started working again. "Yeah, I'm fine. Sorry. It's all coming back to me."

"What's coming back?"

"Memories. She was one of my best clients, as well as one of my closest friends."

"That's sweet. The reason I'm asking is because I need any information you might have about her, her relationships, and people she might've had beefs with. I'm part of the team investigating her murder."

"Are you an undercover cop?"

"No. Of course not. I'm her cousin, Benjamin Becker."

Alicia gasped. "Oh, my God! You're the lead investigator from *The Banshee Busters!* You probably get this all the time, but I'm absolutely in love with your show."

I laughed. "I hear that a lot, but it's always nice to meet a fan." I breathed out when she told me to, so she could get deeper into the muscle tissue.

"I'm sure she told you a lot about her personal life when she saw you," I continued. "I wanted to know if you could tell me what she shared with you."

"Sure thing. What do you want to know?"

"Literally anything and everything you have will help immensely."

"Let's see. Someone she had a beef with was Julie Capp. Something about her being a druggie psycho bitch who wanted revenge over getting fired."

"I met her earlier."

"How'd it go?"

I sighed. "I knocked her unconscious."

"You knocked her out?"

"I had to. She rushed me, and I acted in self-defense."

"Nice. You probably lived out a lot of people's fantasies. Everyone I know who met her would love the chance to beat her ass."

"Good luck with that."

"Tell me about it." She moved her hands to my upper back. "Now that I think about it, Coco Centennial comes to mind."

That sparked some interest. "Who's that?"

"She's a porn star. At least, she is now."

"What does she have to do with Liberty?"

"You remember when Liberty got her breakout role in *Ain't No Mountain High,* right?"

I nodded as best I could with my face plastered against the hole in the table.

Alicia chuckled. "I'll take that as a yes. Coco also auditioned for that role. She and Liberty were the final two women being considered, and they ultimately chose Liberty, paving her way to stardom.

"Coco has been bitter as hell ever since and even blamed the loss of the role on the downfall of her acting career. She got minor parts in B-list movies, but all the films bombed. She left the entertainment industry and went into the sex industry, where she's been ever since."

So a porno bitch apparently blamed my cousin for the decline of her shitty career? I knew her acting was the problem. To keep our friendships strong, Brady, Calvin, and I set aside one night a week to hang out and talk. We left our phones in our rooms, didn't talk with our girlfriends or anyone else, and spent time enjoying each other's company.

One of our favorite things to do aside from video games and drinking was to watch bad movies, like *Octodactyl,* a horrid piece of garbage about a carnivorous pterodactyl/octopus hybrid that escaped from a CIA lab and terrorized a beach somewhere in North Carolina. That was Coco's best nonporn film to date, and it was awful. I never watched any of her porn movies. If the critics said that was her best movie, I couldn't imagine the worst.

"Do you think Coco had enough of a grudge to want Liberty dead?"

She moved back to my lower back. "Absolutely. I honestly don't know if she had any part in the murder, but I have no doubt she's happy to hear that the person she blames for her failures is gone."

She cracked her knuckles when she finished the massage. "There you go. How do you feel?"

I rolled onto my back and sat up slowly, twisting from side-to-side to test. "That feels good. Thanks. What do I owe you?"

"You don't have to pay me. You're dealing with the loss of your cousin who was in the public eye for seven years, which sounds horribly stressful. I wanted to get those kinks out of your back and help you."

"That's very nice of you." I put on my shirt and jeans. "I really appreciate that." I took a business card from my wallet and gave it to Alicia. "Would you call me if anything else comes to mind?"

"I sure will. For what it's worth, I pray whoever did it rots in prison for life."

"Not only that, but he'll burn in hell, too. Thanks again."

I left the room and said good-bye to Wes before walking to the bar and grill where the others waited.

I found them at the bar, and I remembered Brady and Angela scaring me when we left Harley's house, so I sneaked up behind them and leaned in really close to Brady to ask in a demonic voice, "What's up?"

He spat a mouthful of water over the bar. "Bro! What on Earth was that for?"

I sat on the open stool between him and Callie. "Revenge."

"You kind of had it coming," Angela said. "The way you frightened him outside of Harley's house wasn't very nice."

I put a hand on Brady's shoulder to steady myself and leaned back to look at Angela. "You'll get yours, too. I won't forget."

Callie sipped her watermelon margarita. "How'd it go with Alicia?"

"Decent. She gave me another name to look into."

"Really?" Katie asked. "Who?"

"Her name's Coco Centennial. Apparently, she's an actress turned porn star who blames the downfall of her career on Liberty snagging the lead in *Ain't No Mountain High.*"

"Hold on," Brady said. "Coco Centennial? Isn't that the same bitch who starred in that *Octodactyl* piece of shit?"

"That's her. I think we should...."

My phone buzzed on the bar before I could finish. I grabbed it to check caller ID and saw it was restricted. If it was the same person who claimed to be the killer, I had a few choice words to say.

I slid out the keypad and put the phone on speaker for the benefit of the others. "Who are you, and why is your number blocked?"

"I see you've been talking to Alicia Carmichael," a distorted voice said.

In addition to murder, we could add stalking and harassment to the growing list of charges for this person. "Maybe I was, and maybe I wasn't. What the hell is your point?"

"Be sure she watches her back. She might meet the same fate as Harley."

13

The phone went dead, and I set it down on the bar. "I can't believe I'm letting this person get to me."

Brady held up two fingers to get the bartender's attention. She walked over, flipping her towel over her shoulder, and placed both hands on the bar to lean closer. "What can I do for you guys?"

"My best friend here is in a bad place," Brady said, his hand on my back. "He needs a drink or twenty. What would you recommend?"

Staci, the name on her tag, thought about it for a few seconds. "Are we trying to forget things that happened or are we drinking until we don't have feelings anymore?"

Brady looked at me expectantly.

"I guess a bit of both," I said. "It'll be hard to forget what happened no matter how drunk I get, so I'm aiming for drinking until I don't have feelings anymore."

"In that case, you need a special cocktail. It's something I created called the Strawberry Staci Slammer. It contains two parts banana liqueur, two parts strawberry liqueur, and three parts tequila." She shrugged. "That doesn't sound like a lot, but a couple of those will take you where you want to go pretty fast."

I loved everything strawberry and banana, so I decided it was worth a try.

They were very tasty. I would've had twenty if my liver could survive, but we had more people to interview for Operation Justice for the Liberty Belle, which was the weird code name Brady gave our investigation. I restrained myself at just two drinks.

Staci gave me a glass of water afterward to flush out the alcohol and enable me to concentrate on the task at hand.

The six of us walked to our minivan parked in front of the chiropractic office and got in. I called Chief Boone.

"I need a favor," I said when he answered. "I don't know if anybody at the station looks into the addresses for suspects, but I need a couple of those for a woman named Coco Centennial."

"You got it. Is she a possible suspect?"

"Yeah. I talked to Liberty's masseuse. She said we should look into Coco. She might have a serious motive to want Liberty dead."

"All right. I'll have Carl look into it. He should have something for you in five minutes."

"Awesome. Thank you, Sir."

Boone called back five minutes later and gave me her home address. "She works at the Stuff-It-In Studio on Sunset. If she isn't home, try that."

"Sounds good. Thanks." I hung up. "We'll check her house first. Hopefully, she isn't there."

"What if she isn't?"

"Then maybe she's shooting some porn, Dumbass," Angela said.

"Or doing pornographic stuff off camera," Randy added.

We all shared a laugh. I put the van into gear, and we drove toward Coco's house.

Coco Centennial obviously wasn't her real name. When she was a teen, she took part in the "porn star name game," where people took the name of their first pet as their first name and the street where they grew up as their last name. She had a golden retriever named Coco and grew up on Centennial Avenue. She loved the sound of both names.

When she started making a name for herself and starred in some commercials, she ditched her birth name of Zoe Merrill and started using Coco Centennial.

According to Carl, Coco lived in a gated community in the Hollywood Hills. That was surprising for someone who claimed her career was ruined by Liberty Belle when she snatched a leading role out from under her. Maybe she made money in other ways, like as an escort.

We pulled up to the gate and were greeted by a female guard. I rolled down my window to talk to her.

"Good afternoon, Sir," she said. "What can I do for you?"

"We're here to see Coco Centennial."

"I see. Business or pleasure?"

I stared blankly at her, even though she couldn't read my expression through my sunglasses. "What would you consider working with LAPD on a murder investigation?"

Before she could reply, I added, "That's not sarcasm. It's a genuine question."

"I would think that's business," she said slowly. "What does Coco Centennial have to do with that?"

"She's a suspect in the murder."

The guard immediately pressed a button to open the gate. "Good luck solving the case."

I smiled, tipped my baseball cap to her, and drove through.

All the houses in the community were either manors or mansions. Coco lived in a manor. It was easy enough to locate her place. Her name was cut into the yard. I pulled into the wraparound driveway and turned off the engine.

"Let's figure out how best to do this," I said. "I'm thinking we could use the same method we did with Julie."

"You mean pretend to be a magazine reporter and extract information that way?" Angela asked. "I'm in."

"Yeah," Katie said. "That sounds like fun. It'd give me a chance to work on my character acting, plus I can report it at class when we're back."

Katie was taking acting classes at Texas Sate. There was a possibility, however slim, that a casting agent for a TV show or movie might see us on *The Banshee Busters* and want to cast us in a role. Katie wanted to be prepared if that happened.

Brady took a camo backpack from the rear of the van. "If you're doing characters, you should put on some of these disguises Jason loaned Ben a couple days ago."

I got the color-changing contacts and slipped them into my eyes. A bald cap covered my black hair before I slipped on a short red wig. Callie applied the fake red goatee.

Katie chose a strawberry-blonde straight-hair wig, while Angela opted for a fire-engine-red wavy wig.

"We look pretty unrecognizable," I said. "Let's get this done."

Randy loaned me the camera. I grabbed the voice recorder and notepad with my favorite blue pen and walked to the front door with Angela and Katie.

I rang the doorbell, and the door opened to a golden-blonde woman in a sheer red tank top and white short shorts. Her hair was tied in a low ponytail, the tank top showed off plenty of skin, and her shorts barely went two inches below her ass. She had huge boobs, which were hard not to notice.

"Can I help you guys?" she asked.

"Yes. My name is Justin Nunez," I said in my best vaguely Australian accent. "I'm an intern reporter for *Us Weekly* magazine."

"I'm Victoria Vance, the reporter he's interning for," Katie said.

"I'm Rachel Wilkes, the photographer," Angela said.

'You're Coco Centennial, right?" I asked.

"I sure am." She nodded. "Why are y'all here?"

"To interview you. *Us Weekly* is writing a story on some of the new projects you're working on, and they sent me here to get your firsthand account of things."

"That sounds nice. It's been awhile since I've been approached for a magazine interview." She stepped aside. "Come on in and have a seat in the living room."

The three of us walked in and followed Coco to the living room. It wasn't much different from mine back in Texas. The only significant differences were that her fireplace was nicer, she had a faux bearskin rug instead of a faux tiger-skin rug, and the room was significantly larger.

A porn star was bound to make more than a zookeeper, waiter, and bank teller combined.

I sat in a leather chair, while Angela and Katie sat on a bright white loveseat. Coco sat across from us with a coffee table in the center. I placed my voice recorder on it, "Justin Nunez interviewing Coco Centennial, *Us Weekly*."

"Let's see," Coco said, thinking aloud. "A lot of my recent stuff I'm not too proud of, but what else am I going to do to make money now that my acting career has been derailed, right?"

"Hmmm," Katie said, feigning curiosity. "What do you mean your acting career has been derailed?"

Coco chuckled. "That's a long story. I'll need a drink." She lifted a bell from the end table and rang it. A guy who looked like he belonged in a Chippendale show walked in.

"Armando, could you get me a bottle of Barefoot red wine, please?" Coco asked sweetly.

He left and returned a few minutes later with the wine and four glasses.

"Thank you, Boo," she said. "You can take a break now."

He left the room.

Coco poured a glass. "Do any of you want some?"

If she was going to talk at length about Liberty, it seemed like a good idea to partake, especially if she offered. Maybe alcohol would curb my anger if she said something nasty about my cousin.

We accepted her offer, and she poured glasses for all of us. After sipping from hers, she took an e-cig from the drawer on the end table.

"Y'all don't mind if I use this, do you?"

We shook our heads.

"Thanks." She took a drag. "I'm trying to quit, and I heard e-cigs are a good step toward getting there." She blew out some vapor. "Plus, this coconut-flavored cartridge tastes wonderful."

After another drag, she was ready to tell her story. "I started acting when I was sixteen, mostly doing TV commercials. I did everything from Wendy's to Burger King to Huggies."

"Huggies?" Angela asked. "Isn't that a diaper brand?"

"Yeah, it is." She sipped from her wine. "The producers thought I had the perfect mom look despite never having kids, so I was booked for it. Pretty easy money, if you ask me."

I sipped some wine and tried to calm my nerves before asking, "So when did your career start going bad?"

She sighed. "When I lost the lead role in a romantic comedy called *Ain't No Mountain High*. I still can't believe that happened."

"Why'd you lose it?"

"Apparently, they liked some girl named Liberty Belle better. Something about how she was more fit for the part than I was."

"That would fall on the producers, not Liberty herself," Katie said.

"You'd think." She took another drag from her e-cig. "Then tabloid stories starting popping up about how she was talking shit about me, since she snagged the role out from under me."

"You believed them?"

"Of course not, at least, not at first. Liberty seemed like a nice enough girl, and even though I wasn't happy about losing the role of a lifetime, I was kind of happy for her."

She sipped some wine. "Then rumblings came from Hollywood that Liberty really was talking garbage about me, not just in the tabloids. I tried to tune it out as much as I could, but one day, it got to be too much. I couldn't handle it anymore, and I snapped."

"Did you snap so badly, you killed her?" I asked.

Coco became silent. "She's dead?"

"Yes," Angela said. "She was found stabbed to death in Jason Lancaster's beach house."

"Hmmm." She took another drag from her e-cig. "I really don't know how to respond to that. I mean, I resented the rumor that she was talking shit behind my back, but I wouldn't have murdered her over it."

"Do you have any idea who could have been behind it?" I asked.

Coco shook her head. "Sorry. I don't."

"All right." I took a business card from my wallet. "Could you contact me if you hear anything?"

Coco took the card. "I guess I could do that."

"Very good." I stood. "I guess it's time to be going."

"I'll walk you guys out."

Coco opened the door for us, and we walked out. Before I left, I turned. "Thank you for your time, by the way."

"No problem. Have a good one."

"Thanks. You, too."

I walked to the waiting van and climbed in. Callie woke up when I shut the door.

"Oh, good," she said. "Y'all are back. How'd it go?"

"All right, I guess," I said. "This feels like it might have been a wasted lead. She didn't seem like the murdering type."

"That don't mean shit, Puny Man," my bodyguard Sonja said. "She could've been covering her tracks. After all, she is actress, yes?"

"She is, but based on the reviews I read, I don't think she can act very well. If she really murdered someone, I think her mannerisms would have given her away."

I started the engine. "We might as well go check with Travis and see if...."

My phone rang. I picked it out of the cup holder, seriously hoping it wasn't another blocked number. It was Jeremy, so I answered.

"What's up, Bro?"

"Dude, you guys need to come back to the house right now. It's super urgent."

I knew him well enough to know he wouldn't exaggerate about something like this. "All right. We're on our way."

I hung up and drove from the house.

"Who was that?" Callie asked.

"Jeremy. He needs us back at the frat house. Something happened."

"Did he say what?" Brady asked.

"No, but I'm sure we'll find out soon enough."

14

The dead body of Alicia Carbanaro hung from the roof over the entryway. Her arms and legs were stretched out like a star formation, and her throat had been slit. Her pink Polo shirt was stained red, and blood spilled down onto the front steps.

I stared at the body in disbelief, trying to find my voice. "What the fuck happened?"

"I don't have any idea," Jeremy answered. "I found her like this when I got back. I called Boone, and he's coming over with a forensics team right now." He handed me an envelope. "This was in the mailbox addressed to you."

I looked at the envelope. It was the same as the letter that came with Harley's head on the front stoop. It was addressed to me at the frat house with a skull and crossbones for a return address. When I carefully opened it, I found a folded letter inside with the same kind of cut-and-paste letters used.

I hope you liked the surprise. If you keep trying to bust us, you'll receive more of these. That's a promise.

I read it over. The word *us* stood out. More than one person was involved in the murders. Julie Capp was at the top of my list of potential suspects, given her reaction to hearing about Liberty's death. If she did this, we had to focus on her. Maybe that would lead us to her partner.

Boone arrived ten minutes later with the forensics department. As one guy snapped pictures of the scene, Boone asked what happened.

Jeremy recounted the events, and I handed Boone the letter from the killers.

After he read it, he said, "Huh. Us. So there's more than one."

"That's what I thought," I said.

"Do you have any surefire leads?"

"One right now," Brady said. "Julie Capp had the most-intense reaction to the news."

"Yeah, we suspected her, too." He rubbed his chin in thought. "We'll have to set up some surveillance around her. Maybe we can find some definite evidence that will pin her to the crime."

He looked at me. "I'll have this letter run though the tests to see if we find any strange fingerprints."

"That's be nice," I said. "Hopefully, something will come up."

"You'll be the first to know if it does."

The sight of a second dead body being used as a threat against me made me want to hit the bottle again. I was no alcoholic, but the investigation might drive me to it if people kept showing up dead.

We needed to talk to Travis and figure out if he knew anything about Liberty's murder. I decided to have lunch and try to calm down, then we could investigate the psycho ex.

We went back to Jason's place to check on him and try to calm down. Maybe Nina would make something tasty for us again.

I rang the bell, and a different woman answered. She was black, in her late thirties or early forties, had straightened dark hair with bright-red hues that fell to her shoulders, wore glasses and a white sleeveless blouse with a pair of stonewashed jeans.

"How may I help you?" she asked.

"Hi. My name is Ben Becker. I'm a friend of Jason's, and we wanted to see him for a few minutes."

"Of course." She stepped aside and let us in. "He's in the living room."

"Thank you kindly." I tipped my hat and walked inside. We found Jason in the living room, killing zombies with a guitar in the game *Left 4 Dead.* He was so focused on the game, he screamed like a girl when I tapped his shoulder.

He turned and saw us. "Oh, hey, Guys." He clutched his chest. "Dude, you should know better than to scare me like that, especially when I'm playing a zombie game."

"Oops. I thought it'd be funny."

"I guess it was." He laughed. "What's up?"

"Is Nina here by any chance?" Brady asked.

"He wants to know if he can drool over her," Angela added.

"You need to hush," Brady said.

"She is," Jason said. "I can ask her to whip up something if you like."

"That's be nice. Anything that calms nerves would be preferred."

"I know bacon cheeseburgers make me feel at ease." Jason stood. "What happened?"

"A third dead person," Callie said.

He stared at us blankly for a few seconds. "All right," he said slowly. "I'll have Nina get started right away."

Jason walked toward the kitchen. The six of us sat at the dining room table, waiting. He returned with seven bottles of different varieties of beer.

"Do y'all want a specific beer, or does it not really matter?" he asked.

None of us but Katie had a preference. He gave her the only bottle of Miller High Life, and the rest of us took whatever he had.

Jason popped the top off his Coors and drank. "All right. While Nina's preparing the burgers, tell me what happened."

"We just finished interviewing Coco Centennial, trying to see if she had any idea what happened. Alicia told me the other day that Liberty might've had a beef with her over the role in *Ain't No Mountain High*. We figured it would be a good idea to see what she had to say."

"How'd that go?"

"Different than expected," Angela said. "Coco said she wasn't happy that she lost the lead in the movie that could've revived her career, but she was still happy for Liberty."

"She said Liberty was talking shit about her after the fact, though," Katie said. "She admitted the tabloids were running the story into the ground, and she tried her best not to believe them, but she couldn't take it forever."

"She snapped to the point where she murdered my soon-to-be fiancée?" Jason asked.

"Not according to her," I said. "Her exact words were, 'I resented the rumor she was talking shit about me behind my back, but I never would've murdered her over it.'"

"Interesting." Jason drank from his Coors. "Did she say she'd contact you if she heard anything else?"

"Yeah, she did," Angela said. "Hopefully, something will come through soon."

My phone buzzed on the table. It was Boone, and I said a silent prayer he found evidence that would help break the case. "Hello, Sir," I said.

"Hey, Ben. I'm calling to update you on the analysis of the letter," Boone said.

"Did you find anything?"

He sighed. "Unfortunately, no. Not one fingerprint. We're dealing with pros who seriously don't want to be caught."

I screamed with frustration inside my mind. "That's unfortunate. Thanks for calling." I hung up and closed my eyes to take a deep breath.

"Everything OK, Dude?" Randy asked.

I shook my head. "No. Boone said the forensics scan didn't find out piece of evidence we could use to bust these fuckers."

"That's no good. But look at the bright side."

"What could possibly be any good about this situation?" Angela asked.

"We're ninety percent sure Julie had something to do with it, so that gives us some kind of relief."

I clenched my fists. "Dude, I know you mean well, and I appreciate that, but the only way I'll find any kind of relief is when we lock up the dumbasses and throw away the fucking key."

Nina walked in carrying a tray of cheeseburgers and fries. She set it in the middle of the table. Jason thanked her, and we each took a burger and plateful of fries. After praying over the food, something we were trying to make a habit of, we dug in.

"OK, here's a question." Jason drank from his beer. "You said a third person died, but I haven't heard anything about it yet."

"Oh, that's right," I said. "We found Liberty's masseuse hung up on the frat house."

"Alicia? Those fuckers got to Alicia?"

"Unfortunately. They stretched out her arms and legs, tied her into a five-pointed star, and slit her throat."

Jason closed his eyes. "All right. This needs to end. It's bad enough they killed Liberty. Now they're murdering people who had nothing to do with the initial investigation."

"That's what we've been saying," Brady said. "We need to catch these fuckers and lock them up for good."

"For real," I said, taking another bite of my cheeseburger. "I figured that after lunch, we'll talk to Travis and see what he knows."

"Dude, be super careful with him," Jason warned. "He's legit psycho."

"That's what I keep hearing. My cousin said that, too."

"Because it's true."

"We'll see for ourselves when we get there." I finished off my beer. "We should get going if we want to catch him before it gets too late." As I stood, I added, "Tell Nina we thanked her for the food. It was very tasty."

"And that Brady likes her low-cut sweater," Angela said.

"Shut up, Ho," Brady said.

We walked to the van. Once I sat behind the wheel, I called Boone. "Hey, Chief. We need the address of Travis Cain. He's Liberty's ex-boyfriend and another suspect on our list."

"He lives on Rodeo Road. He's in Apartment 14 in the Cloverfield Complex."

I frowned at his instant response. "Are you sure you don't want to call me back with that?"

"No need. Carl pulled it up while we talked."

"Hi, Ben," a voice in the background said.

"Hold on a minute. Am I on speaker?"

"Yes. We figured things would go faster if we got the addresses as soon as you ask for them instead of calling you back."

"All right. I guess that makes sense. Thanks." I hung up. "Well, that was fast."

"You got the address?" Callie asked.

"I sure did. Let's go see if this guy truly is psycho or if it's just a character trait people gave him because of his situation with Liberty."

I wanted to believe it was just a character trait people gave him, because of the situation with Liberty, but that was a lie. The dude was legitimately a fucking psycho.

It started immediately when all six of us got to his apartment. I rang the bell. A shirtless Mexican guy answered.

"Uh, hi? Can I help you?"

That seemed to be the initial response of anyone who opened his door to see six strangers. I didn't really blame him.

"We're looking for Travis," I said. "From our understanding, this is his place."

"Yeah." The guy crossed his arms. "What's it to you?"

I glanced at Brady, trying to get him to say something. I didn't want to start out by saying Travis was a suspect in his ex-girlfriend's murder. That might hinder our investigation a bit.

Brady glanced back and nodded. "We're from the *Banshee Busters.*"

Brady, you dumbass! I thought.

"Oh, really? Why do I care?" the guy asked.

He was the second person who wasn't impressed that we had our own TV show. That was like meeting two unicorns in a row. We felt such creatures didn't exist, then a horse with a fake horn came along and made us question reality.

"We heard Travis is a web designer," Brady said. "We're looking for someone to take over running the website. He sent us an application through Twitter, and we're here to interview him."

The guy looked at us for a second, wondering if he should believe us. He focused on me. "He didn't tell me anything about this."

I feigned surprise. "Really? Apparently, roommates keep things from one another just like couples."

"That better be a joke," Callie said.

I glanced at her and grinned. "Of course, Honey. I loooovvve you."

She smirked. "Nice save."

I looked at the guy in the doorway. "Is Travis here?"

"No, but he should be home a little later. Even though this is super weird, you seem like you've got an honest face, so you can come in and wait if you like." He stepped aside. "My name's Benji Delmonte, by the way."

Benji sat across from Brady and me in a bright-red recliner. I noticed a tattoo on his left pec with a broken heart and the name

Andrea in the middle. In an attempt to gain his trust a bit more, I asked him about it.

Benji looked down at it. "That? It's kind of a memorial thing."

"Is it for a long-lost girlfriend?" Katie asked.

"Oh, God, no. Everybody knows it's a bad idea to get the name of a boyfriend or girlfriend tattooed anywhere on my body."

Randy chuckled. "My ex didn't."

Somewhere in Tacoma, Washington, where Randy came from, was a dumb girl with his name tattooed somewhere on her body. I didn't feel bad for her, because it was her decision.

"It's actually for my daughter," Benji said.

"Huh," Angela said. "But it's a broken heart."

He sighed. "Yeah. My girlfriend and I lost her."

"Oh, Dude, I'm so sorry," Brady said. "It might not be any consolation, since we just met, but I kind of know how you feel. My brother and sister-in-law lost their baby girl a week before she was due."

"It was a real shock," Benji said. "Everything was great until the day Karrie went into labor. My daughter came out blue, because she wasn't breathing. The doctor took her away to try to get her breathing again, but he came back to the delivery room ten minutes later with the news she was gone."

His eyes welled with tears. "I was so damn excited to be a dad, too. I always wanted a little girl, and my dream almost came true. Then God took her away as soon as He gave her to us. I don't understand why."

Brady glanced at me and mouthed, *Here's your chance.*

I nodded and looked at Benji. "Would you mind if I asked you something kind of personal?"

"Sure. What's up?"

"Do you believe in God?"

He nodded.

"Have you asked Him why it happened? I've never dealt with the pain of losing a child, so I can't imagine how badly that hurts, but

I don't think God would do something like that without having a plan for your future."

"I haven't thought of that," he admitted.

"A lot of people don't when faced with something that horrible. I lost my mother to breast cancer when I was eleven. For the longest time, I blamed God for what happened. I believed He took her away from me just to hurt me."

I teared up over how it hurt not to have my mom when I was growing up. Brady placed a comforting hand on my back. "I reached out to the youth pastor in Minnesota, and he explained God didn't allow terrible things to happen just to hurt people. There's always some kind of plan in place. It might take a long time for Him to reveal it to you. I still don't know what He had in mind for me, but I believe He'll tell me what it is eventually."

Benji sat in silence contemplating that. "You know, that actually makes me feel better. Thanks, Man."

"You got it, Bro. I'm kind of referred to as the go-to guy for advice on Christian matters."

"Who calls you that?" Callie asked.

"Everyone."

"News to me," she said under her breath.

"What was that?"

She smiled. "I said I love you."

"That's what I thought."

I glanced at Brady and nodded slightly toward Benji. He raised his eyebrows and nodded back.

We were so close, we communicated with nods. I just asked if we should tell Benji the truth, and Brady said go for it.

I looked back at Benji and took a breath. "All right, Bro. I have to be honest with you. We're not here to interview Travis for a job with the *Banshee Busters.*"

"Oh? Then why *are* you here?"

"If I tell you, you have to promise not to say a word to Travis. Let us tell him."

"You have my word."

"Awesome." I closed my eyes for a second. "Did he ever tell you about a girl named Liberty Belle?"

"The actress? Yeah, I knew about her. Travis brought her back here to bone her once or twice."

The last thing I wanted was to hear about my cousin having sex with anybody, let alone a psychotic like Travis. "That sounds lovely. I don't know how much you follow the news, but Liberty was found stabbed to death in her beach house in Malibu."

Benji fell silent. "You think Travis did it?"

"We never said that. He's on our list of suspects, given some of the stories we've heard about him."

The door jingled, clicked, and a guy with shaved dark-brown hair and a brown chin-strap beard wearing a pastel-green button-down shirt tucked into dark denim jeans walked in.

"Hey, Benji." He set his briefcase on the counter and looked at us. "What's going on here?"

"Come have a seat, and they'll explain it to you," Benji said.

Travis walked to the red-and-black-plaid recliner and sat down. "So what is all this? Some kind of intervention?"

"You could say that," I said. "We're here to talk to you about Liberty Belle."

Travis groaned. "That stupid bitch? What about her?"

"She's dead," Brady said. "We have reason to believe you had something to do with it."

"Way to ease into it," Angela said.

Travis stared. "There's no way she's dead. She's probably faking her death to try to get rid of me, the selfish whore."

"Really?" Katie asked. "How do you explain the fact that Jason found her stabbed to death in their bathroom?"

"Simple. She's lying, and he's enabling her lies."

"How do you explain the cops making the same discovery?" Randy asked.

"The liars always get the cops involved."

"OK, what's your deal with Liberty and Jason?" I asked. "Why are you so hell-bent on thinking they're lying about this?"

"Because Jason stole her from me. I was with her first. Apparently, he decided I didn't deserve her and took her away."

"What do you mean stole her from you? From my understanding, paparazzi caught you cheating on her with some blonde bimbo."

"It wasn't cheating. I just kissed the girl. That's hardly cheating."

Was he misinformed or just monumentally stupid? My money was on stupid. What sane person would think that kissing someone wasn't cheating while dating someone else? "A lot of people would consider that stepping out. You were dating Liberty at the time, weren't you?"

"Yeah." He leaned back in the chair and crossed his arms. "I still don't think I cheated, though."

"All right, then," Callie said. "What do you consider cheating?"

"Penetration. If I stuck it in the bitch, then I could understand that. Anything less is nothing."

"It's not nothing," Randy said. "If you're committed to someone, you should not go making out with every random girl you come across. If what you do hurts the person you're dating, it's cheating."

"Oh, really? If that's the case, then my flirting with other women to get free drinks hurt Liberty, too."

"Were the drinks for both of you or just you?" I asked.

"Just me, but I don't...."

"Then you probably hurt her. How would you have liked it if she went out and made out with another guy when she was dating you?"

"I would've punched a hole in the wall."

"Then why the fuck is it OK for you to do it if you don't want her to do it?"

"Because I'm the man. I can do whatever I want. If the woman loves me and wants to be with me, she'll deal with it."

"That's incredibly sexist," Katie said.

"Yeah," Angela said. "You're lucky I don't snap off your dick."

"Careful," Brady said. "He might like that too much."

Travis got up. "The fuck did you just say?"

Brady stood up, too. "I think you heard me."

I got between them. "If you lay a finger on my best friend, I'll beat your ass," I warned Travis.

He raised his hand for a second, then lowered it. "Whatever. You're just lucky I don't want to go to jail again."

He walked to the window across the living room and looked out. "Liberty had better hope she's really dead, because if she isn't, I'll kill her myself. If I can't have her, nobody can, and...."

Boom!

The window shattered, and Travis fell backward onto the hardwood floor. The girls screamed. I lay on the floor and crawled to Travis to check.

"He was sniped," I told everyone. "Bullet right through the head."

"Do you think it was the same person who did the last two?" Brady asked.

I looked at him. "I don't know who else it could be." I crawled back to the couches and got up in it. "I'm so sorry for your loss," I told Benji.

He shrugged. "It's all right. I can be honest with you and say I didn't like him much, anyway. He was a bit too deranged for me, and I've been trying to get him to move out for months."

"Why'd you let him move in?" Angela asked.

"I put a listing on Craigslist, and he seemed super desperate. I tried to be a nice guy and give him a chance, but he started trying to control everything about this place and me, too."

While the others talked, I pulled out my phone and called Chief Boone. "Chief, I have some bad news for you and your coroners. Travis Cain was just shot dead."

"Shit. We've got another body to take care of," he said to someone in the room. When he came back on the line, he asked, "Are you still at the apartment?"

"Yes. Want us to stick around?"

"Yeah. That'd be nice. We'll be there soon."

I hung up. "Boone wants us to stay here. I don't know why, but we should follow his request."

"He probably wants to know what happened," Callie said. "We're witnesses to the murder."

"This is the first murder I've seen in real life," Randy said. "I have to say, it's fucking terrifying."

15

Boone and the forensics team showed up ten minutes later with some thermoses of hot chocolate for us, presumably to help calm our nerves. We just witnessed a murder, for God's sake. The other deaths we'd seen were killed beforehand. That time, we handled the aftermath.

"Walk me through what happened," Boone said.

I sipped the hot chocolate. "We were talking to Travis about the murder. He was as deranged and psycho as everyone told us. We brought up the fact that she was dead, and his first response was to claim she was faking her death."

"Interesting." He wrote that in his notepad. "What made him think she wasn't dead?"

"He was a psychopath," Benji said, joining us.

Boone gave him a confused look.

"I'm sorry," Benji said. "I'm Benji Delmonte, Travis' roommate."

"Maybe you can give me some insight into what he was like behind closed doors," Boone said.

"Gladly."

Boone glanced at me. "You guys can take off now if you want. Thanks for alerting us to this."

"No problem, Sir."

The six of us walked to the van and got in.

"What do you guys want to do now?" I asked.

"After seeing someone get shot in the head," Angela said, "I need a drink."

"Any excuse to get drunk, eh?" Brady asked.

"Hell, it must be five o'clock somewhere, right?"

I glanced down at the car clock, which read 4:00. "What do you know? It's four o'clock."

"What does that mean?" Callie asked.

"It's five o'clock in Texas. California is one hour behind us."

"That settles it," Angela said. "Let's get shitfaced."

"Sounds good to me." I started the van and drove away. "Only question left is whether we drink with Jeremy or Jason."

"I've never seen Jason drunk," Callie asked. "I vote we chill with him."

"Seeing him get hammered is on my bucket list," Katie said.

"No, it isn't," Brady said.

"Actually, it is," Angela said. "She has an actual bucket list written in the journal she keeps in her dresser drawer. *Witness Jason Lancaster drunk* is on there."

"Wait a minute!" Katie said. "You've been going through my journal?"

Angela, sitting up straight, avoided eye contact. "No."

"Uh-huh." Katie looked out her window. "I'll get you when you least expect it."

I began to think we'd all be alcoholics before the case was closed at this rate.

We pulled into Jason's driveway half an hour later. I rang the doorbell, expecting someone from his staff to answer, but he answered in person.

"Hey, Guys. What are y'all doing back?"

I smirked. "Nice to see you, too, Man."

He laughed. "You know what I mean, Dude."

"I do. I just enjoy poking fun at you."

"Yeah, that's one thing I love about you."

"Uck," Angela said. "Enough mush. You got any booze? We need to get fucked up."

Jason looked at me.

I shrugged. "I'll explain later."

We stepped inside, and Angela walked toward the liquor cabinet. "Do you have any strawberry lemonade vodka?" she asked.

"No."

"How gay. Where's the nearest liquor store? I'll go get some."

"I'll come with you," Katie said.

"I know LA pretty well, considering I lived here for a semester," Callie said. "You'll get lost if I don't show you the way."

"I want to get my own booze," Brady said. "I don't like strawberry lemonade vodka, and I don't feel right drinking Jason's booze."

"I'm coming, too," Randy said. "I'm in the mood for some Fireball."

They looked at me expectantly. I shrugged. "What?"

"Are you coming?" Callie asked.

"Actually," Jason said, putting an arm around my shoulders, "I'll have him stay here with me. There are some personal things I need to discuss."

"That sounds like fun," Callie said.

"Thanks for understanding." I unclipped the keychain from the belt loop of my jeans and tossed them to her. "Be sure to pick up some Patron."

"Got it covered," Angela said, as they walked out.

Once the door clicked closed, Jason locked it. "Follow me to my game room."

I did, and he closed that door, too.

"Wow," I said. "Whatever you need to talk about must be seriously personal."

"Not particularly. I just like keeping my doors closed."

"That makes sense."

He sat in his gaming chair, and I sat in the chair beside it. "You doing OK?" he asked.

I looked at him. "What do you mean?"

"I want to make sure you're all right. I can't imagine how stressful this is for you. You lost your cousin to some sadistic murderer, and instead of taking time to grieve, you're searching for her killer, so she can rest in peace."

"Yeah, well, that's what I feel I need to do."

"You need some time to let it out."

"Let what out?"

"The emotion you've been bottling up." He put his hand on my shoulder. "I'm here for you so you can let it out, judgment free."

Looking into his eyes, I felt tears coming. "Dude, I don't know what's going on here." My voice cracked. "I still can't believe she's gone."

"I know, Man." He pulled me into a hug. "Let it all out."

I needed that time with him. The only time I cried was the night I found out Liberty died. One night of mourning wasn't enough to get everything out.

Thankfully, Jason understood and gave me what I needed to feel better.

Awhile later, I said, "Thanks, Bro." I dried my eyes. "I actually feel a bit better now that I've gotten that off my chest."

"Of course, Man. I had to do the same thing. I could only do it in private, lest it leak to the media, and they label me a pussy."

"That's stupid. You lost your would-be fiancée. What man wouldn't cry when his girlfriend or fiancée died?"

"Chuck Norris?"

I stared at him for a second. "Chuck Norris may be tough as nails and an extreme badass, but I'm pretty sure he has feelings."

"Good point." Jason laughed. "You want to play some *Left 4 Dead* while we wait for them to come back?"

"Sounds like fun."

Jason turned on the Xbox One and handed me the controller. "Now I have to ask why y'all want to drink again. You aren't turning into alcoholics, are you?"

"Of course not." I thought for a second. "I can't really speak for Angela or Katie, but the rest of us are fine."

"What's going on?"

I took a breath. "We witnessed our first murder."

"Who was it?"

"Travis."

Jason fell silent. "Is this for real?"

I nodded. "Someone shot him through his apartment window while we were interrogating him. We think it's the same people who killed Harley and Alicia."

"I can't say I'm torn up about Travis. He was a nightmare." Jason set up a co-op campaign in the game. "I'll pretend every zombie I come across is Travis reincarnated."

"You must have really hated him."

"Yeah. I told you how horrible he was."

"You did." I looked at the TV screen. "I'll pretend all the female zombies are my whore of an ex-girlfriend."

"You had a girlfriend before Callie?"

"One."

"What happened?"

"She cheated on me with sixty-three different guys in the six months we were dating."

"Holy shit. No one would blame you if you suddenly turned gay after something like that."

"That's the messed-up thing, though. I considered it."

"Why didn't you follow through with it?"

"Is that a serious question?"

"Kind of."

I chuckled. "For one thing, I don't think that's what God wants for me. I told my mentor at the time when I was struggling with it all, and he told me to give it up to God and let Him take care of it."

I walked to Jason's minifridge and took out a bottle of Coke. "So I did. I got a sign that told me to wait, that something better was coming."

"That was Callie, right?"

"If you'd let me finish the story, you would know that yes, Callie was the something better. She didn't come into my life until over a year after the Leona incident."

"Leona was the whore of an ex?"

I looked at him. "No. Leona was my mother."

"Really?"

"No." I laughed. "God, you're gullible." I patted his head. "But I still love you."

The doorbell rang, startling us. Jason went to answer and returned thirty seconds later.

"I just thought of a hilarious prank if you're up for it," Jason said.

"Who's at the door?"

"The others."

"Good. I've been meaning to get my revenge of Angela. What's the plan?"

"Pretend to be dead in the pool. Do the dead man's float. I'll answer the door, pretending to freak out. They'll come outside, see you're dead, and lose their shit."

"That's sounds incredible." I laughed. "Let everyone except Angela in on it. She frightened me after Callie and I met Harley, and I swore revenge on her."

"Awesome. Go get ready."

"You got it."

I took everything important out of my jeans pockets, like my wallet and phone, along with my glasses, and set them on an end table in the game room. Walking out to the pool, I pulled off my shirt and dived into the deep end, floating on my stomach.

Two minutes later, I heard Angela say, "Ben! Look what we got!" Her sing-song voice ended, then she screamed. "Oh, my God! He drowned! Someone do something!"

They ran out a few seconds later and pretended to be shocked. Jason warned them about the prank. Angela was screaming her head off, running around the pool, trying to find a phone to call 911. When I was almost out of breath, I shot up and pointed my finger at her like a gun. "Gotcha!"

She stared at me. "What the fuck is going on here?"

"That's payback for frightening me after meeting Harley."

Angela put her hands on her hips and grinned. "You scared the living shit out of me, you ass. You're such a fucker."

I splashed her a couple times. "And you're wet."

Katie sneaked up behind Angela with a finger on her lips. I nodded.

Angela gave me a confused look. "What are you nodding at?"

"Oh, nothing. I have water in my ear."

"Well, it serves you right. I really thought you were d...."

Katie shoved her into the pool. Angela surfaced and glared at her.

"What was that for?" Angela demanded.

"It's a free country. I felt like pushing you in, so I did."

"You whore."

I climbed out to air dry. "What kind of drinks did y'all pick up?"

"Some Svedka, Patron, Fireball, and Southern Comfort," Callie said. "I figured if we planned to get messed up, we might as well do it right."

"Sounds fun. I need to figure out what else we can do for the investigation beforehand, though, so I won't forget when I'm shitfaced."

"I'll come with you," Brady said.

We went inside and sat at the dining room table. I pulled out my notepad where I wrote down all the facts and interviews we had. "With the list of important people Jason gave us to talk to, three of the five are dead," I began. "Harley was decapitated. Alicia's throat was slit, and Travis was shot in the head. That leaves Brooklynne, a second personal trainer Liberty sometimes worked with, and a guy named Reece Lassiter."

"Who's Reece Lassiter?"

"I don't know, but apparently he has a tie to Liberty. Otherwise, Jason wouldn't have included him." I looked at Brady. "We need to talk to one of them tomorrow sometime. The only question is who."

"I vote we try Reece first. We know Brooklynne was Liberty's personal trainer. Unless she was a lesbian, she wouldn't have any romantic interest. Plus, I can't think of another motive for murdering someone unless there was some kind of unrequited attraction."

"What about if she had a thing for Jason? I don't know if that's true, but, like you said, that's a common motive for murder. Maybe she wanted to be with Jason, but Liberty was in the way of that. It'd be like Travis in reverse."

"Huh. I didn't think of that. OK. Let's check out Brooklynne tomorrow afternoon."

"Sounds like a plan to me."

My phone in the game room rang. I figured it was Calvin. "I need to answer that, maybe set up the party when I get back."

I hurried to the phone to catch it before I missed the call. "Hey, Bro. What's up?"

"Hey, Man. Just wanted to see how things are going."

"They're going. I gave Angela a heart attack."

"Oh, dear. I hope she didn't die."

"No, she's fine. It was revenge for when she scared me after we met with Harley."

He laughed. "People shouldn't try to prank you, Bro."

"Tell me about it. I'll get them back ten times worse."

"That's awesome. Here's a weird thing. I was watching the news a bit ago, and they ran a story about some guy named Travis Cain being shot in the head while you guys were interrogating him."

I realized the media worked way too fast at times. "They already have it circulating? It happened only six hours ago."

"How odd. I just wanted to make sure y'all were OK."

"Yeah, we're all fine. I can't say the same for Travis, though."

"I don't care about him as much. It makes me feel better knowing you guys are good."

I smiled. "Thanks for checking on us, Bro."

"You got it, Man. It's really for my peace of mind."

"Calvin, get back here!" a woman called. "Use your jackhammer in my pothole!"

I burst out laughing. "Are you in the middle of having sex with Katelyn again?"

"Yes. She's super horny."

"I have to give her credit for super clever metaphors for whatever it is you're doing."

"Thanks, Ben!" Katelyn said.

"Hold on. Am I on speaker?"

"Yes."

"Dude!"

"Hey, Bro. It's easier to have sex when both my hands are free."

I was silent for a second. "Are you having sex with her right now, while you're on the phone with me?"

"Maybe."

I chuckled. "You're super weird, Bro, but I still love you."

"Hey, I love you, Man. Keep me updated on new developments as they happen."

"I will, as long as you aren't balls deep in Katelyn at that point." I laughed.

"No guarantees."

I hung up and called my dad to give him a quick update. "Hey, Dad. I just wanted to give you a small update."

"I hear Liberty's ex-boyfriend Travis Cain was shot dead in front of you."

"Yeah, he was. We're all fine, except for being temporarily scarred."

"Good to hear."

"Apparently, there are two killers. We're almost positive we know who one of them is."

"Oh, good. A surefire lead. Who do you have in mind?"

"Julie Capp, the girl who was fired from *Coulrophobia* due to excessive drug use and sleeping around with the crew."

"She thinks Liberty was behind that?"

"According to her, it was all Liberty's fault. She claimed she read a story on TMZ that said everyone wanted her gone, but Liberty was the driving force behind it."

"I see. Why do you think she's one of the killers?"

"Because of her reaction to the news of Liberty's death. Julie was ecstatic."

"Huh. Either she's a murderer, or she's one messed-up bitch."

"Even if she isn't one of the killers, she's a messed-up bitch. Anyway, the gang's calling me to get to the party we're having with Jason. I have to go. Love you, Dad. I'll talk to you soon."

"Love you, Son. Stay safe."

I went into the dining room to find a game of beer pong set up with everyone gathered around the table. The night started with Brady and me playing against Angela and Katie. It ended when the sun woke me the following morning beside the pool without my shirt.

I didn't understand. Every time I drank, I ended up in some strange place shirtless. The previous year we had a party at the zoo for a coworker's twenty-fifth birthday, which involved a lot of drinking. I woke up the next day shirtless in the zebra exhibit in the hay trough. I got the nickname "Manger Danger" for an entire year after that.

That story would go into zookeeper history. We had a Hall of Fame/Shame in the break room in visitor HQ as a running joke. My story was on the wall engraved in a plaque, right beside the time Giovanni pranked our coworker Heidi Thurston. He had his girlfriend give him makeup that looked like he'd been mauled by a lion, then he lay beside their meat trough.

Heidi walked past the exhibit on her way to clock in and stopped to say hi to Simba and Nala, the two lions. She almost had a heart attack. She needed a week off to recover from the shock, and Giovanna got slapped several times when she realized it was a prank. It was still hilarious.

Even though I always lost a shirt when I drank, it could have been worse. I could find my way into a tree like Brady did, as he did that morning.

I looked around and saw Randy in the water on the steps leading into the pool, Angela on the floor in the dining room, Katie sprawled across the table, and Callie slumped over in Jason's gaming chair.

Jason was in his room, watching the TV on his dresser. "Hey, Man. Come on in."

I stepped inside, and he scooted over on the bed. "You can sit with me if you want. It's not gay. We're practically brothers."

"I know." I laughed. "I've done more than this with Brady."

I sat down and looked at the TV. "Is that a rerun of *The Banshee Busters?*"

"It is. It's from the second season, when you guys investigated that haunted library in Arkansas."

That was a fun time. One of the main reports of activity was books flying off the shelves by themselves. When Jeremy, Angela, and I walked through the main floor of the library, and Brady and Carmen—his then girlfriend—held an EVP session in the basement, a book flew off the shelf and fell on the floor in front of Angela. She picked it up and saw it was a cookbook. Jeremy joked that the ghosts were trying to tell her to learn how to cook. She smacked him with it.

"What's the plan for today?" Jason asked.

"We figured we'd talk to Brooklynne and see if she has anything to offer our investigation. I know we never met her before this, but Brady and I have a theory that, if she's the other killer, jealousy could have played a factor, like the Travis thing in reverse."

"You mean she had a thing for me?" He thought about that.

"Now that you mention it, she acted a little weird around me when she came here to hold workout sessions with Liberty."

"That's good. Tell me what happened."

"She gave me her sexy eyes, like she wanted to get into my pants." He drank from the water bottle on his nightstand. "She was super touchy-feely with me on more than one occasion. She used me for example poses of what she wanted Liberty to get into when they did yoga. She always took the opportunity to feel me up and down.

"I tried telling her to knock it off, that I loved Liberty and wasn't going to treat her like Travis did. Brooklynne said she understood the words, but her actions showed something else."

"Did you tell any of this to Liberty?"

"Of course. She brushed it off and said Brooklynne didn't mean anything by it."

"You thinks she did, though."

"I do."

"Interesting. What time is it?"

Jason glanced at his watch. "It's ten-fifteen."

"Wow. That's late. I want to see Brooklynne before noon. Hopefully, someone will wake up by then, so I don't have to go alone."

"There you are, Bro," a voice said from the doorway.

I saw Brady wearing only a black undershirt and a pair of leopard-print boxers.

"What's the plan for today?" Brady asked.

"I thought we'd talk to Brooklynne like we discussed last night. If no one else is up in fifteen minutes, you and I will have to go alone."

"Sounds good to me." He looked down at his state of undress and grinned. "I should probably put on some clothes."

He left and returned five minutes later wearing a pair of dark-green basketball shorts, a black sleeveless shirt, and brown flip-flops. He tossed me a navy-blue tank top. "Here."

"Thanks, Dude." I slipped it on over my head. "You ready?"

"I suppose I am."

"All right. We're off," I told Jason. "We should be back in an hour or two."

"Sounds good," he said. "Have fun and don't let her molest you. She has a thing for guys with defined abs."

"That sounds hot," Brady said.

I looked at him. "Dude, think of Vanna."

"Good point. She might not like that too much."

"Gee, you think?"

"Was that sarcasm?"

I grinned. "We've been best friends for eight years. You tell me."

According to Chief Boone and Carl, Brooklynne Grace Donahue, her full name though she went by the first and middle professionally, lived in a manor five miles from Travis' former apartment.

Brady and I pulled into her driveway in Jason's Mustang convertible and discussed how we'd go about extracting information from her. Brady suggested we let our abs do the talking. I reminded him of Vanna again, and we decided we'd pretend we were looking for a personal trainer. If she thought we might hire her to work with us, she might be more willing to answer questions about a deceased client.

We decided to adopt personas, because we didn't want her to realize we were the stars of a TV series.

I rang the doorbell, and it was answered by an attractive woman in her late twenties or early thirties. Her dark-brown hair had caramel highlights and was tied in a high ponytail, she wore a neon purple sports bra, black yoga pants, pink-and-white Nikes, and looked like she spent too much time in a tanning booth.

She waited a couple seconds for us to speak, then said, "Can I help you boys?"

"Yes. My name's Carson Steele," I said.

"I'm Mike Rosario. We're looking for a personal trainer."

She crossed her arms. "What makes you think I'm a personal trainer?"

I pulled out my phone. "For one thing, you look like one. You're wearing a sports bra and yoga pants, which isn't something who doesn't work out would wear." I pulled up her website and showed her the picture. "This is you, isn't it?"

She studied it. "Well, yes."

"That's what I thought." I lifted my shirt to show her my six-pack abs. "I need someone to help me keep this sexiness in check."

Her jaw dropped. "Wow. All right, I see what you mean." She stepped aside. "Come on in. I'll gladly answer any questions you have."

Brady and I stepped inside, where she led us to a pool in the backyard. There was an in-ground hot tub in a gazebo that she wanted to chill in while we discussed the possibility of hiring her as our trainer. She stripped down to a studded dark-green thong bikini and invited us to get in with her. We shared concerned glances, stripped to our basketball shorts, and got into the hot tub. Brooklynne stretched her arms out on the sides of the tub and asked. "What questions do you guys have?"

"Before we get into that," I said, "we wanted to ask you about the client who referred us to you. Her name's Liberty Belle."

Brooklynne became tense. "Yeah? What about her?"

"You realize she was found stabbed to death in her beach house?"

She was silent. "I guess. I've been watching the news lately."

"Her boyfriend, Jason Lancaster, suspects you might have had something to do with it," Brady added.

"Why the fuck would Jason think something stupid like that?"

"He says you had an obvious thing for him and wanted to sleep with him," I said.

Brooklynne laughed. "Are you kidding me?" She rang a bell sitting on the deck beside her, and a young woman in grass skirt and shell bra came out. "Heidi, could you be a dear and ask Pierre to fix me a mango mojito?"

Heidi nodded and walked off.

"Is she your servant?" Brady asked.

"I consider her more of an assistant. She's a native of Honolulu. I told her she could dress any way she wanted while she's here, and that's what she chose."

Five minutes later, Heidi returned with a mango mojito.

"Thank you, Darling," Brooklynne said, sipping from the drink. "She's also a hula instructor when she has the day off from here."

She sipped again and said, "Tell me why the hell Jason thinks I wanted to sleep with him."

"He said you gave him the eye, the kind that conveyed the message you wanted to get into his pants."

"Oh, for fuck's sake, I was glancing at him. I knew he was with Liberty, and I'm not a home wrecker."

"He also told us you used him to demonstrate different poses when you and Liberty did yoga," Brady said. "According to him, you used the opportunity to feel him up."

"Someone thought too highly of himself," she said sharply.

"Whoa! Don't use that tone with me. I'm just relaying what Jason told us. There's no need to get snippy."

She closed her eyes and took a deep breath. "You're right. I'm sorry. I'm just a bit frustrated, that's all. It sounds like Jason's trying to pin her murder on me."

"What makes you think he'd do that?" Brady asked.

"Because he's trying to cover his own ass. I think he did it."

"You're fucking kidding, right?" I leaned back against a jet. "I'd love to hear your reasoning."

"He claims he didn't hear a struggle or even a scream. I can't imagine the beach house is so big that he wouldn't hear his girlfriend being murdered."

"So just because he didn't hear it happen means he one hundred percent did it? He can't be a heavy sleeper, or the real killers couldn't have held her down and stifled her screams. He totally did it, because he didn't hear anything."

"Whoa. I never said he did it one hundred percent. I said I think he did it."

I smirked. "All right. If we're going to throw around statements like that, I think you wanted to be with Jason, and you killed Liberty to get her out of the picture. That's what the media will believe."

She glared at me. "The hell is that supposed to mean?"

I glared right back. "If you keep trying to ruin Jason's reputation by saying he murdered Liberty, I'll ruin yours by telling the media you wanted to ruin his relationship and steal him from Liberty."

"Fuck you. I did not. You'd better not say a damn word to anyone about that."

I got out of the hot tub. "I'm sure you would have loved to do that with Jason. You of all people can't tell me what I will or won't do. I'm done here."

"What the hell?" Brooklynne asked. "I thought you were here to discuss the possibility of hiring me as your personal trainer."

"Yeah, no. That went out the window when you started being a condescending bitch."

"Wow. Nice attitude, asshole."

I laughed. "Do you really think that will make me feel bad? Sweetheart, I've embraced the fact that I'm an asshole. Dealing with stupid bitches like you made me this way. If you don't like it, you can go fuck yourself."

"What did you just say?"

"I believe his exact words were, 'You can go fuck yourself,'" Brady said, getting out and pulling on his muscle shirt.

"Now wait a minute. I don't appreciate your...."

"You can shut the fuck up right now," I said. "I don't want to hear another word out of your damn mouth." I picked up my jeans and slipped on my sandals. "Let's go, Dude. We're done here."

Brady followed suit.

"You'll regret being rude to me," Brooklynne shouted.

I flipped her off without turning around and walked out to the car.

"Well, that went well," I said sarcastically, revving the engine.

"Tell me about it," Brady said. "I'm sure Jason will love hearing this."

I started the drive back to the beach house. Halfway back, a black Chevy Tahoe in an oncoming lane swerved into ours and came within inches of hitting us.

I slammed on the brakes and laid on the horn, flipping the driver off. "Learn to drive, you old bat!"

"How'd you know the driver was old?" Brady asked. "The windows are tinted. I couldn't see a damn thing in there."

"I don't know. I was guessing." I parked the car and stopped to catch my breath. We almost had a collision while driving someone else's car. My insurance was based in Texas. If we had an accident in California, it would be a real pain to deal with. The car I was driving wasn't in my name, and the owner was under house arrest for the murder of his fiancée. I didn't know what might happen even when it clearly wasn't my fault, but it was a pile of stress I didn't want to add to my plate.

After I calmed down, I put the car back into gear and drove to Jason's.

I pulled into Jason's driveway, parked the Mustang, and headed inside with Brady to find the others playing Monopoly. They looked up when we came into the dining room.

"Look who decided to show up," Angela said. "How'd things with Brooklynne go?"

I sighed. "About as expected."

"Did she try to sleep with you?" Jason asked.

"She better not have laid a finger on you," Callie said. "I've never been in a fight, but if that woman tried to get in your pants, I'll beat the whore out of her."

"It seemed like she wanted to at first." I sat at the table. "Brady and I used the façade we were looking for a personal trainer to keep us fit."

"Like what you and Callie did with Harley?" Katie asked.

"Yup," Brady said. "She seemed interested at that point, led us to a hot tub in her backyard, stripped down to her bikini, and invited both of us in with her."

"Then a threesome happened," Angela said.

"Don't joke about it," Callie said.

"No sex happened," I said. "We told her about Liberty and how Jason thinks she had something to do with it, then she laughed and more or less called him an idiot who thinks too highly of himself."

"Seriously?" Jason asked. "That stupid bitch wanted to break up my relationship, and she fucking knows it."

"She claims otherwise," Brady said. "We didn't believe her."

"It was around that point that Kilabenjaro showed up," I said. "Nobody talks shit about someone I care about and gets away with it."

That was the name of my alter ego. It was a play on the word Kilimanjaro, the mountain in Tanzania. Friends in high school gave me that nickname, and it stuck after I left college. Every time I had to put someone in his place for any reason, my friends and I, and even some of the fans, referred to it as a Kilabenjaro moment.

"What did you say to her?" Randy asked.

I grinned. "She said she thought Jason killed Liberty and wanted to blame her to cover his own ass."

I saw anger in Jason's eyes and held out a hand toward him. "Calm down, Bro. I set her straight."

Getting a bottle of Mountain Dew from the fridge, I walked back to the table. "My response was, if she wanted to throw around bullshit like that, I'd tell the media she wanted to ruin his relationship by sleeping with him. She then said, 'Fuck you, I didn't do that.' Seeing as I don't like being cussed at by anyone, I ended it and got out of the hot tub.

"Then she wanted to know what happened to the whole thing about hiring her as a trainer. I told her the possibility went out the window when she became a condescending bitch." I took a swig from my Dew. "She called me an asshole, which didn't faze me at all. I told her dealing with dumb bitches like her made me that way. If she didn't like it, she could go fuck herself. Then we left."

No one said a word. Angela started applauding.

"Amazing," Angela said. "I wish I'd been there to witness such savageness."

"You could have come," Brady said, "but you were passed out on the floor when we left."

"That's because we needed to get drunk to forget what happened to Travis. It's not my fault I had a little too much to drink."

"Oh, really?" Katie asked. "Whose fault is it?"

"Mine," Angela said.

"Sometimes, you make no sense," Callie said.

My phone buzzed. I pulled it out of my pocket and saw it was Chief Boone. "Yes?"

"Ben, where are you and your friends?"

"At Jason's. What's going on?"

"We need you at Brooklynne Grace's house. There's a situation."

"All right. We'll be there soon."

I hung up.

"What was that?" Brady asked.

"Chief Boone. Apparently something happened at Brooklynne's house after we left. He needs us to meet him back there."

"This isn't related to what you said on your way out, is it?" Callie asked.

"I doubt it. I didn't touch her or even threaten to. Besides, it's not illegal to call someone a condescending bitch or yell at her when she's clearly wrong."

"Even if it were," Angela said, "I don't think Boone would do anything about it. He seems like the kind of guy who'd take your side over hers."

"Mostly because we're working with him," Brady said. "She's a psycho bitch."

"We need to go back and see him," I said, taking the van keys from the key ring. "We'll keep you updated," I told Jason.

"Sounds good, Bro. Stay safe."

Getting into the van, we drove to Brooklynne's.

A Black officer who seemed a few years older than me met us at the door. "Good. You guys are here." He offered his hand. "I'm Officer Vince Ajaria."

I shook it. "Good to meet you, Officer. What's going on?"

"Follow me, and I'll show you."

He led us to the backyard. The first thing we noticed as the crime-scene tape around the gazebo. EMTs were there, and two guys in forensics jackets were surveying the scene. Boone stood to one side, letting them work.

He looked up when we came into view and motioned us over. "You're probably wondering what's going on."

"Kind of," Brady said.

"I'll make it short and sweet. Brooklynne Grace has been murdered."

16

Boone raised the crime-scene tape, so I could step inside and see for myself. It was worse than the three previous murders. Her body floated face up in the tub, and she had a frozen expression of horror on her face. Her throat had been slit, and blood filled the hot tub. Whoever did it also turned on the jets, so blood and water bubbled up constantly.

"Dear God." I covered my mouth with one hand. "This can't be real."

"Unfortunately, it is," Boone said. "Obviously, we know you didn't do it. We just wanted to talk to you and whoever else was here to get your side of what happened before this."

"It was just Brady and me. Everyone else stayed behind."

"I see. Get Brady and bring him inside with us, so we can talk."

Brady and I followed Boone and Vince to the bar Brooklynne had in her manor. We sat on stools.

Boone took out his notepad. "Tell me what happened when you guys met with her."

"Where to begin?" I asked. "Things seemed OK at first. We told her we were looking for a personal trainer, so she might open up to us."

"Makes sense."

"We got into the hot tub and asked her about Liberty," Brady said. "We told her Liberty was dead, and Jason suspected she had something to do with it. Then all hell broke loose."

"Did she admit to any involvement?"

"No," I said. "She adamantly denied it. Then she threw out an idiotic theory that Jason murdered Liberty and was trying to pin it on her. Naturally, I wouldn't let anyone say anything so defamatory about someone I knew, so I defended him."

"You didn't hit her, did you?" Boone asked.

"Of course not. I brought up the fact that Jason told us she wanted to sleep with him, which she also denied to the nth degree. She claimed Jason killed Liberty. I told her if she was going to try to ruin Jason's reputation with such bold-faced lies, I'd spread the word she wanted to steal him away from Liberty, which has some truth to it.

"Then she said, 'F you, I did not,' and told me not to lie about her. I told her she didn't get to tell me what to do and got out of the hot tub. The last thing she said before we left was, 'You'll regret being rude to me.'"

"What about that black Tahoe?" Brady asked.

"Tahoe?" Boone asked, looking up from his notes. "What about a Tahoe?"

"I don't know if it's directly related to Brooklynne's murder," I said, "but on our way back to Jason's from here, a black Chevy Tahoe swerved into our lane and came within inches of hitting us."

"It seemed like someone did it on purpose," Brady said. "They drove fine on their side of the road until they were close to us."

"Do you think there's a chance the driver had something to do with this?" Vince asked.

"Honestly, I do," I said, "but even if the person was directly involved, I don't see how we can locate him. I didn't get the plate number, and there must be hundreds of black Chevy Tahoes in LA alone."

"Hundreds isn't that many," Vince said. "If there was any significant detail either of you remember about that car, I'm positive Carl can find it."

"All I remember is that the windows were tinted super dark," Brady said. "I didn't catch the plate number, but I remember it had a K in it."

"That helps a bit," Boone said. "That's enough for now. Thanks for your time, Guys."

"No problem. Let us know if you need anything else."

"We will."

Brady and I left and went to the others, who waited for us outside. For some reason, Angela was in the pool.

I looked down at her and grinned. "Is it that hot out here?"

"Yes, it is, but my whore of a roommate pushed me in here again."

"I told you I'd get you back for reading my journal," Katie said.

"This is the second time you did this!"

"Yeah, but the first one was for fun."

"We talked with Boone," I said, "and told him everything we know about this. The only thing that's left is to get hold of Reece and see what he has to do with the case."

"Let's take care of that after lunch," Callie said. "I'm super hungry."

"So am I," Randy said.

"After seeing the crime scene in the hot tub, I lost my appetite," I said, "but if y'all want to grab something yourselves, I'm fine with that. Just let me go back to the frat house first. I'll give you the keys to the van, and you can pick up something to eat."

"Sounds good to me," Brady said.

We were back at the frat house twenty minutes later. Everything was ordinary—no threatening letters in the mailbox, no dead bodies, no suspicious packages. We walked inside to find Jeremy on the couch, watching a rerun of *The Banshee Busters*.

"Hey, Guys," he said. "Long time no see. Where'd y'all go last night?"

"Jason's," I said. "Katie had a longtime goal of partying with him and seeing him drunk, so we decided to fulfill that for her."

"None of you would know that if Angela hadn't read my journal."

"Oh, come on," Angela said. "If it's that big a deal, you can tell them one of my secrets."

"That seems fair." Katie grinned. "Angela once made out with a stripper."

"That's the big secret?" Randy asked. "It's not such a big deal."

Katie looked him in the eye. "It wasn't a male stripper."

"Oh." Randy thought about that for second, then his eyes popped open. "OH!"

"Yeah," Katie chuckled.

"In my defense," Angela said, "she was hot as fuck, and I had some drinks."

"That's different," Brady said sarcastically.

Angela glared at him. "Watch yourself."

"Let's go get Chinese or something," Callie said quickly. "You want anything, Jeremy?"

"Yeah. I'd like sweet and sour chicken on rice."

"Got it," Callie said, walking up to me with her hand out. I gave her the van keys, and she said, "We'll be back soon."

The door opened and clicked shut, and Jeremy glanced at me. "What are you doing still here?"

I glanced at him. "Nice to see you, too, Cuz."

He grinned. "You know what I mean, Bro."

"I do." I laughed. "I don't really feeling like eating."

"Really? What happened?"

"I saw something worse than the surprise we got here a few days ago."

"Which one, the decapitated head in the box, or the girl with her throat slit strung up from the roof like a star?"

"Both."

"That sounds awful." He paused the TV. "Tell me about it."

"You've heard of Brooklynne Grace, right?"

"The personal trainer Liberty worked with sometimes?"

I nodded. "That's her." I took a breath. "Brady and I talked to her about her possible involvement in the murder, which she denied. She claimed Jason killed Liberty and tried to pin it on her, and I told her to fuck herself and left. Boone called soon after that and said we needed to return to Brooklynne's house due to a situation. We got there and saw she'd been murdered. Someone slit her throat and let her bleed out in the hot tub."

"Oh, goodness. Is there a pattern here?"

I squinted in thought. "What do you mean?"

"Think about it. Every person you talked to about Liberty's murder ended up dead. Call me crazy, but that can't be coincidence."

"You think the same person who murdered Liberty got to the other four, too?"

"It's possible."

"I never thought of that."

"That's why I was the brains of the group during the first two seasons of *The Banshee Busters.*"

I grinned. "Yeah. To hell with you for leaving us for LA."

"Was that a joke?"

I punched his shoulder. "Of course it was."

Ten minutes later, the door opened, and the others poured it carrying bags of Chinese food.

"Surprise, Dudes," Brady called. "We're back, and we come bearing gifts."

He pulled out a bottle of Mountain Dew Code Red and handed it to me. "We remembered you, even though you said you weren't hungry."

I smiled. "Thanks, Dude."

We walked into the dining room, where the food was distributed. Jeremy said grace for us. As the others ate, I looked through my notes from the investigation. It appeared that Jeremy was onto something concerning the pattern of the murders. Each person we spoke with had a connection to Liberty. Harley was her personal trainer. Alicia was her masseuse. Travis was her deranged, obsessive ex-boyfriend. Brooklynne was a second personal trainer Liberty worked with.

Micki, Brian, and Dinah, various costars who worked with Liberty, were still alive, and we were certain they didn't kill anyone. That left only Julie Capp with a very high probability of being involved in the initial murder, and, therefore, the subsequent murders.

"Bro, what are you thinking about?" Brady asked, snapping me back to reality.

"I'm thinking about all the murders we've come across. Jeremy thinks there's a pattern."

"That's what I thought, too," Callie said. "There's no way these killings are random, given they all have Liberty as a common denominator."

"Exactly," Jeremy said. "Whoever killed Liberty got to those four, too."

"The only question is who," Brady said. "We're agreed that Julie Capp has a high probability of being directly involved, but is she working with someone or working alone?"

"She's working with someone," Angela said, taking a bite of her General Tsao chicken. "Don't you remember the note Ben got after we found Alicia's body. It said, 'If you keep trying to bust *us*.'"

"True," Randy said. "Who else would want Liberty dead badly enough to kill her?"

"What about Coco Centennial?" Katie asked. "She had motive with the tabloids spreading the story about Liberty's supposed shit-talking, and I'm sure she had the opportunity, since she's a party girl porn star. There's no way she's home before four in the morning on a given night."

"Remember when we talked with her?" Angela asked Katie. "She seemed super genuine when she answered our questions, and she swore she didn't have anything to do with the murder."

"Come on," I said. "She could be acting. People guilty of murder say anything to throw others off their trail."

"Dude, you've seen *Octodactyl,*" Brady reminded me. "Based on her performance in that shit show, she doesn't have a good acting bone in her whole body. There's no way she could convince anyone she was innocent of murder if she did it."

"That may be, but something about her doesn't sit well with me."

"Why's that?" Callie asked.

"It feels like she's hiding something. I've dealt with a fair share of psychos and horrid people who put up a good-person front, and in every case, there's something very subtle that threw me off. Sometimes it was a particular word or phrase that sounded weird, or a body gesture, like an eye twitch."

"What does an eye twitch have to do with anything?" Randy asked.

"It generally means the person is lying," I replied.

"Did Coco say or do anything that seemed off to you?" Katie asked.

"Now that you mention it, she did. Her tone changed when she talked about the tabloids spreading that rumor about Liberty talking shit about her."

"I didn't catch that. It must've been super subtle."

"It was, but it wasn't subtle enough to slip past my radar." I pulled out a phone. "I'll call Boone and ask him to keep a close eye on her. I can't shake the odd feeling I have about her."

I dialed the LAPD and waited for someone to answer. "Hi, Mandi. This is Ben Becker. Is Chief Boone available?"

"I'm sorry, he's not at the moment. Would you like to leave a message for him?"

"Yeah. That'd be fine. I was reviewing my notes about the Liberty Belle murder investigation, and something about Coco Centennial seems off to me. I suspect she played a major role in the murder. I wanted to ask Chief Boone if he would keep an eye on her."

"Sure thing. I'll relay that message to him and have him call you back when he's available if you like."

"That sounds great. Thank you. Have a good day."

"Thanks. You, too."

I hung up. "She'll inform Boone about Coco," I told everyone.

"Awesome," Randy said.

"I propose a bet," Brady said. "I still don't believe Coco had anything to do directly with this, but it seems you do. If you're right, and she played a direct role in the murder, I'll give you $2,500 and take you out anywhere you want for a weekend. If you're wrong, and she's innocent, you owe me $2,500 and a weekend out anywhere I want to go."

I thought about that. Working at the zoo full-time brought in $9.75 an hour, or about $1,600 a month. The work we did on *The Banshee Busters* earned us $5,000 per episode, plus $250 per million viewers for the première. If I was wrong, I wouldn't be out too much money, but if my hunch was right, I'd have an extra $2,500 to put in the bank. It was a win-lose situation, but I wouldn't lose that much.

I grinned. "You're on."

Brady opened his arms to seal the bet with a bear hug. Normal people shake hands to confirm a deal or bet, but Brady and I hugged. We weren't normal.

"Ben, are you sure about this?" Callie asked.

"Trust me, Honey. I'll be fine either way. Think of it this way. If I win, you'll benefit, too."

"How so?"

"Remember that $2,000 diamond tennis bracelet you've been eyeing at Zale's?"

Her eyes lit up. "My God! You'd get that for me?"

"Of course, Baby Girl."

"Uck," Angela said. "Enough mushiness. Let's get on with this."

"Spinster," Brady said, covering it with a fake sneeze.

Angela glared daggers at him. "Shut up."

"Gee, I wonder what time it is?" Katie said, trying to break the tension.

I checked my phone. "One-thirty."

"Good. We have time to check out Reece if we want."

"Yeah," Callie said. "Maybe he's the one we need to finally solve this case."

"Hopefully he won't end up dead like the other four," Randy said.

"Dude, don't jinx it," I said, only half-joking.

"What are we waiting for?" Brady asked, standing. "Let's go see what the guy has to say."

"Sounds good to me." I pushed my chair back and stood. "Let's do it."

17

As we piled into the van, I called the station again. "Hi, Mandi.
It's me again. If Boone isn't available, is Carl? We need an address for
Reece Lassiter."

"The DJ?"

"I guess so."

"Sure thing. Give me a second, and I'll transfer you."

"Awesome. Thank you."

I was on hold for twenty seconds before Carl came on the line.
"This is Carl."

"Hey, this is Ben Becker."

"Oh, hey, Bro. How goes it?"

"It's going all right. How are you doing?"

"I can't complain. What can I do for you?"

"We need an address for Reece Lassiter. He's the last person
on Jason's list of super-important suspects, and we want to talk to him
to see if he had any insight into the investigation."

"Reece Lassiter the DJ?"

"How is it that everyone knows this guy? I never heard of him
before this investigation."

"He's an up-and-coming DJ. You wouldn't know him unless
you were into underground rap or a devout follower of celebrity gossip.
He's had a couple run-ins with the law that made tabloid headlines."

"Ah. I'm not into any kind of rap. While I follow celebrity
gossip at my own level, Katie's the devout follower."

"Did you guys hear that Reece was arrested for attempted vehicular manslaughter?" Katie asked. "Apparently, he tried to run over his ex-girlfriend when he found out she cheated on him."

I realized I might have something in common with Reece. I never tried to run Leona over with my car, but I strongly considered it. Even though it was super illegal and immoral to hit anyone with a car, regardless how much she deserved it—cheating on me with sixty-three different men constituted deserving it—I wouldn't be overly upset if someone did it.

I'd be celebrating, which probably made me a terrible person. *To hell with decency when it comes to whorish ex-girlfriends,* I thought.

"I have a couple addresses," Carl said. "The first is RAX Studios on Rodeo Drive. The second is his private residence in the Abercrombie Apartments complex. He's in number twenty-five. No relation to Abercrombie the clothing chain."

"Thanks, Carl. We'll look into those right away."

"No problem. Give us a call if something comes up."

I hung up. "We'll check out RAX Studies first. Carl said that's where Reece makes his music. If he isn't there, we've got his home address."

"Where does he live?" Brady asked.

"The Abercrombie Apartments."

"Oooh, those are nice!" Callie said. "Each unit has its own Jacuzzi bathtub."

"I love Jacuzzi bathtubs," Randy said. "They're great for having sex in, a lot roomier than regular bathtubs."

We all fell silent and gave Randy nasty looks.

"So I've heard," he said quickly.

"I'm sure," Katie said.

We pulled up to RAX Studies ten minutes later. A Hispanic guy in a red-and-white valet uniform walked up.

"I can park this for you if you like," he said.

I put the transmission in Park, turned it off, and gave him the keys. "I appreciate it."

The six of us got out and walked into the building, while the valet parked the van. We entered an immense lobby with bright-white carpeting, onyx black marble walls and desks, a two-tier fountain in the corner, five bright-white chairs on each side of the lobby, and awards on the wall behind the main desk.

A Black woman wearing a bright purple pantsuit, her hair tied up in a professional-looking bun, sat behind the desk. She looked up and smiled warmly when we came in.

"Hi. How may I help you guys?"

I smiled back. "Hi. My name's Ben Becker."

"Of the *Banshee Busters?* I'm a huge fan of your show!"

"Thank you." I chuckled. "We're here, because we're working with LAPD on the Liberty Belle murder investigation. We have reason to believe that a DJ who records here might have some connection to the victim."

"You must mean Reece Lassiter," the woman said. Her name-tag read *Kendra.*

"Right," Brady said, his brow furrowed. "How'd you know that?"

"I overheard him talking to Liberty on and off the past couple of weeks. He had a huge crush on her occasionally bordering on obsession."

"Oh, dear," Callie said. "We didn't know it was that bad."

"That's why we need to talk to him," I said. "Is he here?"

"Unfortunately, he's not. If you want to catch him at home, I can give you his address."

"No need. We got it from the police. Thank you for your time." I slipped her a business card. "Could you call me if something comes up?"

Kendra took the card. "I sure can."

"Awesome. Thanks again. Have a good day."

"You, too."

We walked back outside to the valet area, where I told the attendant which car was mine. He brought the minivan back in five minutes. As we got in, I gave him a $20 tip.

"All right," I said once I was inside, "he isn't at the studio. Let's go check his apartment."

"How will we do it?" Callie asked. "I don't think it's wise to give the real reason we're there."

"Good point," Brady said. "We need a plan before we get there."

"He's a DJ, right?" Angela asked. "Maybe we could pretend to be clients looking for a DJ to spin at a party."

"That's a great idea," I said. "Maybe if we offered him plenty of money, he'd be all over it."

"Then we can say that talking to him about Liberty is a requirement," Brady said. "Let's do it."

As far as we knew, Reece Lassiter lived alone in Abercrombie Apartment unit 25. We pulled into the guest parking lot and parked. I turned to look at everyone. "Who's ready to do this?"

"I am," Callie said. "I've always wanted to see what an apartment here looked like on the inside."

"Who'll do the talking?" Brady asked.

"I will. I have an idea how to go about this so it's a bit more convincing."

We got out of the van and walked toward the complex together. A sign in the lobby listed the apartments and floors. The building was eight stories, with four apartments on each floor. Reece's was on the seventh floor.

Brady and Angela decided to race up the stairs to fuel their competitive fire, while the rest of us took the elevator.

When the doors opened on the seventh floor, Angela was leaning against the wall, catching her breath. Brady arrived five seconds later.

"You whore," he told Angela. "You cheated."

"I did no such thing. You just suck."

"That's not what you said last night."

"That doesn't make sense."

"Your mom doesn't make sense."

"Your mom's a ho."

"Let's return to this later," I said. "We have something more important to do right now."

"You're right," Brady said. "Sorry."

We crept to the door for Apartment 25. I turned my hat backward, looked at the others, nodded once, then knocked. I waited and was ready to knock again when a Latino guy wearing a black undershirt, jeans, a bright-white ball cap on backward, and a gold necklace with a cross on it opened the door.

Instead of asking if he could help us, he stared at us and didn't speak.

"You're Reece Lassiter, right?" I asked.

He nodded. "That's me."

"Good to know. I'm Benjamin Becker of *The Banshee Busters* on Syfy."

His eyes lit up. "I knew you guys looked familiar! I'm a huge fan of that show."

I grinned. "Thanks. We love meeting our fans. We're here, because we wanted to ask you a favor."

"Sure thing." He stepped aside. "You can come in if you'd like."

We walked in and removed our shoes, marveling at how nice the apartment was. It looked like it had two bedrooms, one bath, with a large kitchen and dining room and living room. The walls were painted half snowflake white and half robin's egg blue. A fireplace with a brick mantel stood in the living room, with a sixty-inch flat screen TV hanging over it, a black velvet couch, cobalt-blue loveseat, a black-and-white coffee table, and a neon-blue shag rug in the middle of the room.

I sat on the couch with Brady and Callie. Angela and Katie took the loveseat, while Reece pulled up two chairs for himself and Randy.

"What's up?" Reece asked.

"I know you work with a record company, but I wondered what kind of DJ work you do," I began. "We plan to throw a *Banshee Busters* première party in a week, and we hoped to hire you to spin a couple hours for us."

"That sounds really fun. Do you guys have a preference on the kind of music?"

"Whatever you have should work just fine," Brady said. "We do have a requirement before we can hire you, though."

"What's that?"

"It involves an actress named Liberty Belle," I said. "We need to ask you a couple things about her."

Confusion showed in his eyes. "Liberty? What does she have to do with my playing your party?"

"Well, the thing is, she's been murdered. We're working with LAPD to solve it."

He fell silent. "She's dead?"

I nodded. "Her body was found a couple weeks ago in Jason Lancaster's beach house."

"Wow. I need a drink." He walked to the fridge and took out a bottle of Red's Apple Ale. "Do you guys want one?"

"I'll take one," I said. "What do you have?"

"Let's see." He looked in the fridge. "I have a couple more bottles of Apple Ale, some Miller High Life, some Coors, three strawberry wine coolers, a pitcher of water, some OJ, a gallon of whole milk, and some Coke."

"I'll have one of those Apple Ales," I said.

He took out a bottle. "Anyone else?"

"I'd like a High Life," Katie said.

"I'll have a wine cooler," Callie said.

Reece set his ale on his chair, handed me mine, and went back for the other drinks. He gave drinks to the two women and opened his.

"Let me see if I have this right," he said, taking a drink. "Liberty Belle was murdered in Jason Lancaster's beach house, and you guys are working with the police to solve it."

"That's right," I said.

"You want me to spin at your party, but before I can, you have to ask me some questions about her."

"Yeah."

"Is this an interrogation?"

"I guess you could see it that way."

"I don't have a problem answering what you ask. I'd like to cooperate to the fullest extent possible."

I mentally sighed in relief. Perhaps the interview would be easier than expected. With a smile, I said, "I think we can arrange that."

It was interesting to go into the interrogation banking on an unknown person, but I realized Reece was cool and wanted to cooperate with us regardless of whether we hired him for a night. Maybe we should make the party a reality. It would be easy enough to get guests. All we had to do was send a tweet to our 800,000 followers about a première party.

I love fans for their loyalty and willingness to do anything for us. When Randy's grandmother passed away, he had a hard time coping, because he'd been really close with her. He was usually in charge of our Twitter and social media accounts and was the tech manager for our show. All of us had access to our official series accounts on Twitter, Facebook, and Instagram.

I sent a message on Twitter and Facebook, asking our fans to keep Randy in their prayers after his grandma's death. Within a week, Veronica, the lady at Syfy who gave us the chance to have our show in the first place, contacted me with the news that the fans were sending tons of gifts and cards addressed to Randy to their headquarters. It took two UPS trucks filled to the brim to deliver all those gifts from New York to Texas. The support really helped Randy through his mourning and grief.

Reece leaned back in his chair. "If you have any questions about Liberty, feel free."

"Awesome." I took out my notebook. "Thanks for being so willing to cooperate with us. I wish we had the same luck with Julie."

"Who?"

"Julie Capp," Callie said.

"It doesn't surprise me that she was a bitch."

"You have a problem with her, too?" Brady asked.

"I do. Everyone does. She's a cunt. My girlfriend once asked for her autograph, and that stupid, stuck-up bitch told her bodyguard to 'get that thing away from me.' It took every ounce of willpower not to beat her ass."

"I believe you," I said. "I had a similar experience when we interviewed her. She was ecstatic to learn Liberty was dead, claimed she was the reason she was fired from *Coulrophobia*, and had the audacity to claim she was the real victim when I told her off."

He spat out a mouthful of ale. "Sorry about that. You should know better than to say something funny when I've got a mouthful of drink."

I chuckled. "Sorry."

"It's all good." He capped his bottle. "What did you say back?"

"She said our show couldn't have been all that good if she never heard of it, so I told her we didn't broadcast to druggie bitches. She said she wasn't one, so I corrected myself and called her a druggie cunt. Then she threatened to hit me and rushed me. I blocked it easily and knocked her the hell out, hopefully breaking her nose."

Reece applauded. "That is awesome! Dude, you probably lived out the dream of half of Hollywood by punching that bitch in the face."

"The best part is he won't be charged with assault," Angela added. "That's assuming she's stupid enough to file a report. Randy had his camera running, and it clearly showed Ben acting in self-defense."

"Nice."

"It is now," I said. "We should get back to Liberty. She's the one I'm concerned about at the moment."

"Sure thing. Sorry."

"No worries. I just want to solve this as soon as possible."

"You were a big fans of hers?"

"You could say that. She was also my cousin."

"Wow, Bro. I'm really sorry."

I nodded slowly. "It sucks donkey ass, but what can I do? I feel the only way to get through this is figure out who did it, so she can rest in peace."

"And the pieces of dog shit can rot in jail where they belong," Brady added.

"That's a plus, too."

Callie handed me a pen, and I prepared to take notes. "Back to the case at hand. We talked to Kendra at RAX Records, and she told us she overheard you talking about having a huge crush on Liberty."

"Yeah. She was a good-looking woman. Regardless of how beautiful I thought she was, the thing I really liked was her personality. I had the pleasure of meeting her a couple times in passing. Once was at a party after the première of her movie *Christmastime Is Fear*, and she was such a sweetheart."

I wrote down his response. "So this was just a harmless infatuation?"

"Absolutely. I knew she was dating Jason, and I'm not a guy who steals girls from other men. Besides, she wasn't within my ideal age range."

"What's that?" Callie asked.

"I'm twenty-four. I prefer to date women my age, plus or minus three years."

"Liberty was only twenty-nine," Katie said.

"True, but that makes her five years older than me. I don't know what it is, but even that was weird to me."

"Interesting," I said. "Kendra also said something about how your crush on her was, in her words, 'borderline obsessive.'"

"Where the hell did she get that idea?"

"She claims she overheard you talking about it with other people."

"I wasn't obsessed with her. I only talked to her at parties when we crossed paths. It was mostly small talk. I think I'm allowed to have a crush on a nice woman without making myself out to be some obsessed stalker."

"Nobody said you were. We certainly don't think that."

"Thanks."

"No problem." I took more notes. "When was the last time you saw Liberty?"

Reece thought for a moment. "There was a club event downtown I was guest DJ for in the middle of April. She was there with Jason."

"How did she seem that night?"

"What do you mean?"

"Was she calm, cool, and collected, like everything was all right with the world? Did she appear fidgety and showing signs of paranoia, such as looking around to make sure nobody could get to her?"

"Now that you mention it, she seemed a little off. It wasn't super obvious, and it could have been the couple drinks she had during the night, but she showed some repetitive nervous behavior, like wringing her hands and brushing off her shoulders."

"That's weird. It seems like she was expecting someone to sneak up on her."

"Or she could've just been a little tipsy, as Reece said," Angela said. "People do things that are out of the ordinary when they're under the influence. It's like Brady with his obsession for passing out in trees, or Katie using anything tall and upright for a stripper pole."

"Damn." Reece laughed. "I need to drink with you guys."

"You can when we have that party," I said. "It'll be a good time."

"For real."

I closed my notebook. "That's all we need for now. Thanks for your time, Bro."

"Glad to do it, Man." Reece stood and offered his hand. We shared a bro hug, clasping hands and putting the other hand on each other's backs. He walked us out, and I gave him my card, asking him to call if anything else came up.

"Keep me up-to-date about that party," he said.

We took the elevator down and went back to the van.

Jeremy was watching something on Hulu when we arrived. "Hey, Guys. How'd it go with Reece?"

"Better than expected." I sat beside him.

"Really? That should be a relief after your last couple of encounters."

"You're telling me," Brady said. "It was nice to talk to someone sane who didn't threaten to beat our asses or call us derogatory names."

"What did he say?"

"He said he had a crush on Liberty, but it was just harmless infatuation," Callie said. "He never planned to act on it."

"Isn't that what Harley said, too?"

"Yes," Angela said, "but Reece seemed super genuine with his answers."

"He was super willing to cooperate with us," Katie added, "and he wasn't standoffish or disrespectful in any way."

"That's a lot more than we can say about anyone else," Randy said.

"Except Alicia," I added. "She was super cooperative, too, and wanted to see the murderers behind bars as much as we did."

"Harley wasn't that bad, though," Callie said. "He may've had odd mannerisms, but he wasn't rude or mean."

"That's true."

"Julie was a nightmare," Brady said. "Travis was an asshole. Brooklynne was also a huge bitch, and I'm kind of surprised how Ben kept his cool for the most part." He glanced at me. "No offense."

I grinned. "No worries. Not to brag, but I'm proud of myself, too. If I were faced with a similar situation to the one with Brooklynne, I probably would've released Kilabenjaro right away."

"Didn't you?" Callie asked.

"I did eventually, but I kept him caged as long as possible. As soon as that bitch tried to pin Liberty's murder on Jason, I opened the door. He got out the minute Brooklynne said the two words that are guaranteed to unleash him."

"What are those?" Angela asked.

I looked her in the eye. "Fuck you."

Her eyes widened.

"Those are the words that summon Kilabenjaro," I added.

Angela's eyes returned to normal. "Oh."

"Wait a minute," Jeremy said. "I'm confused. Who the hell is Kilabenjaro?"

"That's a nickname I picked up in high school," I said. "Every time I snap and become an asshole, it's known as unleashing Kilabenjaro."

"That's clever. Props to whoever gave you that name."

"I know, right?"

"What do you guys want to do tonight?" Brady asked. "We need to take an evening out to relax and regain our sanity."

"Sounds good to me," Jeremy said. "How about we go to Wrecking Ballz? It's a bowling alley with a bar that has karaoke every night."

"That sounds like fun," Callie said. "Maybe Ben can show off his singing voice."

"Yeah!" Brady said, slapping my back twice. "He almost sounds like Elvis Presley when he sings *Can't Help Falling in Love.*"

"I don't think I sound like him that much," I said, chuckling.

"Maybe we'll let the bar patrons decide that," Jeremy said. "When did you want to go?"

I looked at my watch. "It's only three right now. When does karaoke start?"

"Eight-thirty on weeknights, nine on Fridays and Saturdays."

"Let's go at five," I suggested. "That'll give us enough time to play a couple games before we hit the mic."

"How about a little later, like six-thirty or seven?" Angela asked. "I need a nap. I'm super tired."

"That sounds good, too," Randy said. "Then I'll wake up refreshed and kick some ass on the lanes."

"Good luck with that," I said. "My average is 160, and I score 140 on a bad day."

"Oh, a challenge, eh? Maybe I'll come back with steaks when we wake up."

"Sounds good. I'll lie down a bit, too. It's long overdue."

We agreed taking a load off for a couple hours was best. We would regroup downstairs in the dining room at 5:15 and go to the bowling alley.

"What doesn't kill you makes you stronger, stand a little taller, doesn't mean I'm lonely when I'm alone...."

Kelly Clarkson's anthem woke me at five o'clock. I sat up slowly, rubbed sleep from my eyes, and looked at my phone after shutting off the alarm. To my surprise, I saw I missed ten calls from an unlisted number, all from 4:00 to 4:45.

Shit! I thought. *Was this Reece, and the people who killed Harley, Alicia, Travis, and Brooklynne got to him, too.*

I shot out of bed like a rocket, put on my glasses, and called the number.

"Hello?" asked a guy I didn't recognize.

"Hi. This is Ben Becker. I got a lot of calls from this number, and I'm returning them."

"Hey, Ben. Thanks for calling back. I'm Reece Lassiter's brother, Wes. There's a bit of a situation, and we need you at the hospital."

18

My heart sank to my stomach. "What happened?"

"Two masked assailants attacked him this afternoon. He was knocked unconscious, sliced in the arm, and stabbed three times in the abdomen. I'm with him at the East LA Hospital on Whittier."

Fuck. They got to him. "Oh, my God. Is he OK?"

"He's still out cold, but his heart's beating."

"Good. That's a huge relief. We'll be right down." I hung up and called Chief Boone. "Chief? Urgent situation. I need you to meet us at the hospital on Whittier Boulevard. Reece Lassiter is there in critical condition."

"He's alive?"

"Yes. It sounds like it. I just spoke to his brother, and he said Reece is unconscious but still has a heartbeat."

"I'll be there in fifteen."

I hung up, slid my phone into my pocket, and sprinted downstairs. The others were waiting for me.

"Whoa, Dude," Brady said. "What's the hurry?"

"We need to reschedule the karaoke time." I almost jumped into my flip-flops. "Reece is in the hospital."

"What?" Callie asked. "What happened?"

I grabbed the van keys from near the door. "The killers got to him."

"Shit," Randy said. "Did they kill him, too?"

"No. I talked to his brother. Reece is out cold, but the doctors found a heartbeat."

"Thank God," Angela said.

"My thoughts exactly. We need to go now."

Ten minutes of lead-foot driving later, we arrived at the hospital and ran in to the front desk.

"Where's Reece Lassiter's room?" I asked the Black woman at the desk.

She looked at her computer. "He's in 217. Are you folks here to see him?"

"Yes. It's super urgent."

She looked around. "Normal visiting hours ended half an hour ago, but since I recognize you from *The Banshee Busters,* I'll make an exception."

That wasn't the first time our fame paid off, though we never tried to use it often. Not everyone knew us, anyway.

The woman pressed a button under her desk, and the doors on the right swung open. "Go see him. I have a favor to ask, though."

"Sure. What's that?"

"I have a friend who owns the property a church was built on, and she thinks it's haunted. She would love it if you guys could go there and walk through it some night."

"We can arrange that." I put an arm around Callie. "Have your friend send her contact info and the details about the property, and this girl will look it over and get back to you soon."

"I'll have her do it right away. Thank you, Sugar."

"No problem. Have a good one."

"You, too."

We walked quickly into Reece's room, where another Latino guy in a black T-shirt, jeans, and a white beanie cap leaned on the wall beside the door. He looked up when we approached.

"You Ben?" he asked.

"Yeah, that's me."

"Awesome. I'm Wes. Please come in."

The six of us followed him into the room. Reece lay in a hospital bed attached to a heart monitor. Gauze was wrapped around his head, covering a cut on his face. He also had bandages on a left shoulder and abdomen. The steady beeping of the heart monitor revealed he was still alive. I thanked God the killers didn't know he survived the attack.

"Praise the Lord he's alive," I told Wes. "I have to be honest with you. I was really scared he was dead after you called so many times."

"It was a close call. Reece and I are super close, given we're the only family each of us has. If I got to his apartment only a few minutes later, the doctors said he would've died."

"Wow," Callie said. "It's a good thing you got there when you did."

"Tell me about it. We hang out all the time."

"Do you have family anywhere outside the city?"

"Yeah, but not much. Our dad died when we were little. Our mom's a coked-out whore and wasn't there for us when we grew up. We have a sister in Miami and an older brother in Oklahoma, as well as two aunts and a uncle on Dad's side. One aunt is in Minneapolis, the other lives in Texas. The uncle doesn't stay anywhere for long."

"Is your uncle a couch surfer?" Brady asked.

"No. He's actually pretty wealthy. He was on an episode of *Deal or No Deal* when it was in its prime and won $200,000. He made some good investments that paid off over time, so he's worth over five mil now. He has homes in three different states and lives in each one for a season. He has a spring and summer home in Colorado, a beach condo in Hawaii during the winter, and a place in Delaware for the fall. He loves watching the leaves change color."

"Sounds like fun," Randy said.

"Yeah, it is. The best part is, he chooses to host all of us family at his place for Christmas each year, so in addition to seeing everyone I don't normally see, we don't have to worry about snow or ice."

Chief Boone walked in with a notepad in hand. "Hey, Guys. Sorry I'm late."

Wes looked suspiciously at me. "What's this about?"

"For one thing, your brother was assaulted," I said. "Obviously, there's the need for a police report. Two, we have reason to believe the attack wasn't random."

"What do you mean?"

"We're working with LAPD to solve the murder of Liberty Belle. Reece was never a suspect per se, but he met her at parties a couple times he either attended or spun for, so we thought he might have some insight into what happened. Before we met him, we talked with four other people, and they all ended up dead."

"Oh, Man. You think the people who murdered everyone else tried to kill my brother, too?"

"Exactly," Callie said. "Thank God he survived."

"I need some information from you about what happened," Boone told Wes. "Could you step into the hall with me for a minute?"

"Sure." As he walked out, he looked back at us. "If my brother wakes up, be sure to comfort him and make him feel at ease until I'm back."

"You got it," I said.

Wes and Boone stepped outside and closed the door. I sat in a chair beside the bed, waiting for Reece to wake up. I sent a tweet from our *Banshee Busters* account asking the fans to pray for Reece.

Ten minutes later, Reece opened his eyes.

Maybe the power of prayer does *work,* I thought.

"Hey, Guys," he said slowly. "What happened?"

"You were attacked and knocked unconscious," I said. "Your brother called 911, then us. We came down as soon as we heard."

"Why does my stomach hurt?"

"They stabbed you in the abdomen," Katie said.

"Those bitches."

I blinked in surprise. "Bitches? Is that a generic term, or were they women?"

"Unless guys have developed giant boobs and high-pitched voices, I'm pretty sure I was attacked by females."

That gave us one part of the attackers' identities. All we needed was to know who they were.

"What did they look like?" I asked.

He thought for a second. "I didn't see much. Both wore black from head to toe. They had black ski masks, black turtleneck sweaters, black sweatpants, black combat boots, and black gloves. I didn't see their hair or eye color. Their hair was tied up under their masks, and they wore sunglasses."

They sounded like pros who knew how to cover their tracks.

"As I fought them off, I pulled off one of their gloves. They might have left it when they rushed from the apartment after they thought they killed me."

If I weren't already a follower of Christ and gave Him my life, I would have fallen to my knees and done it in that instant. That glove might be what we needed to find and convict the killers.

"Good," Brady said, as if reading my mind. "That could be the breakthrough we need to convict whoever the fuck did this once and for all."

That happened more than once, when Brady and I shared the same thought. We sometimes used our "best-friend telepathy" to mess with people's mind. Their reactions were hilarious.

"Hopefully, that will do it," Randy said. "The letters we got didn't yield any results from diagnostics testing."

I sat up straighter in the chair. "Where's the glove?"

He looked at me. "It must be still on the floor of my apartment. I was out cold. Wes may've thought it was mine."

"We need that glove," Angela said.

"No shit, Sherlock." Brady said.

Angela glared at him. "That kind of talk will get your ass beat." She smiled. "It's a good thing we're already in a hospital. You won't have to go far to get the medical attention you'll need."

"That's enough, Children," Katie said, then turned to Reece. "I apologize for our idiot friends. That's how they flirt."

Angela walked up behind her. "Keep talking like that, and you'll get the bed beside Brady's."

Reece looked at me. "Your brunette friend scares the shit of me," he said softly.

I leaned closer to him. "Welcome to the club, Man."

"Y'all better be discussing case details over there," Angela told us.

I grinned at her. "Of course we were." I leaned back toward Reece. "She's usually very nice, but I think it's her time of the month."

He nodded.

"What did you just tell him?" Angela asked.

"Nothing. We were discussing the set list he'll play for our party."

She crossed her arms. "Right."

After talking with Reece a little more, we decided to visit his apartment to get the glove. I promised Reece we'd visit him later and left after getting the apartment key from Wes.

When we reached the apartment, it was closed and locked, which was good. I opened the door, and we slowly stepped inside. Randy turned on the lights, revealing the aftermath of the struggle Reece put up for his life. Blood dotted the hardwood floor, the table was flipped over, the couch had a large gash in it, and, five feet from the counter, lay a black glove.

"There it is," Brady said. "That thing will let Liberty rest in peace." He walked over and reached for it.

"Brady, no!" I shouted. "Don't touch it with your bare hand. You'll contaminate the evidence."

I reached a hand to Callie, who sighed and pulled a pair of rubber gloves and a plastic bag from her purse. I handed them to Brady. "Put these on first."

"What are you kids doing in here?"

An older man from the apartment across the hall stood in the doorway.

"You realize this is a crime scene, right?"

The sarcastic asshole in me wanted to say, "No shit, Sherlock," but I decided to be polite. "Yes, we do. We're working with the police to solve a murder. This was a bump in the road."

"You're working with the police?" He clearly didn't believe me. "Yes."

"Prove it."

I sighed and pulled out my phone, as the man stared at me.

"Who are you calling?" he demanded.

I held up my hand. "Shut up a second." I scrolled through my contacts, dialed the number, and turned on the speaker.

"Hey, Chief. It's Ben. We're at Reece's apartment picking up some evidence that we're positive will be the breakthrough we need."

"Did you use rubber gloves?"

"Yeah. We got that taken care of."

"Good."

"Anyway, the reason I'm calling is because there's a geezer here who thinks we broke in to steal something. He wanted me to prove him wrong."

"Geezer?" the man exclaimed. "I'm forty-seven!"

I looked at him. "Well, I'd apologize if you didn't look like seventy-four." I focused my attention back on Boone. "Tell this man why we're here, so he can get off our case, and we can go back to solving Liberty's murder."

"I got it. Put me on speaker."

"Way ahead of you."

I held the phone out so the man could hear better. "This young man and his friends are working with me. I'm Police Chief Alexander J. Boone. We're investigating the murder of the actress Liberty Belle."

"Is she the lady in that movie about seven people being hunted down in an airport by a deranged, machete-wielding man on Christmas Eve?"

"You mean *Christmastime is Fear?*" I asked. "Yes, that's her."

"I love that movie." He stepped back. "Sorry for bothering you."

"It's all good," I said. "Sorry I called you a geezer."

He went back to his apartment and closed the door. Brady held up the bag with the glove in it.

"We have what we need, Chief," I said. "We'll bring it to the station right now."

"Sounds like a plan. See you shortly."

I hung up and looked at the others. "We ready?"

"I think so," Callie said.

"Very good." I looked around the room. "Hold on. Where's Angela?"

"She's in the massage chair," Katie said.

"What massage chair?"

"Oh. Sorry. I meant the visage chair."

I stared blankly at her. "The visage chair?"

Katie nodded.

"So she's sitting on someone's face?"

"Wouldn't be the first time," Brady said.

"For fuck's sake, I can hear you!" Angela said, coming out of the bathroom. "I was in the bathroom, you big bunch of bitches."

"Hope you sprayed it with Febreze," Brady said. "Wouldn't want Reece walking into a literal shit storm when he comes back."

Angela punched his chest.

"Ouch! You whore! That hurt."

"It was supposed to."

"That's enough, Ladies," I said. "We need to take that glove to the police station."

We were there in ten minutes. Since all we wanted to do was drop off the glove and leave again, Brady and I decided to run inside, while the others waited in the van. Brady wanted to talk to me, mostly about how much of a violent bitch Angela was, and he didn't want anyone to hear him.

We walked up to Mandi at the front desk. She smiled at us.

"Hey, Guys," Mandi said. "How goes it?"

"Better." I held up the plastic bag. "We got evidence."

"Oooh, how fun. I'll let Boone know you're here."

"No need, Mandi," Boone said. "I already know."

"That was quick." Laughing, she went back to her work.

Boone looked at us. "I hear you have a glove for us to inspect."

"We sure do, Sir." I handed him the bag. "Reece pulled that off one of his assailants. They ran off and forgot to take it with them."

"Thank goodness for the idiocy of criminals, right?" he joked. "I'll run this through DNA testing and let you know the results."

He studied the glove. "I assume Reece's fingerprints will be on this too, right?"

"I'd think so," Brady said.

"Very good. I'll alert the crew, so they won't think he's a suspect."

"I didn't think he was," I said.

Boone looked at me. "The forensics team won't know that."

Brady and I walked back to the van and got in. As I started the engine, I said, "I hope things went well while we were gone."

"They did, Dad," Callie said sarcastically.

I looked at her in the rearview mirror. "You're asking for a spanking with that sass, Young Lady."

"Sounds kinky," Brady said.

I chuckled. "Dude, you're hilarious."

"I know. Every time Vanna sasses me, I paddle her."

"So I hear. She isn't quiet."

"Maybe I'll invest in a ball gag."

"Or just shove your sausage in her mouth while you paddle her. It's cheaper."

"Then she might bite it by accident."

"Then you'd be a lady. We'd call you Bailey, not Brady."

"For God's sake, have you two forgotten we're still in the van?" Angela demanded.

"Oh, my God, Darling. You scared the piss out of me," I said. "You really should put a bell around your neck. You make no impression whatsoever."

"You bitch."

"I thought my name was asshole."

"That, too."

Angela and Katie wanted to go to the spa after we gave Boone the evidence, so we decided to split up for a bit. While those two took a day at the spa, Callie, Randy, Brady, and I went to visit Jason.

I rang the doorbell twice, and the same Black woman answered it again.

"Hi," she said. "Welcome back."

"Hi. Is Jason here?" I asked.

"I'm sorry. He's out for a bit."

"Really?"

"Of course not." She grinned. "He's in his game room if you'd like to come in."

"Why, thank you. I'd like that quite a bit."

The four of us stepped inside and removed our shoes as Jason came out wearing a black undershirt and bright-red basketball shorts.

"Hey, Guys," he said. "Any particular reason you're here?"

"Not really," I said. "We just wanted to see how things are with you."

"We think Angela's on her time of the month," Brady added.

"I wasn't going to mention it in her presence," Callie said, "but I agree. She's got all the signs."

"Like what?" Jason asked.

"Mostly the bitchiness. While Ben and Bready met with Boone, she complained about cramps."

"At least we know she isn't pregnant," Brady said.

I looked at him. "She hasn't slept with anyone the entire time we'd been in California." I thought for a second. "Come to think of it, none of us have."

Jason cleared his throat.

I looked at him.

"I was just clearing my throat."

"Good." I grinned. "I thought you were going to say you slept with someone."

"Would it be a problem if I did?"

"Well, not, but I'd think you'd want to wait a little out of respect for Liberty before jumping into the sack with another woman."

"OK. You got me there."

My phone rang. I pulled it out and saw it was Chief Boone.

I slid the keypad to answer. "This is Ben."

"Hey, Ben. This is Chief Boone."

"Yes, Sir. How's it going?"

"Pretty well, I'd say. How are you?"

"Can't complain."

"I'm calling to say we finished running the DNA test on that glove."

"Good. Anything pop out?"

"We found Reece's fingerprints, which we expected, but we got another one, too."

"Excellent. Who was it?"

"Let's just say your initial instincts were spot on. The prints belong to Julie Capp."

19

Thank You, Lord! I thought. "That's awesome. Finally something shows up. I'll tell the others. Thanks for calling."

"No problem. Have a good one."

I hung up and saw them all looking at me. Taking a deep breath, I walked to the front door. "Excuse me for a moment."

I stepped outside and closed the door behind me. "Yes! Yes! Yes! Fuck, yes!"

I walked back in. "I'm better now."

"My goodness," Callie said. "That was loud. What was that about?"

"We have a definite suspect?" Randy asked. "Who is it?"

"Boone ran the glove through DNA testing. The results came back. In addition to that, they checked the prints. They found some from Reece. A second set on the glove belongs to Julie Capp."

Jason clenched his fists. "That stupid bitch. I knew she had something to do with it."

"We figured that from the start," I said. "Thank God she's such a shitty actress. Her attempt to throw us off the trail failed miserably."

"When did she do that?" Brady asked.

"She pretended she didn't know when Liberty died until we told her. Then she celebrated like it was 1999. That made me suspicious." I sighed. "From the beginning, I suspected she had a direct hand in my cousin's murder, but until this moment, all I had was a suspicion. Now that we can prove she's one of the murderers, the whole innocent-until-proven-guilty mantra goes right out the window."

"So let's go nail the stupid whore," Randy said.

"Believe me, I'd love to do that, but she's working with some-one, and there's no way in hell she'll tell us who it is. I want to get them both, so the case is completely finished."

"That makes sense," Brady said.

"You know, it's weird, but right now, I feel like having fun." I pulled off my shirt. "I plan to jump into the pool in a celebratory fashion."

"Ahem." Callie held out her hand. "Give me your phone, wallet, and glasses. You don't want them to get wet."

"Good point." I fished my wallet from my back pocket and handed it to her, along with my phone and glasses. I knew if I wore my jeans into the pool, they wouldn't dry very fast.

I glanced at Jason. "I'd like to borrow a pair of your shorts."

"Go for it, Bro."

I walked into his room, slipped out of my jeans, and pulled on a pair of his bright-white basketball shorts. When I stood at the edge of the pool, taking in the beautiful day, I felt as if the sun shone brighter than before. The water looked clearer, and the temperature felt extra warm. I didn't know if that was because I hadn't noticed all that before, or if I was relieved that we finally confirmed the identity of one of the killers.

I was shaken out of my daydream by someone tackling me from behind. I barely had time to take a breath before I hit the water.

I surfaced sputtering and saw Brady treading water nearby.

"Dude, what was that about?"

He grinned. "Just to help you get into the pool like you said you were going to."

"Hilarious." I splashed him, and he splashed me back and dunked me.

We resurfaced and saw Callie, Randy, and Jason standing at the edge of the pool.

"If you boys are done with your bromance, how does a bit of celebrating tonight sound?" Callie asked.

"Honey, our bromance will never end," I replied.

"For real," Brady said. "We've decided to be best man in each other's weddings. There will be plenty of sexy bro dancing at the receptions."

"That would be super close to being gay," Randy said.

"We've done plenty of things that could be misconstrued as gay," I replied. "A real friend makes your family question your sexuality."

"Is that so?" Callie put her hands on her hips. "What else have you two done?"

"That's for us to know and you maybe to find out eventually. What are we doing tonight?"

"I'll have dinner catered," Jason said. "I'll also ask Nina to make a huge cake. We can figure out entertainment later."

"Yoo-hoo!" a female voice called. "Helloooo."

"We come bearing gifts of booze to celebrate the confirmation of one of the bitches," a second female voice said.

The gate in the bright-blue fence around the backyard opened, and Angela and Katie walked through carrying two bags each from a liquor store. They walked to the edge of the pool and set the bags down gently.

Angela saw Brady and me in the pool. "Having another bromance moment, are you?"

"Yes, we were," I said. "At least we're comfortable enough with ourselves and each other to express our brotherly love in ways that might get weird looks in public."

"And sometimes more," Katie said. "Remember that time in Decatur?"

In the third season of *The Banshee Busters,* we were called to Decatur, Illinois, to investigate a haunted movie theater with a possible connection to Mafia activities in its heyday. We usually filmed 18-22 episodes a season, with a new episode every weekend.

If we were in Texas, depending on how far the city was, we either made it a night trip and returned home in the morning, or we stayed overnight in a hotel and returned the following day. If we went out of state, we spent a weekend at the location.

We usually settled in on Friday night, did the investigate on Saturday night, and went home Sunday. During the Decatur investigation, we decided to go out to dinner to unwind from the plane and to pump ourselves up for the walk-through the following night.

Brady and I were usually touchy-feely in a joking way, and, while we walked around downtown after dinner, we playfully jostled each other and touched a lot. A guy walking toward us thought we were in a gay relationship and stopped to ask if he could have a threesome with us.

Looking back, it was pretty funny. Once we explained we weren't gay, he seemed disappointed, but he understood. He apologized and asked to give us hugs, which we agreed to.

Randy took a picture of me embracing the guy and posted it on Twitter. It went viral for being a sweet moment. Angela and Katie, though mostly Angela, wouldn't let us live down the fact that we were offered a threesome with another man. For some reason, they found that hilarious.

"That was the funniest thing in the world." Angela laughed.

"That sounds super awkward," Jason said. "I'll put in our catering order. Do you have a preference?"

"Does B-Dubs cater?" Brady asked.

"What's that?"

"It's what a lot of people call Buffalo Wild Wings," I answered. "I think they do."

"That's what I'd like," Brady said. "I'm in the mood for wings."

"Wings do sound tasty," Callie said.

"Sounds good," Jason said. "I'll order three platters of wings, two bone-in and one boneless. I'm thinking honey BBQ boneless, garlic parmesan, buffalo bone-in, and a huge order of onion rings and cheese curds. That sound good to everyone?"

We agreed. Brady and Katie wanted mango *habanero* hot wings, so they gave Jason money to buy a fourth platter of bone-in wings for them. He also asked Nina to come over and make cakes for us —one half-chocolate, half-vanilla sheet cake, one round red velvet cake, and one German chocolate, which I hated.

She got the cakes baked in ninety minutes. The wings arrived forty-five minutes after that. We spent the night celebrating that after a week of nonstop stress and people threatening us left and right, we finally had confirmation of one of my suspicions.

The next morning, I woke in an apple orchard without a shirt on. It never failed. Every time I drank, I lost my shirt somewhere. The apple orchard wasn't familiar, though. I stood slowly to avoid dizziness and looked around, seeing rows of apple trees to the horizon.

I walked for a little bit, trying to find out where I was, when I heard snoring. I couldn't locate the source until I looked up and saw Brady passed out in a tree—again.

I kept walking for five minutes and finally saw Jason's beach house in the distance. He must live next door to an apple orchard. I wished he told me, though it wasn't relevant until that moment.

With my hangover, I struggled to get back to his house. I found Callie passed out near the edge of the pool and was tempted to push her in, but I decided against it.

If it were Angela, I would've done it without a second thought, but I hoped to marry Callie someday. If I shoved her drunk ass into the pool, she'd hold it over me for the rest of our married lives, then get her revenge when I least expected it.

Callie never forgot things like that. She wouldn't let go of a prank until she pranked the other person back. She told me a story about going to school at UCLA. She was accepted into a sorority and lived there for a semester. The girls got along well and occasionally played harmless pranks on each other, like whipped cream pies to the face or dumping ice water on someone in the shower.

Callie's biggest fear was snakes. She was terrified of them for as long as I knew her. Unfortunately, her sorority sisters knew it, too. They put some giant rubber snakes on her and around her bed while she slept.

Callie woke up, saw the snakes, and freaked out. She eventually realized they were fake and laughed with her sisters, but she waited until the end of the semester for her revenge. Out of the five girls who pranked her, three were terrified of spiders, especially tarantulas, one was afraid of scorpions, and the last one had a fear of mice.

She recruited three sorority sisters to help her get some tarantulas, scorpions, and mice, but she mixed live ones with fake ones. At least the scorpions had their stingers removed, so no one would be hurt.

She planted them around her sisters' beds while they slept. When they woke up, some just laughed.

"Very funny," they said. "Using rubber tarantulas to scare me. That's pretty good."

When they realized some of the things were real, there was a shit storm of screaming. Five sets of sheets had to be washed and bleached when it was over.

I didn't want to wake up in bed someday covered in tarantulas, so I decided to let her sleep off her drunk. I didn't need a heart attack.

In my groggy state, I walked right into the plate-glass sliding door leading into the house. His housekeeper did too good a job at making it spotless.

I opened the door, stepped inside, and closed it. Angela was sprawled on the table like the last time. Katie was on the pool table holding a cue between her legs, and Randy was nowhere to be found. I hoped he was still alive.

I walked into Jason's room and found him in bed, watching TV.

"Hey, Man," he said. "Come in."

I stepped in, and he slid over, so I could sit beside him.

"Watching another episode of *The Banshee Busters* again?" I asked.

"I swear. It's so weird watching you in the first two seasons. You look so young."

"I know." I laughed. "Having a goatee makes me sexier."

"Conceited."

"Normally that's true, but the fans say I look better with facial hair."

"How do you know?"

"*People* ran a poll in a recent issue asking 100 random people in Times Square whether they thought I looked better with a goatee and facial stubble or completely clean-shaven. Seventy-six percent voted for the facial hair."

"Interesting. Women do enjoy facial hair."

"On men at least."

"True dat."

"What the hell happened last night?"

Angela appeared in the doorway and leaned against the frame. "Ugh. I feel like death incarnate."

"That's because you drank a shit ton of vodka," I said.

"You hit the beer keg pretty hard, too," Jason added.

"That explains the empty bottles all over the place. What's the plan for today?"

"What do you mean?"

"Are we going after more people to find the second murderer?"

"We could, but I need time to power through this fucking hangover." I looked around. "What time is it?"

Angela looked at her phone. "Ten-thirty."

"Good. That's not too late. I want to get to the frat house and give Jeremy an update."

"We can do that. First, we need to find Brady and Randy."

"Brady's in an apple tree in the orchard next door. I have no idea where Randy is."

Angela grinned. "That stupid boy lives in trees."

I laughed. "It sure seems that way." I looked at Jason. "Whose apple orchard is that?"

"It's owned by a convent. The nuns there love apples and pick them once a week."

The doorbell rang. Since Jason said he wasn't properly dressed to answer, I went there with Angela. We found three nuns on the doorstep, supporting Brady.

"I believe he belongs to you," the one on the left said.

I took his arm and helped him inside. "Thank you, Sisters."

"We'll make sure this doesn't happen again," Angela said.

"You'd better, or God will rain judgment down on you like a monsoon," the one on the right said.

They walked away, and I closed the door.

Brady dusted himself off. "Geez, what bitches."

"Tell me about it. God won't be raining down any judgment on us. If anything, He'll forgive you for trespassing if you ask Him to."

"You think so?"

"Duh? It's not like you're going to hell for drunkenly finding your way into a convent's apple orchard. You'd have to do a lot of messed-up shit to be sent down there."

"Like murder someone?"

I thought about it. "Yeah, probably."

"Then we know where Julie's going," Angela said.

We shared a laughed. When my phone rang, I took it out and checked caller ID. It was Calvin, probably wanting another update on the case. I hoped he wasn't having sex with Katelyn again.

"Excuse me a moment." I walked into the dining room and answered the call. "Hey, Dude."

"Hey, Man. How are things?"

"Can't complain. How's it going back in Texas?"

"About the same. I wanted to know if there are any new developments in the case."

"As a matter of fact, yes. You know who Reece Lassiter is, right?"

"DJ Peanut Butter Cup? Yeah."

I stifled my laughter. Of all the DJ names he could have chosen, Reece took DJ Peanut Butter Cup. "That's news to me."

"I also heard he was knocked unconscious by two armed assailants."

"He was, but he's in stable condition and should be released from the hospital sometime today."

"That's what TMZ reported."

"Interesting."

"So give me details, Bro. What's the new development?"

"It's super exciting. After days of nonstop stress and multiple threats of people wanting to murder us, we finally confirmed one of the killers."

"Oh, my God. That's amazing. Who is it?"

"Julie Capp."

"That bitch."

"Calvin, get back here and eat your dinner!" Katelyn shouted.

I chuckled. "Did she make dinner for you?"

"In a way."

"Dude."

"Yeah?"

"Don't tell me you're having sex with her gain."

"OK. I'm not having sex with her again."

"He's lying!" Katelyn shouted.

"Thank you for being honest, Katelyn."

"It's what I do."

"I don't know if I should feel special or weirded out," I told Calvin. "Every time you ask me for an update on the case, you're having sex."

"Not every time. I'm not inside her right now."

"Either way, it's super hilarious. This will be part of my stand-up monologue on open-mic night at Hula Hilarity."

Hula Hilarity was an upscale comedy club in downtown San Antonio. A strip on the street consisted of restaurants, bars, and clubs with different themes. Hula Hilarity had a Hawaiian theme. The strip club next door was called the Queen of Hearts and featured everything heart-related. The strippers wore heart pasties, their thongs had giant hearts on the front, the tables were heart-shaped, and the VIP rooms had heart-shaped sofas. I didn't know that from experience, and no one could prove otherwise.

"You're funny, Bro," Calvin said. "Be sure to give me a fake name, so no one knows who you're talking about."

"OK. What name do you want?"

"Brian Porter."

"You're serious?"

"Yeah. Why? Is that a bad name?"

"I never said that."

My phone beeped with an incoming call. I looked at the screen and saw a text from Carson, asking me to call him.

"I was just wondering where you got the name," I said.

"I thought of it out of nowhere."

"That's interesting."

"Calvin, your supper's getting cold!"

"I'll be right there, Sugar Pop. I have to go, Bro. You heard the lady. My dinner's getting cold."

"Yeah. I need to call Carson, anyway. I love you, Man. Have fun eating out."

"Love you, too. Hopefully dessert tastes good this time."

"Are you implying I don't taste good?"

"Good luck on damage control," I said.

"Thanks. I'll need it."

I hung up and called Carson.

"Hey, Man," he said. "How's life out west?"

"Getting better every day. How are you doing back in Texas?"

"I'm all right. I realized I haven't talked to you since you left, and I wanted to know how the investigation's going."

"It's about time. Have you been keeping up with the news? I heard TMZ is going crazy with updates."

"Yeah, I have. Last I heard, DJ Peanut Butter Cup was attacked in a home invasion and is in the hospital in stable condition."

"There's more. While fighting the intruders, Reece pulled off one of their gloves. We got it to the forensics team at the police station."

"Oh, really?"

"Yup. The best part is, they confirmed the identity of one of the murderers."

"That's incredible! Who is it?"

"Julie Capp."

"Isn't she the druggie bitch who was fired from *Coulrophobia* for always being high?"

"That's her."

"She sounds disgusting."

"Trust me. She's worse in person, but sweet lady justice will nail her soon."

"Do you have any leads on the second one?"

"Nothing definite, but we figure Julie will get together with the bitch again. We're keeping close tabs on her for now."

"Good deal. I have to get going. The girl here is signaling for me to wrap it up."

"Ooo-la-la. Are you with a new lady friend?"

"I'm at All the King's Women getting a lap dance."

"You answered the phone in the middle of that?"

"Why not?"

My friends were sexual weirdos. "All right. Have fun with that."

"Jade has a big ass. Of course I'm having fun."

I laughed and hung up. Brady walked into the dining room, also on the phone. He hung up and sat down across from me.

"What's up, Bro?" he asked.

"I just talked to Calvin and Carson. They wanted details and updates, so I gave it to them." I took an apple from a silver platter in the middle of the table and bit into it. "Who were you talking to?"

"Your dad. He tried calling you, but your phone kept going to voicemail."

"Probably because I was on the phone with Calvin and Carson." I took another bite of the apple. "I hope Jason stole this from the orchard."

"It's be nice revenge for the way those old bitches dragged me out of there. Did you know being grabbed by bony old lady fingers hurts more when you're hung over?"

I stared at him. "That's good to know for future reference."

We went back to the frat house to update Jeremy on the new findings. I felt like a record on Repeat, telling everyone the same news. It was a good thing, because it meant Liberty was one step closer to finally resting in peace.

Pulling into the driveway, I saw an unfamiliar car parked in front of the house. It was a magenta Lexus convertible with black exterior and the top down. I wondered if Jeremy had a lady over for some sexy time, but, when we went inside, we found him sitting on the couch with Micki. I was partly right.

He looked up at us when we came in. "Hi, Guys." He paused the program they were watching. "Come in and take a seat. We were just watching your show."

"I loved the one where you guys investigated that plantation in Louisiana," Micki said. "It was funny how Angela and Katie reacted to the ghost in the master bedroom."

For our third midseason finale, we walked through Myrtle Plantation, the most-haunted plantation in Louisiana and possibly the entire South.

While Angela and Katie were doing EVP work in the master bedroom, a door slammed shut, making Angela scream at an octave higher than a dog whistle. Katie called the ghost a whore and yelped three seconds later when someone pinched her.

When we reviewed the evidence the following day, we found a woman's voice on the recording saying, "How dare you," right before Katie yelped. We still laughed at that one. According to a couple top-ten countdown videos on YouTube featuring the funniest moments in our investigations, we weren't the only ones who felt that way.

"That ghost was mean," Katie said. "It pinched me."

"Probably because you called it a whore," Randy said.

"Only because it scared Angela."

"Oh, come on," Angela said. "I wasn't that scared."

"Give me a break," Brady said. "You had a higher pitch than a dog whistle."

"Hush," she snapped at him. "You weren't there."

"Yes, but the video doesn't lie."

"Anyway," I said. "I have some news."

"Oooh!" Jeremy said. "I love news. What might that be?"

I put my hand on Callie's leg. "Callie and I got married."

She elbowed my ribs. "We did not!"

"Not yet, but eventually we will."

"Well, of course, Hon."

"Gross!" Angela shouted. "Tell them the real news."

"Spinster," Brady said, faking it like he sneezed.

Angela glared at him. "Shut up."

"The real news has to do with Liberty," I said. "The police confirmed the identity of one of her murderers."

Jeremy stared in shock, then said, "Excuse me for a moment." He walked outside, closed the door behind him, then shouted, "Yes! Yes! Yes! Fuck, yes!"

Brady looked at me. "He really is your cousin."

"Yup. I had the same reaction when I got the news."

The door opened, and Jeremy returned. "I'm good. Who is it?"

"Julie."

Micki groaned. "Of course it is. She's fucked up in the head."

"Tell me about it. Forget jail. She needs a mental asylum." I stood. "I'm getting a drink."

"Get me a Coke while you're up," Jeremy said.

"You got it." I went to the fridge and opened the door, taking a Coke for Jeremy and a bottle of Mountain Dew for me.

Bang!

The window behind me shattered, and an intense burning sensation went through my right arm.

Bang!

I felt the same burning in my shoulder. Jeremy tackled me to the ground, then came darkness.

20

I woke in a hospital bed with gauze bandages around my biceps and shoulder. Everyone was there, including Chief Boone and Reece.

"Wha...what happened?" I asked, disoriented.

"You were shot, Bro," Reece said. "Twice."

"Was I really?"

"Yeah," Jeremy said. "I had to get you on the ground pretty fast, so whoever it was wouldn't kill you."

"Good thing he did, too," Callie said. "Whoever it was shot the fridge six times."

I'd been in a couple fights in my life, but nothing compared to being shot and almost killed. My dad would lose his shit when he found out. Since I was already semifamous for *The Banshee Busters,* the news would be online soon, maybe with TMZ.

"Did you get a look at whoever it was?" I asked.

"No," Brady said, "but I saw the car. It was the same one that tried to run us off the road when we left Brooklynne's."

"So that's the car Julie has?" Callie asked.

"Did you get the license plate?" I asked.

"I caught more," Brady said, "but not much. All I could remember was 6KV something."

Boone jotted that down in his notepad. "Good. That'll help us find the car a lot faster. There can't be that many black Chevy Tahoes with that plate number."

"Awesome," I said. "Then we can finally nail the punk bitches who murdered Liberty and put all this behind us for good."

I was kept in the hospital overnight for observation. Callie refused to leave my side, and Brady and Reece hung around for extra comfort and support.

I was cleared to leave at noon the following day. Jeremy came to pick us up and take us to the frat house. The only thing I wanted after coming so close to death was to relax with my friends, maybe drink a little later if I felt up to it.

The six of us, along with Jeremy, Micki, and Reece, spent the afternoon playing games on Jeremy's Xbox one and Wii U consoles. The favorites were racing games like Burnout/Mario Kart, Super Smash Bros, and any installment of Halo.

In the middle of that, my phone rang. It was my dad. I knew what it would be about, so I excused myself and went into the kitchen to answer.

"Hey, Dad."

"Oh, my God, Ben. Are you all right?"

"I'm fine now."

"Thank goodness." He sighed in relief. "*ABC News* ran a breaking story that you were shot. I thought you were dead."

I didn't think I had enough fame to be worthy of a news segment on ABC, but apparently, I was. "No, Dad. I'm OK. I was hit in the biceps and shoulder. The hospital took care of me. I was released earlier today."

"At least the shooter didn't hit any arteries."

"Yeah. I would've been screwed."

"I just wanted to make sure you're all right."

"Yup. I'll probably get a ton of calls and texts about this in the next few hours."

I heard a crash in the background like glass breaking.

"I have to take care of that," Dad said. "Brandi danced her way into the coffee table and broke it."

As best I understood, Brandi was on a *Just Dance* kick recently. Apparently, she wanted to lose ten pounds and figured the best way was to dance.

It was too bad she had two left feet, though. So far, she broke the piano when she kicked it too hard, knocked over some picture frames and broke them, and threw a vase across the room by mistake doing an arm gesture. The vase shattered against a wall. She could add the coffee table to the long list of things she broke while dancing, although ironically, none of her bones were on the list.

"All right," I said. "Have fun with that. Make sure she doesn't break anything else."

"Ha. No guarantees."

I hung up and took only two steps before it rang again. "Yo."

"Dude, you aren't dead, are you?" Calvin asked.

I considered messing with his head but decided against it. "Of course I'm not dead, Bro. I'm talking to you right now, aren't I?"

"OK. That's a good point."

"Is he OK?" Katelyn asked in the background.

"Yes, he's good, Sweets," Calvin replied.

I chuckled. "Are you living with her?"

"Of course not." He laughed. "We're at the Bromance Bungalow playing badminton."

"Better than having sex, I suppose."

"Yeah. I figured it would be nice to switch it up once in a while, even though sex feels amazing."

"How thoughtful of you to spare me this time."

My phone kept beeping while I talked to Calvin. At first, I thought the battery was dying, then I realized I had a bunch of Twitter and Facebook notifications.

Randy must have posted a message on our social media accounts about the situation. A lot of our fans were wishing me a speedy recovery and tagging me in Twitter posts and retweets with get-well messages.

I sat on the couch in the living room with everyone else, holding a Miller High Life. Callie, Angela, Katie, and Micki were embroiled in a heated Halo battle. A lot of playful smack talk was thrown around, mostly involving jokes about each other's moms. Angela sliced Katie's character with a sword, and my phone beeped again with an unregistered number from New York.

"Callie, could you turn down the volume?" I asked, then answered hesitantly, "Hello?"

"Hi. Ben?"

"That depends on who's asking."

"This is Veronica from Sy-Fy."

"Oh, hi. How's it going?"

"Pretty well I'd say. How are those bullet wounds healing up?"

"Better with each passing hour."

"The reason I'm calling is to let you know that since last night when the news of your shooting broke, we've been flooded with cards and gifts from fans. We're forwarding them to your home address."

"That's awesome. Thanks for letting me know and doing that."

"No problem, but there's one more question."

"Shoot. No pun intended."

Veronica laughed. "Good to see you can keep your sense of humor even after almost being killed."

"It gets me through the tough times."

"That's awesome. The question is, when I confirmed I got the right number, you said it depends on who's asking. What would you have done if someone you didn't want to talk to tried to contact you?"

"I'd either tell them I wasn't the one they were trying to get or pretend to speak only Spanish."

"Hilarious. I just wanted to let you know to expect a lot of packages when you get home. All of us in the office are praying for a speedy recovery."

"Thank you. I really appreciate that."

I hung up. Brady looked at me and asked, "Who was that, Bro?"

"Veronica. She said our fans sent me a ton of gifts and cards in response to the situation I got into."

"That's nice of them."

"Yeah, that's one reason I love our fans. They're super loyal."

I looked down at my bottle of High Life. "The hell am I doing with this?"

"I probably shouldn't be drinking," I said, handing the bottle to Brady. "I'm on painkillers, and everyone knows mixing those with alcohol would lead to death."

"That wouldn't be so bad if alcohol was the death of you," Brady said, taking the bottle.

"What do you mean? I would still be dead."

"Yeah, but at least Julie wouldn't have a hand in it."

Jeremy broke out the liquor around 5:30, and everyone with the clear exception of Reece and me started drinking.

Even though I couldn't partake in the alcohol, hanging out with those closest to me and laughing at their drunken shenanigans helped me forget I had psycho bitches hunting me down. It's nice to let loose once in a while, even if liquor doesn't play a part in it.

I woke up the next morning and saw I missed five calls from Jason. I guessed he didn't know about the attempt on my life until he tried to contact me. I got some water from the kitchen and called him back. He answered on the first ring.

"Ben?"

"Yeah, Bro. It's me."

"Thank God! I thought you died!"

"My dad had the same reaction, but I'm fine. Two bullets hit my biceps and shoulder. The rest went into Jeremy's fridge. All of us are alive and well, though I can't say the same for the fridge."

"I doubt anyone cares about the fridge," Jason said. "The more important is that you're all OK."

"That means a lot. Thanks for checking on me."

"Yeah, Bro. You know I care about you."

"I do."

"Could you guys stop over later? What happened the other day scared the shit out of me, and I'd rather not let you die without hanging out with you one more time."

I chuckled. "Ouch. Laughing hurts.

"Hangover?"

"No. I didn't drink last night."

"Then why does it hurt to laugh?"

"Gee, I don't know. Maybe the two bullets that were lodged into my arm have something to say about it."

"I see your sarcasm is still alive and well."

"Heh. As am I." I took a drink of water from the glass next to me on the nightstand. "But these cretins aren't going to kill me, trust and believe that. I'd sooner die from alcohol poisoning than let one of them take me out."

"Alcoholic," Jason whispered under his breath.

"What was that?"

"I said can you guys come by later?"

"I'll let you believe that," I teased. "Sure, we'll be there in half an hour. Love you, Bro. See you soon."

"I love you, Man. Please stay safe."

I hung up and sat at the dining room table to wait for everyone else to sober up or wake up. Jeremy came downstairs wearing only his silky red boxers and one white sock. His usually neatly spiked black hair stuck out all over the place, his facial stubble was more spread out than usual, and he had huge bags under his eyes. He was obviously hung over. He came over and wrapped his arms around me from behind in a hug.

"Hey, Cuz. How you feeling?" he asked.

Smiling, I patted his arm. "I'm OK. Looks like you had plenty of fun last night."

"I don't remember much, but I woke up with Micki in my bed."

My smile vanished. "Dude, you didn't."

"I did. I don't know if anything happened, but I rolled over this morning, and there she was."

Micki strolled in, her medium-brown hair a mess. She wore a pastel-pink T-shirt that barely reached her knees and a pair of matching slippers. "Good morning, Guys. Last night was fun." She winked at Jeremy.

I smiled wider. "Oooo-la-la."

"I guess it was," Jeremy said. "What exactly happened?"

Micki giggled. "You don't remember?"

He shook his head.

Well, I do. And if you didn't catch feelings, don't worry. Neither did I."

"Uh...good to know."

She grinned and opened the fridge for orange juice.

Jeremy leaned closer to me and whispered, "Dude, I think I fucked up."

"Apparently that's not the only thing you fucked," I whispered back.

"Normally, I would appreciate a well-timed joke like that, but I'm freaking out."

"Why? Do you have feelings for her now?

"No. I'm afraid she might be pregnant."

I almost burst out laughing. "I doubt it, but if she is, look on the bright side. She's making enough money with her acting career that you won't have to pay child support."

"I don't want a fucking kid, though. I'm not ready to become a father."

"I'm on birth control guys," Micki whispered from behind us. "No worries.

"I didn't know you could hear that," I said. "Sorry."

"No problem." She patted my head twice. "I thought it was funny that you thought you were whispering quietly enough that I wouldn't hear you.

I grinned. "Well, I have been told I'm funny."

"Yeah, but don't quit your day job."

"Are you implying I'm not funny?"

"Of course not." She took a nonchalant sip of her orange juice. "I'm just saying you make enough money with your TV show that you don't need to do anything comedy-related for money."

"Uh-huh. I'll just have to take your word for that."

"Good choice." She opened the bullet-ridden fridge again. "Do you guys want something to drink?"

"Yeah," I said. "Give me apple juice."

"Make that two," Jeremy said.

Micki pulled out a jug of apple juice, poured two glasses for us, and handed them over.

I thanked her and drank. "Before I forget, Jason wants to see us all soon."

"Why?" Jeremy asked.

'I looked at him. "What do you mean, why?"

"Why all of us?"

"Why not? You and I were related to his fiancée, Mickie knew her personally from shooting a movie with her, and the rest of the gang met him when we got here."

"Good point. He's a pretty cool guy."

"He is," Micki said. "I haven't talked to him since Liberty died, let alone seen him. I want to make sure he's all right."

"Then it's a plan," I said, looking around. "Where is every-one else?"

"Where you would expect?" Jeremy asked. "They're passed out in various places throughout the house."

Reece staggered into the kitchen five minutes later clutching his stomach. "Ugh, fuck whoever shanked me," he muttered. "When I figure out w ho it was, I'm going to give it back to them tenfold."

When he saw us sitting around the table, he smiled. "Oh, hey Guys."

"What's up, Bro?" I asked. "How you feeling?"

"My stomach still hurts like absolute hell, but I'll survive." He opened the fridge and got out a pitcher of water. "Apparently, you weren't lying. Your friend really does like passing out in trees when he drinks."

I laughed. "Yeah, it's one of his drunken quirks."

"Kind of like Katie magically transforming into a stripper is one of her drunken quirks?" Jeremy asked.

"Yup."

"She reminds me of Cinderella," Reece said. "Except instead of a fairy godmother, she has dark liquor. And instead of getting a beautiful ball gown, she loses her clothes. And instead of meeting a handsome prince, she has the rest of you to wake up to."

"I heard that," Katie shouted from the living room. "Ah son of a *whore*, my head! It hurts like a bitch!"

Micki leaned forward on the counter, resting her hands on it in front of her. "Oh, and do Brady and Angela bet on everything?"

"Well, *everything* is a bit of a broad statement."

Actually...that's not entirely true. When our African elephant got pregnant at the zoo, Brady and Angela bet on whether it was a boy or a girl. The zoo welcomed a baby girl elephant two years later (elephants have ridiculously long pregnancies), and Angela ended up acting as Brady's personal butler for a week.

I took a drink of my apple juice. "What did they bet on this time?"

"Something about how many shots of Captain Morgan they could take before blacking out."

"Who won? And more importantly, what were the stakes?"

"I did," Angela said, stumbling into the kitchen. She only had on her black and white pajama pants with a strapless red and white bra. "But I don't know if it was worth the fifty bucks now."

She glanced at Jeremy. "You might want to replace that toilet."

Jeremy gave her a confused look. "Which one? There's six bathrooms in here."

"How am I supposed to know? I was really fucked up last night."

"Anyway, we should get going soon," I said, pushing back my chair. "Jason's expecting us. Apparently, my near-death experience at the hands of a sadistic bitch like Julie scared him. He wants to make sure he sees us one last time before she kills me."

"Oh, come on, dude," Reece said. "She won't kill you."

"I know. That's what I told Jason, but I think he's using it as an excuse to see me again." I finished my apple juice. "Not that there's anything wrong with that. I love spending time with him."

"Should we wait for the other three to wake up?" Angela asked.

"There's no time," I replied. "We're already late." I glanced at Jeremy. "Could you wait here for them and bring them to Jason's once they're sober?"

"You got it. I'll text you when we're heading over."

"Awesome. Micki, how much space does your car have?"

"It fits five, like most cars. You want to ride with me?" she asked.

"That's the only choice we have." I chuckled. "I don't care that it's pink."

"Same here," Reece said. "It takes a real man to wear pink and ride in a pink car."

"Just as long as you keep the top down," I added. "It makes me look hot."

I looked down and saw I wore a black muscle shirt, jean shorts, and my favorite white hat turned backward. "I am."

"Then let's do it."

Five minutes later, Micki, Angela, Katie, Reece, and I were on the road to Jason's place. I called him as we left the frat house.

"Hey, Man," I said. "We're on the road now. Just thought I'd let you know."

"Awesome. Thanks, Bud. Who's with you?"

"Jeremy's still at the frat house, waiting for Callie, Brady, and Randy to wake up. We partied pretty hard last night. It's me, Angela, Katie, Micki, and Reece."

"Reece? Wasn't he on the list of important people to interrogate?"

"Yes, but he's a super cool guy, and we're one thousand percent positive he had nothing to do with the murder. He was attacked by the people who killed Liberty. Because of him, we were able to confirm Julie is one of the killers."

Glancing in the side mirror, I saw a black Chevy Tahoe closing in on us. My first paranoid thought was that Julie was back to finish what she started, then logic set in. California is the most-populous state in the country. There are hundreds, if not thousands, of black Chevy Tahoes running around.

I sighed in relief, then I saw the license plate, and my relief vanished. The first three digits were 6KV.

21

Julie was back to finish what she started.

"Micki, go faster," I said.

She glanced at me. "I'm already five miles over the speed limit."

"I'm sure the cops will forgive you this time."

"Why should I go faster?"

"Look in the rearview mirror."

She glanced up and turned pale. "Fuck! Is that who I think it is?"

"If you think it's Julie Capp, then yes."

"Shit, shit, shit, shit, shit!" She mashed the gas pedal to the floor. The Tahoe sped up, too. It swerved into the left lane, cutting off a Ford F-250 pickup. It pulled up beside us, and the passenger window rolled down.

I still had Jason on the phone, so I said I'd call back. He understood, and I hung up.

The passenger in the Tahoe was dressed all in black, like Reece described his assailants.

"What the fuck is wrong with you?" I shouted.

The person didn't answer and aimed a polished silver revolver at us. I ducked down, as did everyone else. Micki hunched over the wheel and went faster, just as the person fired five rounds.

Three of them hit the side of the car, one hit Micki's side mirror, and the last one missed entirely. The Tahoe sped off.

I dialed Chief Boone. "Chief, this is Ben Becker. It's an emergency. We were just attacked by the same people who shot me a couple days ago. We're in pursuit."

"Where are you?"

"On US 101 north. It looks like they're headed toward that Hollywood sign. Dispatch a couple cops to that location. We're right behind them."

I hung up and called Jason back. "Hey, Bro. Sorry about that. We were visited by the Wicked Bitch of the West again."

"Julie? She didn't shoot you again, did she?"

"She missed. Four bullets hit Micki's car, though."

"That's not a problem," Micki said, speeding to catch up to Julie. "My net worth is seven million dollars. If the insurance won't cover it, I can get a replacement car. Then I'll scrap this at the junkyard and get cash for the metal. I'll give the money from that to charity."

"How thoughtful of you," I said. "Anyway, we're now in pursuit of her and whoever is with her. Hopefully, this nightmare will be over after today, and Liberty can rest in peace."

"Seriously, Bro, be careful," Jason pleaded. "I don't want to lose you in addition to Liberty."

"I'll be good, Man. Chief Boone is dispatching officers to help us. They'll meet us at the Hollywood sign and help us take those bitches down."

"Good. I love you, Man."

"I love *you*. I'll call you once this is over."

I hung up and stared at the sky, as Micki sped down the highway. Clouds were rolling in, and the sun was covered. It looked like a storm was coming.

What a way to set a scene, I thought.

"Uh-oh," Mick said, glancing at the sky. "I'd better put the top up. Looks like rain."

She pressed a button beside the headlight switch, and the white convertible cover came over us. It was a good thing. The first raindrops hit the windshield a few seconds later. We screeched to a halt at the observation area for the Hollywood sign, where we saw the Tahoe already parked.

I beat the shit out of the Tahoe when I got to it, not because I thought the bitches were in it, but it made me feel better to beat on *something.* I wouldn't be allowed to beat up the murderers, because the cops would frown on that no matter how justified I might be. Taking my frustration out on something related to them was good enough.

The other four ran up to me, and Reece had to pry me away from the van before I injured myself. I shattered all the windows and made some sizeable dents in the sides.

Weeks of grief over losing my cousin to a senseless, heartless murder, coupled with rage from a week of being threatened by psychos, finding three dead bodies and some body parts, watching someone be shot in the head, and getting shot twice made me stronger than normal. That surprised even me. When I finished, the Tahoe looked like the pretty little souped-up, four-wheel-drive Carrie Underwood destroyed in her music video for *Before He Cheats.*

Angela looked up toward the big sign. "There they are!" She pointed toward a clearing in the woods.

We looked up and saw three people dressed in black from head to toe sprinting for the Hollywood sign. Seething with rage, I took off in a dead sprint after them.

Reece and Angela, the most-athletic of the others, ran their hardest to catch up and make sure I wouldn't do anything stupid, like push them off the top of the sign. I knew I wanted to do that.

Micki and Katie jogged after them.

As I ran through the canyon, I saw rain falling harder and harder with each passing minute. Hearing police sirens, I glanced back to see three cop cars screech to a halt, lights flashing and sirens blaring. Two cops jumped out of each car and ran after us.

Good, I thought. *At least there's more backup.*

The Hollywood sign is at an elevation of 1.578 feet, and it is a couple thousand feet more to get there from the main observation area. I was in such a flaming rage, I sprinted the whole way, and it didn't feel very far.

I reached the large H and saw the last of the three culprits climbing a workman's ladder to the top. Once the last person had a good foothold, he kicked the ladder down.

They were clearly all idiots. Not that would I commit the same crimes, because I wasn't a heartless psychopath, but if I were trying to escape someone I had already tried to kill, who wanted to beat my ass at the very least and possibly murder me, I wouldn't have kicked the ladder down. I would have dragged it up with me, so no one could follow me up.

They certainly didn't think like I did. I grabbed the ladder and set it back in place.

Angela and Reece caught up with me, as I stepped onto the first rung.

"Dude, don't do it!" Reece shouted over the rising wind.

I turned and faced them. "Give me one good reason why I shouldn't climb this fucking ladder, beat their fucking asses, and shove them off to their deaths!"

"Because that's not who you are!" Angela shouted.

"Normally, you'd be right, but these fuckers have it coming. They murdered my cousin for no good reason, so they need to die."

"Bro, you need to listen to me for a second." Reece walked up and placed his hands on my shoulders. "Can you do that for me?"

Sighing heavily, I nodded. "I guess I can do that."

"Wait," Angela said. "I just thought of something. How do you know they won't get away again?"

"Trust me," Reece said. "Once they're up on that H, they won't go anywhere. The O is too far for any sane person to risk jumping onto."

We heard a helicopter and looked up. Boone must have dispatched a chopper in addition to the officers on the ground. A searchlight came on and shone on the H.

"Freeze where you are!" a voice commanded.

Five shots rang out.

I grinned. "Good. They've been shot. Hopefully, they're dead."

Reece shook me. "Dude, please listen to me and be completely honest with me."

"You got it, Man."

"You're a Christian, aren't you?"

I nodded.

"Think about what God wants you to do. Do you think He wants you to break one of His commandments just to get revenge?"

"I guess not."

"Of course, He doesn't. Look, Man. I know these past weeks haven't been fun for you. I can't imagine how rough it must be to deal with everything you've gone through on top of losing your cousin in a highly publicized news story. God doesn't allow bad things to happen just to hurt you. It's not fun right now, but trust me. God knows what He's doing.

"Maybe it was time for Liberty to go home to Him, even though you, your family, and the people close to her weren't ready for her to leave. It definitely wasn't the ideal way for her to go, but it's God's will.

"Remember that she's now in Heaven with Him. She's no longer in pain. She isn't suffering, and she won't have to deal with the negativity that surrounded her on Earth. She still loves you very much, and now she's watching over you as your guardian angel."

"She's with your mom now," Angela said. "You have two special women watching over you who love you a lot. You'll see them both again someday."

I stood there with rain pouring down, as Reece held onto my shoulders. My eyes filled with tears. "Thanks, Guys," I managed, fighting to keep my composure. "I needed to be reminded of that."

"Of course," Angela said. "That's what friends are for."

Reece looked at me. "Would you mind if I gave you a hug?"

I grinned. "Not at all. Lucky for you, I love hugs."

He smiled and wrapped his arms around me, as rain poured down. The wind rose even more. "God wanted me to give you this," he said in my ear. "He wants you to know how much He loves you, and He has your best interests at heart. Please remember that."

I nodded. "Thanks, Man. That means a lot." I looked skyward. "Thank You, God. I love You, and I pray You opened the pearly gates to welcome Liberty home. Treat her well."

Reece released me, and a feeling of warmth bubbled up from my stomach and spread throughout my body. It was like God telling that everything would work out in the end, and that warm feeling was His comfort and life, something I seriously needed after the month I just had.

Six cops ran up to us, followed by Chief Boone, Officer Vince, Katie, and Micki.

"Good," Boone said. "You guys are still down here. The suspects were shot with darts from the helicopter and are paralyzed. They can't escape. They're fully conscious and coherent, but they can't move for a few hours."

"Awesome," I said. "Now we can officially nail them and end this nightmare of a week."

"How will we get up there?" Officer Vince asked.

"The dumbasses left us a ladder." Angela pointed at the ladder.

"Then let's go apprehend them," Chief Boone said.

I checked that the ladder reached the top of the structure. The officers went first, followed by me, Angela, Reece, Katie, and Micki.

The three suspects lay on the structure, paralyzed. Officer Vince walked to the first one and hoisted her up by the armpits.

I glared at them. "Let's unmask them and see who they really are."

Vince kept the person up and tore off the mask to reveal Julie Capp.

I narrowed my eyes. "You."

"Yeah, me." She smirked.

"You're a heartless bitch, you know that?" Micki shouted.

Julie laughed. "It's cute that you think I care about your opinion of me."

"Why the fuck did you murder my cousin?" I demanded.

"She ruined my career. She spread lies around the studio and got me fired from *Colrophobia.*"

"You got yourself fired, you stupid cunt," Micki said. "FYI, literally everyone in production wanted your dumb ass gone. Liberty was simply the mouthpiece who said what all of us were thinking."

"The fact that she was the one who said it and went to the producers and director about it ruined me."

"What if you knew everyone wanted to get rid of you?" Angela asked. "Would you kill them all?"

"Probably."

Micki looked at Angela. "You really ask that of a psycho bitch?"

"Who the fuck are you calling a psycho bitch?" Julie shouted.

"You!" I shouted back. "You are! Who the hell murders someone in cold blood, because she supposedly ruined your career, even though you brought it on yourself?"

"She did. I told you I need medical marijuana."

"That's horseshit."

"You don't know my life."

"I don't have to. If you're going to kill someone, because you don't like what she said or supposedly did proves you're mentally unhinged. You seem like the kind of person who would lie about early onset arthritis just to score free weed."

"Because she is," Officer Vince said.

"What the fuck do you know, Pig?" Julie sneered.

"Carl did some research," he replied. "If there's no family history, it's highly unlikely you'd develop arthritis by yourself at an early age. How old are you, anyway? Thirty-five?"

"I'm twenty-eight, you stupid bastard."

"Close enough."

Lightning flashed twice, and thunder rolled. Below us, more flashing lights lit the canyon. Some news vans arrived, hoping to catch the drama live.

I looked back at Julie. "So you killed my cousin, because you ruined your own career."

"She did."

"No, you did. You're pathetic."

"Like I give a damn what a nobody asshole like you thinks?"

I gave a bark of laughter. "First off, I'm not a nobody. I have a bigger fan base with my TV show than you ever did with your shitty D-list movies. Secondly, you can call me any fucking name you want, Sweetheart. It don't faze me at all."

Brady, Callie, Randy, and Jeremy climbed the ladder to join us. I glared at the second person clothed in black. "Now that we've nailed the first one, let's see who the second one is."

An officer stepped toward the motionless form, who wasn't as paralyzed as Julie. The person raised a hand.

"I can do it myself," she said.

I recognized the voice. The mask came off, and we were looking at Coco Centennial.

Brady's jaw dropped. "Fuck. I lost the bet."

Angela nudged him hard. "This isn't the time to be concerned about that."

I narrowed my eyes against the pouring rain. "Seriously?"

Coco flipped her hair and looked at me. "Yup. What's so hard to believe."

"The fact that you almost put on a good enough act to fool me into thinking you were innocent. I saw that piece of shit you starred in."

"Which one?" Micki asked behind me.

I pointed a finger at her. "Good one." I turned back to Coco. "Watching you in any movie you took part in proves you don't have a good acting bone in your big, fat, whore body."

"Clearly I do, if you believed I didn't play any part in the bitch's murder."

"You really don't. I saw right through your bullshit. I've dealt with plenty of stupid women like you before. I could tell you were hiding something."

"What I want to know is what the hell Liberty ever did to you," Micki said. "Why the hell did you want to kill my best friend?"

"Because she ruined my career, too. I lost out on the role of a lifetime. That part in *Ain't No Mountain High* would have revived my career. I could've gotten roles in A-list movies, but that stupid whore stepped in and stole that part from me. Then she had the nerve to talk shit about me afterward."

"I swear to God, if you're stupid enough to believe those tabloid stories enough to murder her, you deserve to die," I said.

"Which is exactly what she'll do," said a voice behind me.

We turned and saw the third person remove his ski mask. It was a blond guy none of us knew. Apparently, the paralyzing darts wore off faster than Boone thought.

"I'm sorry," I said. "Who are you?"

He looked at me. "I'm Alex Merrill, Zoe's brother."

"I told you to refer to me as Coco!" she snarled.

"No. That time of your life is over." He stepped closer to Coco, and she got to her feet and stepped back, almost losing her balance in the wind and the ridiculous six-inch steampunk boots she wore.

"You realize everyone hates you, right?" Alex asked.

"What the hell are you talking about?"

"Our entire family. Mom and Dad disowned you when you got into the porn industry. Our sister is embarrassed to call you her sibling, and the extended family wrote you off when you roped me into your bullshit."

"Wait," Chief Boone said. "How were you involved?"

"If I tell you, you have to promise I won't be in as much trouble as these two whores," Alex said.

"We'll see about that once we know what you did."

He sighed. "I didn't play a direct part in any of the five murders or the two attempted ones."

Reece and I exchanged glances.

"After Coco and Julie decapitated Harley, I overheard them planning on the phone how to keep tabs on who the *Banshee Busters* crew interviewed and how they would kill Alicia next," he confessed. "Coco saw me. I walked out, threatening to go to the cops to turn them in. She forced me to be their getaway driver."

"How did she force you?"

"She cornered me and said I would be their driver from then on. If I refused, she'd cut off my head like she did to Harley."

"You were the one who almost ran us off the road five miles from Brooklynne Grace's house?" Brady asked.

"Yes, but only because Julie had a knife at my throat and told me to do it. It was the same knife that sliced Brooklynne's throat."

"I see," Chief Boone said. "Walk me through who each of them killed."

"They both got Harley. They broke into his manor an hour after the *Banshee Busters* left. Julie tackled him from behind and held him down, while Coco sliced the machete through his neck."

"I don't have time for this." Coco turned to leave, but Officer Vince hit her with his taser.

"You aren't going anywhere except prison," he said.

"Alicia was solely Julie's victim at first," Alex continued. "After the massage parlor closed, Julie broke in, sneaked up on Alicia, and sliced her throat with a dagger. Then she and Coco worked together to string up the body at the frat house.

"Travis was Coco's target. She stole a sniper rifle from my friend's dad and set up on the roof of the gym across from their apartment complex. She waited for him to step in front of the window and killed him with a headshot.

"To kill Brooklynne, Julie hopped the fence and gave her the same treatment as Alicia. She sneaked up behind her, slit her throat, and let her bleed out in the hot tub."

"That one was disgusting," I said. "You turned me off Bloody Mary cocktails for the rest of my life."

"You don't drink those," Brady said.

"Again, not the time to worry about that," Angela said.

"For Reece," Alex said, "I waited in the car, while Julie and Coco did the dirty work. They came out in five minutes and told me to lead foot it. I did."

"Too bad I'm still alive," Reece said.

"Same thing for the shooting of Ben," Alex said. "I honestly feel bad about it all. I don't have any excuse for the part I played. I'll take whatever punishment you give me with dignity. I can't believe I let this bitch of an estranged sister manipulate me like this." He narrowed his eyes at her. "That's why she must die."

He stepped toward her again, and she backed up another step. "Alex, what the hell do you think you're doing?"

"I'll be going to jail, anyway, for the role you forced me to play. I might as well give them a good reason to take me." He walked toward her menacingly, and she stepped back.

"I'm not fucking kidding you, Alex. You'd better get the hell away from me before I...." She stumbled at the edge, arms flailing, then she lost her balance and fell backward to the canyon.

We all stepped closer and saw her lifeless body sprawled out on the canyon floor.

Alex raised both hands. "You saw I didn't actually touch her, right?"

"Yes, we did," the chief said. "That'll be considered an accidental death instead of murder."

Vince cuffed Julie while reading her Miranda rights. "You have the right to remain silent. Anything you say can and will be used against you in a court of law...."

He led her past me when he finished but stopped for a second. "Did you have any final words you want to say to her?"

I thought for a second. "Yeah, I do."

I looked her in the eye. The rain and wind slacked off a bit. "You're the worse piece of human scum I ever met. You're a washed-up druggie, psycho bitch who deserves to rot in jail for the rest of your miserable life. Even though you killed my cousin in a senseless, heartless act of murder, I still choose to forgive you."

She stared in shock. "Are you kidding? I murdered a member of your family, and you're just going to forgive me?"

I nodded. "I don't know what it is. I seriously want to hurt you for revenge, but I'm sure the police would frown on that." I glanced back at my friends.

Reece smiled and nodded, so I turned back to Julie.

"Plus that's not who I am. It's not who God wants me to be.

"God calls us to forgive those who trespass against us, regardless of what he does. He forgives us even when we don't deserve it or want it, and the only reason I'm forgiving you is for my own good. You don't deserve forgiveness. Hell, you probably don't even want it, but I don't give a flying fuck about that.

"God calls me to forgive, so I can be forgiven by Him and can begin the healing process for myself. Call me anything you want and say anything you like about me. I know who I am in Christ. I know He has forgiven me, and I know He'll be with me every step of the way for the rest of my life. That's all that matters to me."

I nodded to Officer Vince. "You can take her away now."

He led her to the ladder, where another officer helped her climb down to a waiting cop car. Another officer escorted Alex down.

The gang walked over to me after I finished speaking.

"Dude, that was amazing," Randy said. "I bet what you did took huge balls."

I grinned. "It wasn't balls, Man. That's called being a Christ follower."

Callie gave me a big hug, which turned into a group hug.

"Isn't this a sweet moment?" a voice asked.

We parted and stepped aside, and Jason came forward with the biggest smile I ever saw since Liberty died. He wrapped me in a huge bear hug.

"Dude, thank you soooo much for your hard work and help this week." Tears flowed freely from his eyes. "It still sucks to lose my fiancée and your cousin, but you don't know what a weight has been lifted off my chest now that her killers will face justice. She can finally rest in peace."

I hugged him back. "You got it, Bro. It wasn't easy, but, by the grace of God, we did it."

As we released each other, the storm clouds parted, and the sun broke through. It was almost like God told us we'd done a good job. I looked at the sky and saw a cloud that vaguely resembled Liberty from the waist up. She was smiling from ear-to-ear and appeared to be waving at me.

My eyes welled, as I waved back. "Have fun in heaven, Cuz. You can finally rest in peace. I love you."

Brady came up and put an arm around my shoulders. "You did great, Bro."

I smiled at him. "I couldn't have done it without you guys. Along with God, your emotional support is the only reason I didn't put a bullet through my own head."

"That's what friends are for," Callie said, walking up and putting her arm around me from the other side.

One-by-one, the rest of the gang came up and stood shoulder to shoulder. We stared at the city of Los Angeles for ten minutes, musing over how far we'd come.

Going into the investigation, I didn't think we'd face as many challenges as we had. I considered giving up almost every day.

Then I thought about Liberty and the reason I took the time to fly to California and what God wanted me to do. With His love and support, and the same from my friends, I made it through a week of hell on Earth relatively unscathed. Try as they might, Coco and Julie didn't break me. They could do anything imaginable to my body, like break my bones, shoot me, or beat me to a pulp, but it wouldn't have affected me that much. Those things were just my body. Physical wounds heal. They wanted to break my spirit, but God didn't let them.

The saying, "Sticks and stones may break my bones, but words will never hurt me," was true in my case, especially with God on my side. If He was with me, who could be against me?

"We did it," Brady said. "Liberty is officially resting in peace."

"Yeah. That's a huge weight off my chest," I said. "The feeling is indescribable."

"I'd guess we'll be on the next flight out in the morning," Angela said. "We completed what we came here to do. I can't lie. I'm starting to miss my home state."

"Sounds good to me," Callie said. "I can't wait to share the news with Sierra and Calvin."

"I know Calvin will want to see us again," I said. "It sounds like he misses us like crazy."

"We need to live it up one last time," Jason said. "Tonight at my place. I'm officially off house arrest, and we can party like it's 1999."

"I can spin for you, too," Reece said.

"That sounds awesome," I said. "Let's go set it up."

We slowly climbed down the ladder one-by-one, walked through the canyon with our heads held high, and drove to Jason's beach house to set up for our final night of partying.

Randy got on our Twitter account and sent out a message telling our fans who lived near to Malibu that they were invited to a house party, so we could meet some of our California-based fans.

We had room for roughly 500, and we filled it to capacity in the first half hour.

The next morning, Jeremy drove us to the airport, while Jason, Micki, and Reece met us there to see us off. I promised Jason and Micki I'd stay in touch. After I gave Reece a hug, he said he'd fly to San Antonio soon to see me. I said I'd hold him to that. I got his phone number before they let us board the plane.

When the stewardess called for boarding to begin, we got on. I looked out the window and waved one last time at the four great people who were there for us every step of the way—Jeremy, who gave us a place to stay in LA; Jason, who provided us with comic relief when we needed it and a place to party; Micki, who helped with the case and supported us as needed; and Reece, who was the reason we finally nailed Julie, which led us to Coco.

I wiped off tears, as the plane taxied down the runway and took off for home.

22

Vanna, both Calvins (Brewster and Harrison), Katelyn, Sierra, Carson, and my father were waiting for us when we deplaned in San Antonio. They had a huge *Welcome Home* banner and plenty of balloons.

We met monstrous applause when we entered the concourse. The place swarmed with paparazzi and news reporters asking questions and congratulating us for our hard work in delivering justice for Liberty Belle. We walked through a storm of camera flashes into the arms of our loved ones.

Brady lifted Vanna in a hug and spun her around. Callie received a warm embrace from Sierra and Calvin H, and I walked into my dad's open arms.

"Congratulations, Son," he said, holding me. "I'm so freaking proud of you."

"Thanks, Dad. I'm relieved Liberty can finally rest in peace."

"So am I."

Calvin B hugged me so hard, I had to take two steps back. "Dude, I'm so fucking happy to see you!" He buried his face against my shoulder. "I was so worried you wouldn't come back to us, especially when you were shot."

I laughed and rubbed his back. "Bro, I promised I'd come back. I don't go back on promises."

Katelyn smiled warmly and opened her arms to me. I hugged her.

"Welcome back, Hero," she said.

Carson lifted me off the ground with his fierce hug.

We walked to the parking lot, and I put my luggage in the trunk of my dad's BMW, although I rode back to the Bromance Bungalow with Calvin, and Dad followed.

Brady went with Vanna to spend some much-needed alone time with her. Callie went home with Sierra and Calvin H, and Angela and Katie returned to the Confetti Condo with Brady and Vanna. Katelyn drove herself home, and Randy rode to his apartment with Carson, where they hung out for a while.

On the ride home, I told Calvin more about what happened in LA.

"You missed a lot here," he said. "The day after you were shot, two UPS trucks pulled into the driveway full of cards and gifts for you. It's amazing what your fans do for you guys."

"Yeah." I chuckled. "Veronica warned me about that."

"Just so you know, there was so much stuff, it wouldn't all fit in your room. About a quarter of it is in the living room."

That sounded like a lot more than I expected. I needed to get on Facebook and Twitter and thank everyone, as well as update them on my condition. They probably still thought I was in the hospital recovering from bullet wounds, unless one of the others updated them on social media, or the news broke somewhere else.

"Thanks for signing for me, Bro."

"You got it, Man. You want to have some bro time tonight?"

I looked at him. Brady would be spending time with Vanna for all that "catching up" they needed to do. "I'd love that."

"Awesome. Let's kick some Halo ass."

I laughed. "Sounds good to me."

Julie and Alex were served different doses of justice. Because Alex was roped into the situation after two murders and hadn't played a part in the subsequent ones, he got 200 hours of community service and a year and a half of probation. Julie was sentenced to two life terms in prison with no chance of parole for the five murders she carried out, as well as for conspiracy, attempted murder, and evading arrest. I was glad she was put away for life, so she couldn't hurt anyone else.

Two weekends later, Brady and I went to Schlitterbahn, a water park resort in New Braunfels, for the weekend away Brady and I bet on. Since he lost, and Coco was the main player in Liberty's death, as I suspected, he gave me the $2,500 we agreed on, and we spent the weekend at the resort. We brought along Vanna and Callie to have fun with us.

We were taking a small break from the water park to get a bite to eat when my phone rang. I looked at the number and saw it was Dad, so I answered. "Hey, Dad."

"Son, I have someone from the *Tonight Show* on the house phone. They want to know if you and the gang can fly to New York within the next couple weeks to appear on the show."

I tensed up with shock and excitement. I loved Jimmy Fallon, and it would be amazing to be on his show.

Callie waved a hand in front of my face. "What's going on, Hon?"

I covered the phone with one hand. "My dad's talking to someone from the *Tonight Show*. They want to fly us out to New York and be on the show sometime in the next couple weeks."

"Oh, God, that's exciting," Brady said. "Tell him we'd love to."

Callie nodded vigorously. I grinned and uncovered the phone. "Dad, tell them we're definitely doing it. Do they have a specific day in mind?"

"No, they just said whatever is best within the next couple weeks. They asked that you call them to let them know when you get a set date in mind."

"We will. Thanks for letting me know, Dad." I hung up and looked at the other three with a huge smile. "Well, Guys," I said, spreading my arms, "looks like we're going to be on the *Tonight Show.*"

Aaron Amadeus has always been an avid reader. His favorite activities growing up in the Midwest have been reading a wide range of books, creating cartoons, and in his own way preparing to write novels. To entertain himself, he started writing short stories and on special occasions would create a custom card and a short story based on the interest of those receiving his gifts. He enjoys visiting with friends and family and loves going through haunted houses in the fall.